Black Pandora Box

By Jack Williams

Jack Williams

Contents

"People are hungry for stories. It's part of every being. Storytelling is a form of history, of immortality, too. It goes from one generation to another." – Studs Terkel"

"Trust in God's timing. It's better to wait a while and have things fall into place, than to rush and have things fall apart."

Acknowledgements

Thank you, Grandma, aka Chief. I miss you every single day more than words can describe.

When I tell people, this novel took me eight years to finish, they immediately ask me why. I usually just shrug it off. The answer is simple. This is inspired by real events so I needed to experience more life. I needed to experience more happiness, and more tragedy. I didn't want to release anything premature. I'm really sensitive to everything around me. The noises I hear. The things I see and experience. I truly believe everything in life happens for a reason. Especially when it comes to the people you cross paths with. I want to thank my brother and sister in law for showing me a different side of life. My sister for always encouraging me. My mother and father for giving an unforgettable childhood. My best friends. My lady for everything she does and my niece and nephew who I want to be a role model for.

A very special thanks to Ms. Margo who introduced me to Ms. Raed who would not let me not complete this novel. I couldn't have done this without you. Words cannot explain my gratitude. Your energy and support has been exceptional. I hope that you are willing to work with me on my future projects.

Thank you all for reading. It means the world to me.

What Are We Doing Here?

"I'm never doing a 14-hour flight again man," I said to Vince. "My legs feel like wet noodles."

"Well, this was your idea so deal with it. I hope they're not on bullshit in this country," he responded. "You know how them foreign countries be."

But I didn't know. This was my first time really leaving Chicago in a big way. Vince on the other hand was from the Philippines. We just got off a layover flight from Miami, Florida to Frankfurt, Germany.

"What the hell are we doing here?" I kept whispering to myself every time I remembered why we were here. After so many thoughts about the possible downfall of this random mission I just wanted to go back to my normal life, my home, and school, but I am in too deep. Vince and I were walking through this foreign airport without a trace of German in our language, looking like lost kids in a giant toy store. We were looking for a little German man named Maxi to pick us up and take us to our destination.

"There he is, I think," Vince said, pointing to a small man about 5 feet 8 inches tall and weighed 165 pounds, wearing an 'I love America' t-shirt and waving an American Flag as if he has just shot the last soldier to win an American war. Pretty bold I thought to myself, considering people hate America.

"He has to be looking for us," I told Vince, as we were getting closer to approaching him.

"Hello!" the small German man screamed as if we were deaf.

"Yo!" Vince and I screamed back. "Are you Maxi?"

"Yes, I am. The boss awaits you. Follow me," he replied. I thought to myself, what is this, a movie?

Navigating us through and then out the airport, he took us outside where his luxurious white BMW 745LI awaits.

"Shotgun!" Vince yelled laughing that I had to sit in the back, but I didn't mind because the car was so cozy and luxurious throughout.

Back home in Chicago, my bullshit car had to be cranked at least three times before it even thought about starting. This guy's BMW started instantly at the push of a button. The thought of the finer things in life pushed me further in our decision to pursue our random mission.

"Get some rest! Next destination is Berlin!" Maxi shouted in his broken English accent almost excited.

"Great, sounds like this will take forever," I whispered to myself.

Before falling into a deep daydream, my phone rang from a text message. As I looked up, I saw Maxi looking at me through the rearview mirror. To avoid a lot of discomfort or confusion, I hurried and looked away and back down on my phone. It was a text from Vince.

I hope we don't end up on a meat hook like in the horror movies.

I thought about all the horror movies I've seen, and for some reason, one of the victims always ends up dead and swinging from a hook of some sort. I laughed at the thought then replied,

Me either man.

After I had sent that text, I sent him another text letting him know to put his phone on vibrate or silent because of the look Maxi gave me. Since Maxi didn't talk much and Vince and I didn't really feel comfortable speaking aloud, I threw my MP3 player on to listen to my favorite tunes while finishing my daydreams and attempting to catch some sleep before we met with the boss. It always seems like when you are about to fall asleep, someone or something interrupts you. I was about 10 seconds away from dreamland when I received another text message from Vince.

Who is this boss guy anyway?

I forgot I never really informed him on what exactly we were doing here or details on who we were meeting and why. I basically asked him if he wanted to take a trip to Germany to make some big money and he said sure. I got both our plane tickets to Germany courtesy of Viktor, that same day. Vince was always a spur of the moment type of guy like me. That's why I chose him to go with me and to do business with, not to mention he was my partner in crime beforehand.

*I'm about to email you because the
text is too long to send. Plus, it's easier
to read on your Blackberry anyway.*

I text messaged back to Vince. I made it kind of lengthy to
answer any questions he may ask me.

*Remember that guy I told you about
when I was at the dealership a while back?
The weird foreign guy who kept observing me?
Remember I told you he tipped me very well
and gave me his card after watching my work
with the cars, more specifically his car and
told me if I wanted to make more money to
give him a call? Viktor Halle was his name,
a guy from Germany making a life here in the
US, looking to buy a car at the dealership.
Or so I thought. So anyway, I took him up on
that offer. I got fed up with all the
bullshit at work, not making no real money,
getting treated like shit when I work my ass
off and I didn't want to even think about
the fact that I may be working there full-
time if my school loans don't clear. The
dude tipped me a hundred dollars for
detailing his Benz, so I kind of knew he
wasn't pulling my leg on this one. Pissed
one afternoon after work, I called Viktor up
and explained to him my situation and how
much I hated the way I was being treated at
the dealership. We set a date to meet and
discuss business that same night. We met at
a café not too far from the dealership
actually. I brought my notebook and pen
because I was almost certain I would be
doing something way more important than
delivering and detailing cars for people and
I was right. Here I am thinking I'm about to
land a job in an office with advancement
opportunities and this guy is talking about
a heist. I laughed loudly in his face at the
thought of me doing a robbery. This guy is a
nut job I thought to myself.*

*Then it kind of hit me. I asked myself
who gets their Benz detailed at a dealership
that doesn't sell Mercedes. He asks me if we*

could go for a quick ride and he could explain things some more. I said cool, so we hopped in his 07 SL55 AMG and hit the road, heading towards the dealership. As we pull up to the dealership, he explains to me what we could do with all the cars on the lot and the money we could make doing it. He wants to hot-wire all the cars and export them back to Germany via semi-trucks and cargo ships to sell them to people there. It's like a hot-list of cars sort of speak, but mainly American made cars, since they are rare over in Germany but not any American cars, he wanted the American cars with authority. The Muscle Cars. This guy clearly has money, and you and I need a little bit of that. A lot actually. The meeting between us was coming to an end as I had to let him down. I wasn't about to go to jail for some stupid shit. He understood where I was coming from and told me I had 8 months to change my mind about the job, as he would be leaving for Germany in that time.

As you know, I got great grades last semester, but my financial aid didn't come through which is why I didn't go back to school for my last year. Six months set in and those student loans companies were knocking at my door looking for their money which I didn't have because the dealership wasn't paying half of what I was asking! I never understood why the government just doesn't let people get their education for free. The 7th month of being out of school was a rough time for me. I was spending more than I was making and all my colleagues were advancing, and I couldn't take it anymore. I refuse to be a broke and ordinary ass sucker in these streets, living in my mother's basement or something equivalent to that.

I pulled that card Viktor gave me out of my wallet and gave him another call. After discussing the details of what needs to do be done to get to the cars, Viktor

told me I needed to fly to Germany to meet
with him at one of his nightclubs, and we
would go from there. I felt like I didn't
have anything to lose and everything to gain
so why not? I also felt like this could be a
blessing in disguise because I work at an
American muscle dealership and Viktor just
happens to be on the prowl for American
muscle cars. They say everything happens for
a reason, right? You and I have sold stolen
parts online from the dealership for years
so I figured you would be down for this even
though this is way bigger than a few stolen
parts, this is serious. This is the ultimate
heist. Get caught, and we could go down big
time for this, but if we pull this off, we
don't have to work no more and I can go back
to school. What you think?

I sent a text to Vince saying that I sent the email to him.

I'm about to read it.

He replied. About fifteen minutes went past in which five of
those minutes I was enjoying the scenery of Germany and the other ten,
I was starting to doze off. Suddenly, my phone vibrated with an email
from Vince,

Bro, I can't lie to you. After reading
that email, I'm kind of scared but I'm down,
and you know that. Besides, I'm here now.
It's not like I can hop in a cab and go back
home, lol, so what's next? How much money
can we make anyway? You know my Mom never
asks questions about my whereabouts, and
sometimes I don't think she even cares but
anyway what did you tell your Mom, and how
are you or we gonna get these cars?

My face lit up with excitement as I read the message from Vince.
I was happy to have my wingman with me.

My mom thinks I'm down in Daytona
Beach for a college vacation. I told her and
Toya once I got situated, I would call them
and let them know I made it in safely. I may
even Skype with them just so they can see me

once we get a room. So, I don't have to worry about them on my back you know?

I don't know how much money we can make from this, but I'm sure it beats $6.25 an hour back home by a light year. I'm sure it beats most college graduate's salary by a long-shot too. As far as what lies next for us, I don't know that either. After we meet with Viktor, we both will know a lot more.

As for getting the cars, that's gonna be easy. I own that car lot without owning that car lot you know. They give us something called key plugs to the master board which holds all the car keys to the lot, used and new. I have a few in my position now, but we'll need more than the few I have. Mines are tagged with my name anyway so I can't use mines now that I think about it. They keep a bucket of untagged plugs behind the desk in the General Manager Office that we use to organize the car positions on the lot but the office is loaded with cameras so, I'll have to think of something when I get back to work. I'm glad you asked me because I just thought of something else. When I get back and go to work, I will have them help me re-organize the lot, and from there I'll steal a handful of plugs somehow. From there, a day's work is over around 9 or 9:30 pm and all the managers leave around 10:30 pm after they finish documenting everything and counting the cash on hand from sales. The mechanics are the ones who actually close the place up, and they don't leave till around midnight. During that time frame, I will grab keys for the list of cars Viktor wants. I don't know how we're going to drive more than 1 car at a time, but I'm sure we'll work something out because we need somewhere to store them and everything. It's gonna be kind of difficult because we'll only have roughly an hour and a half to get everything right and in order with no practice drill

```
and for them not to trace everything back to
me. I need to make sure I don't use my
tagged plugs and keep my job despite the
money we make, so I don't make things look
suspicious or at least keep the job for a
little while after the heist.
```

I was almost sure Vince was reading my message without a clue of what I was talking about. Then he texts me

```
        Dude it sounds like you've already
done this before but alright, sounds good.
```

"About thirty more minutes before arrival guys!" Maxi shouted out with excitement.

To me, that meant I got thirty minutes to rest. I got my last views of the scenery a few more seconds before I closed my eyes.

"Yo! Wake that ass up! We are finally here," Vince said while tapping my leg to wake me up from my short slumber.

"I'm up, I'm up," I replied irritably. Gaining my focus, I realized it was dark, and we weren't at a location that I thought we would be at. "A nightclub!?" I questioned Maxi aloud.

"Yes American! A nightclub, now come forth! Viktor awaits you," He replied.

"Whatever," Vince and I both uttered.

Walking towards the entrance of the club seemed like suicide with all the bouncers guarding the door. It had to be at least five guys outside the door, and they all appeared to be at least 6 feet 8 inches tall and weighed about 270 pounds and all muscle! Vince and I were about 190 pounds and about 6 feet 2 inches tall. Although insanely intimidated by the bouncers, we started joking and clowning to ourselves about the thought of getting into a fight with them.

"They would break me in half just by staring at me!" I whispered to Vince.

"I bet they are dumb as bricks, though," Vince joked back causing us to both erupt in laughter.

"What is so funny to you two?" Maxi quickly asked.

"Uhhh nothing," we both quickly responded out of fear and straightened up.

"Americans! Follow me," Maxi instructed, as we approached the front entrance of the club.

"Maxi!" The bouncers and nearby people shouted at him. Maxi was like a celebrity or fan favorite at this club. Everyone was waving to him, ladies running for hugs.

"Who are your new friends? I don't think they can come in," the main bouncer said in his German accent.

"They are longtime friends of Viktor, and he is awaiting them," Maxi replied.

"Fair enough, Viktor is in his office," The bouncer said as he granted us entrance to the club. Finally, we were at our real destination.

The scene on the inside was completely bananas crazy but in a good way. The walls were covered with red and gold striped carpets I supposed to absorb some of the noise in there. There were purple lights hung from the ceilings and strobe lights flashing every which way I looked giving off different illusions of everything you focused your eyes on. Every chair and table seemed to be trimmed in gold with red tablecloths and red and gold flowers as centerpieces.

I looked left, there were beautiful women. I looked right, there were more beautiful women. Slim ones, tall ones, shapely ones but all beautiful! Then there were the really scantily clad one's dancing on some of the tables seductively, but not strippers and they too were literally drop dead beautiful. I don't understand how they can get anything done with all this beauty around, I was thinking to myself.

Looking over at Vince, his mouth was wide open and looked as if it been that way since we entered the club. Surprisingly, we made it to the back room without any trouble or distractions. Walking through the club was unlike any nightclub back home in America that we had ever been too. The feeling was so surreal. I didn't know what to expect behind this thick steel door we approached. It seemed like Maxi did a secret code knock as he knocked on the door. Two quick knocks then a pause and then a final knock. *Boom! Boom!* Pause. *Boom!* Was the sound of the knock that kept replaying in my head. Vince and I both looked over at each other and shrugged with a look of nervousness like two best friends who were approaching an unavoidable death together as we knew for sure there was no turning back now.

"Come in Maxi," a voice said from behind the steel door.

"I knew that was a secret knock," I whispered to myself. As we walked in we saw a few more women in the room in which again all were very attractive and dressed in their tightest black mini-skirts but different colored midriff tops and stilettos seemingly six or seven inches high. I often wondered how women could balance themselves in these high heeled shoes but they seem to manage very well, and they always added to their sexiness. Two of the ladies were counting money at a table using counter machines, and one very gorgeous woman was preparing drinks at a private bar. She stood out as she was the only one in a red dress. This red dress was the kind of red dress that got much attention, and I stared at her probably longer than I should have but I was sure no one could blame me for doing so. Another woman with a measuring tape around her neck was fitting Viktor in the black tailored suit he was wearing. Yes, she was beautiful too.

"Viktor, your guests are here,"

"Thank you, Maxi. If I need you I'll call you okay?" Viktor said facing the other way. Maxi nodded and proceeded to leave the room.

"I really feel like Armani makes the best damn suits! I love a great suit!" Viktor said with excitement.

"I must say, they do," I added. I knew nothing about suits, hell I didn't even own one, but I remember my dad always saying there was nothing like an Armani suit when I was younger.

"Guests? I only sent for one, not two," Viktor said calmly, but with a sense of urgency in his foreign-accented voice. He raised the back of his jacket up and pulled out a berretta. The money machine noise ceased. There was no more talking. All eyes were on this moment. It was serious.

My father wasn't around much growing up, but the time we did spend with each other, he always told me,

"In life, people will always test your fear factor. Fear shows weaknesses so no matter how much you may be afraid of something, never show fear to any man but the Lord himself," I always took my father's advice for as long as I could remember. Vince and I both looked at each other again. It looked as if Vince was a mouse being an approached by a python. I lightly smirked, and looked away. Viktor turned around, facing us with the pistol to his side.

"Well, I hope you didn't think I was going to come alone, did you? It wouldn't be wise to step into foreign territory alone, right?"

"Correct you are. I knew I made the right decision by choosing you for this job. You're a smart kid," Viktor ejected the clip and handed the gun to the woman that was fitting him.

Vince let out a huge sigh of relief as Viktor discarded the gun.

"Thanks," I uttered.

"Who is this friend of yours anyway and why is he so quiet? Is he trustworthy?" Viktor asked. The question felt like an insult to both Vince and me; I felt awfully disrespected. I slighted twisted my face in a frown and replied calmly but mild and respectful at the same time.

"What do you mean is he trustworthy? Do you think I would travel across the world to come do business with someone I don't know and with someone who isn't trustworthy? With all due respect Viktor, on behalf of me and my partner, I feel disrespected. This is my best friend Vince if you must know. Blood couldn't bring us any closer and-"

"I apologize to you both, in no way did I mean to offend either one of you, but in my line of work, I'm sure you can understand why I asked. Let's get down to business, shall we? Drinks?"

"Business first, drinks later," I responded.

"Very well then," Viktor quietly responded. "If you didn't know, I own a ton of nightclubs throughout Germany. This very club you are in is my most popular. The Steinburg which in English is the Castle," Viktor explained as he stood proudly. "I have made a decent living from them, and I am thinking of expansion. Not more nightclubs but something more exciting. Blacklisting, which is the pursuit of the most wanted cars, is what I plan to get into. People are paying top dollar here to get the exact car they want. Imagine if I got the cars from one place to another for less than...half the price and charged top dollar here. Great Profits! Not for just me but for both of you too," Viktor explained.

"Now, you said people are paying top dollar for the exact car they want but what if they want a car that's not on the lot? How do we get those cars?" Vince asked.

"That's a great question, Vince!" Viktor said with enthusiasm as he turned around and pointed at him. "Let me go deeper into detail about that for you. When you two go back to The States, you will provide me with the list of cars that you have on your lot, and from there I will get it to those looking to buy. They will pick from the list I give them. The buyers pick the cars. I give the word back to you guys, and you get those cars," Viktor explained.

"Understood, but what if you have two people picking the same car from the list?" I asked.

"That is exactly what we want! From there, a bidding war is started in which the highest bidder of that vehicle wins and the higher the sale, the higher the profit for the team!" Viktor answered with excitement.

"Why not just set up shop here? Why from one country to another?" Vince asked.

"Besides having the cars, we desperately want, America is the land of the careless, and it is much easier to get the job done there. Not to mention with all the open land there versus here where it is heavily clustered. This will not be an easy task, but with the team, I have configured and put together, things will go smoothly," Viktor assured.

"What kind of team?" Both Vince and I responded with concern.

"Follow me," Viktor told us as he took us to another room.

The room we were now in had a huge projector and open space with plenty of seats not necessarily in any order. You could sit where you choose or move your chair elsewhere. As he pulled a little remote from his back pocket, he motioned for us to sit and the projector began to play.

"Watch and listen closely," He had just about every aspect of this plan mapped out. This intrigued me because I didn't like things out of order or confusion. I preferred everything to be laid out A to Z, so there is no mistaking any of the decisions or orders to be carried out. This aided in things running smoothly and precisely with a positive outcome and hopefully financial windfall in this case. Everyone knows their jobs so no mistakes should be made, even though, shit happens. We all know this to be true no matter how well plans are laid out. There is Murphy's Law, and when you are dependent on others to make things happen, there must be order. With Viktor's plan, I decided to be optimistic and positive and follow his plan to the tee. Seemingly, so far from what we had heard and were seeing, there were no loopholes and this plan could and would work. At that moment, I told myself…I'm in.

The Math and Mastermind

Usually, I'm easily distracted during any presentation no matter what. I'm just not good at following lectures. The old retro sound of the projector Viktor chose to display his plan with didn't help my case but I was doing my best to maintain the focus I had. I wanted to be fully attentive just in case I had to go over anything to explain to Vince or just in case if anyone tried to screw us over during this venture. The plan was complicated but simple. I could tell Viktor thought this plan out for a while. The only factor that the plan was missing is me or someone in my position. He already had a team assembled to play specific positions before I was brought into the picture. My mission is to get back to Chicago, send pictures of the cars on the lot with their specifications to Viktor to choose from and then present to prospective buyers.

Viktor had someone to purchase an old abandoned building with a garage to host all our operations and store the cars until it was time to move them out by semi-trucks and cargo containers. Once we got the building to host operations, he had someone to disguise the building with a dummy company name to stay inconspicuous. One of his men was in charge of creating fake documents good enough to make the company look legit in case things got hectic. By the time it would take the authorities to find out that the dummy business front was really something else we would have enough time to lose them. He also has henchmen to fix and polish any of the cars that needed work done. One would build custom frames inside the shipping containers using wood to evenly fit four cars in a container if need be. Once we knew what cars we were stealing, we needed to go find and purchase those cars at a junkyard and remove the vehicle identification number (VIN) tags and dispose of those cars again. Those VIN tags would be used to replace the VIN number tags in the cars we were stealing so if a customer wanted to check that car's history, an actual record of that car comes up instead of the stolen or the deceased vehicle. That way, everything looks legit. With Viktor putting semi-truck drivers on payroll, getting a semi-truck to hold containers full of cars and a cargo ship ticket to ship the containers of cars to Germany was easy. The set-up for the plan was actually starting to sound perfect. The hard part was keeping the heat off the cars especially since we were planning to strike at night and that's when cops tend to be most busy.

After the projector presentation, he asked us for questions. I didn't really have any, but I did have something important to add, and Vince was curious.

"One issue. Hotwiring these cars won't work. They put some special coating on the wires that prevents them from being hotwired. We had someone try to boost the lot a few years back, and they failed," I informed Viktor. He looked defeated for a second.

"I have to make a call to my people to see if there is a way around that...schiesse!" He yelled.

"Don't worry Vik. I got a way around it. I got access to all the keys. I'll have to just come up with a plan. I'll handle it, put that phone down. No need to call anybody. Don't worry," I assured Viktor. He instantly looked like he found his lost dog as he ran his fingers through his hair, sighing with relief and a smile spread across his face, once again.

"So, Viktor, how much money is everyone going to take home?" Vince asked.

"I put it like this, as stated, once I get the list of cars, I can show my buyers that list and they will pick the car they want from the list and if two people decide they like the same car, they will have to bid on that car in which, the highest bidder wins of course-" Vince cut him off which caused Viktor to make a face that stated is he's serious right now.

"But how much money," Vince asked irritably.

"Hey, be easy bro, he's getting to that part," I said to Vince, trying to calm him down.

"No, it is fine, I will give you an example of an average pay rate, okay?" Viktor responded as his face returned to normal.

"Let's say we get a 68' mustang which will cost us nothing to steal and just a little change to ship it but nothing compared to what it will sell for. So, we get the mustang in the States, a classic car like that will go for what on an average, about $20,000 right? Here in Germany, that will sell for €45,000. That's about $50,000! Say we get a container full which holds about four cars, but two cars for sure so let's use two cars as the example here...ok now times $50,000 by two and what do you get?"

"A lot of fricking money I presume," I said.

Viktor chuckled a bit.

"Precisely, that's about $100,000 roughly. Now say we get two containers, that's $200,000 and three is $300,000 and so forth. Now that is an average example, but let's say those cars get a bidding war started...that average of $50K could turn into $70K or even $100K so imagine those numbers attached to those containers! And this a bit of a stretch but we possibly could net anywhere from $500K-800K a container!"

Vince and I high fived out of excitement as if we had just introduced ourselves for the first time from thoughts of the potential money we could make.

"Who takes home what cash wise?" I asked while doing my best to keep calm from my excitement.

"Well, since we can't do this job without one another, I thought we'd split it right down the middle...20/80! 20 percent for you guys and 80 percent for me!" Viktor said with a serious face. Vince and I looked at each other in total! Viktor erupted in laughter,

"You should see the look on you guys faces! I am just pulling a leg," He shouted.

"Funny!" I Said while giving the stalest face I could give.

"Sorry, I couldn't resist," Viktor replied.

"So, what are the real numbers?" Vince asked.

Viktor paced around the room like a college professor, giving a lecture in the process. "Well...ok all jokes aside, we can't do this job without one another, and we all want to make money, right? And no matter what, I want to be fair to avoid any bad karma understand? I am thinking 65% me and 35% you. I know you all are thinking 50/50 is half and half and that is what is really fair but before you two get fed up, know that I am taking 15% out of my 65% to pay my little henchmen and to pay the shipping fees for our transactions as well as any account wiring fees when transferring money. I'll send an advance when the cars are delivered here, and I'll send the balance to you guys once the customers pay, and then we rinse and repeat! The cars should make it here in about 3 weeks, and by week 4, everyone will be paid in full," Viktor explained. There was a brief moment of silence as if we were mourning someone's death while Viktor looked at us, awaiting our response.

"I think we got ourselves a deal here Vince. We good?" I asked.

"Looks like gold to me!" Vince responded with another ear to ear smile on his face.

"Great, let's shake on it," Viktor said. I had to be clear on my contingency before I shook hands and sealed the deal.

"I only want to do this to one, get back into college and two, put enough money in my pocket to be comfortable. I don't need a bajillion dollars. With the example you gave us earlier, that's more than enough for us. I just want to make sure there aren't any locks on us. After this deal, we are free to go?" Viktor gave me a blank gaze before looking at the ceiling in deep thought.

"Sure. No contracts! You are free to go as you please," He responded. It was a huge weight off my shoulders. I knew in this line of work, there is no way out and if there is, it's usually in a body bag. The three of us shook hands and confirmed our deal.

"Let's party!" Viktor shouted. After a toast of champagne brought over by the pretty lady that was behind the bar, we proceeded to the party floor on the lower level.

The party scene was crazy. Unlike anything, we had ever seen before. Women were everywhere, just stalking and waiting for a chance to talk to us, as if we were celebrities. The woman to man ratio was like four to one, unlike being at home where the woman to man ratio is one to four and the women are all anti-social and stuck-up further than a push-up popsicle. It was all love and all sociable here. After mingling with the women and making up tons of stories as to why Vince and I were in Germany and where we were from, two of the ladies from the meeting room where Viktor had been briefing us, pulled Vince and I to the bar. I didn't really want to go because I was enjoying myself so much, but the sexiness of their attire made my eyes control my mind.

"C'mon, shots for you guys," the woman in the black dress said.

"I don't know, I don't drink too much," I responded.

"No fun, ehe!" I heard Viktor's voice say from behind.

"I know right, he's no fun," the woman in the black dress uttered flirtatiously.

"But I'm fun!" Vince shouted with his hand in the air as if he was waiting to be called on by a grade school teacher.

"He is a smoker anyway. Cannabis at least," Vince continued.

"Yo, don't be telling my business dude!" I said aggressively.

"Don't worry, nobody will judge you here," Viktor added as he laughed at our bickering. "Interesting. Sasha! Renee! Show these gentlemen to their room when you guys are done. Don't forget to water the plants," He chuckled.

"Anyway, I won't take no for an answer kid. Barkeeper! Funf Wodka Aufnahmen bitte! Catch you guys later. Have fun and enjoy your existence while it still exists," Viktor said before downing his of the five shots of vodka that he just ordered, heading into the sea of people on the dance floor.

I didn't remember agreeing to a shot, yet a shot glass found its way to my hand. Viktor was right, though. I needed to enjoy life while it still exists because where we are from, I know first-hand that in the blink of an eye, life could be taken away, which was why I didn't do the bar scenes at home. Vince and the two women were looking at me as I looked up, waiting on a confirmation to toast and down the shots.

"Eh, what the hell, why not," I uttered to myself. "To success!" I shouted.

"Yeahhhh!" The three of them shouted.

With another five shots finding their way into my liver, the night was beginning to become a blur. I remember dancing around the club with various women and then sitting down from the dizziness which was best for me because knowing me, I would have thrown up if I continued down the road I was traveling on. Vince and the two girls we were originally with found me and gave me a bottle of water.

"I told you guys he liked to party. Just gotta know how to persuade him," Vince said grinning.

"Let's take the party to our room boys," the beautiful woman in the red dress who I believed to be Renee said, sounding drunk while still sexy.

"Let's do it! Get up man, round two!" Vince said to me all excitingly.

"Oooookay," I agreed. We drifted off into the back and up some more stairs with the ladies leading us to our room. Things were starting to spin for a second as I was walking up the stairs. I was so drunk it felt like I was in a Dali painting. Luckily, it was only two flights of stairs, otherwise, I just may have decided to sleep in the stairwell for the night.

The two ladies opened a door in the hallway which looked like an abandoned building, but once we entered, I remember a lot of colors and two huge beds on opposite sides of the room. Without warning, Renee pushed me on the bed and climbed on top of me. "Ready to water the plants?" She said right before pulling a joint and a lighter from her bra. Her voice was so sexy and seductive. By plants, she wasn't talking daisies. It was a joint filled with grade A smelling cannabis. I knew cannabis was a worldwide thing, but I never would have guessed I'd be smoking it in Germany with my best friend and two incredible looking women. She lit the joint, took a hit and passed it to me. Although I was sobering up, I knew I still drunk and was thinking, I probably shouldn't smoke right now, but my mind and body were separated from each other. I looked across the room to see Vince and the girl in the black dress making out and thought to myself…

I'm happy he's enjoying himself.

After the joint was finished Renee started kissing on me. This isn't right I kept thinking, considering one of my rules is I never mix business and pleasure and more importantly I had a girl I loved back home or at least I thought I did. But, with the alcohol and cannabis in my system, I could probably be talked into hugging a gorilla. She kissed again, I kissed back, and she laid me all the way back on the bed, and I closed my eyes.

The Morning After

"Rise and shine kids!" Viktor shouted, pulling the curtains back.

'Dang! Ten more minutes grandma' is what I felt like screaming as his good morning gestures reminded me of my childhood. I did not remember too much of the night before, but somehow, the four of us were in the same bed together. I don't recall if we had a movie night or a foursome. I was fully clothed so either nothing happened or someone was very nice to re-dress me. Vince and Sasha were topless and red dress was in her bra and panties. I stared at Renee's body as I ran through what could have happened in my mind. Part of me didn't want to know. I grabbed my phone from my back pocket.

Five missed calls

my screen displayed, followed by a dramatic drum pattern in my head. Four from my girlfriend and one from my mom. Oh boy, I got some explaining to do, I thought to myself.

"Well! Looks like you guys had a blast of a time. Splendid! Time to get down to business. Ladies, go freshen up, your driver will be here shortly. Gentlemen, towels are on the table, the showers are in the back. Meet me downstairs in 30 minutes. Breakfast will be served, your flight leaves in 3 hours," Viktor informed us.

"Alright, we're up. See you in 30," I said.

"Good," Viktor replied, walking away. I turned my head and looked at the red dress, cracking a smile at her. I wanted to speak, but I didn't want to blast her with early morning dragon breath. She cracked a half smile back and buried her face into a pillow. Damn, she must have smelled it already, I thought.

"Bro, wake me up in 10 minutes. I can barely keep my eyes open," Vince pleaded.

"Dude, get your ass up, I'm not messing around here. Viktor is not playing around with us. One wrong move and we are swinging from meat hooks," I said with authority. "We don't need to give any entertainment to a reason why Viktor shouldn't trust us. Now get up!" I continued.

"I'm getting up. You right," Vince replied.

"I know," I said walking towards the showers. After we showered and threw on some fresh clothes, we met Viktor downstairs.

"On time! I love it!" Viktor shouted with enthusiasm. I gave Vince a quick side eye. "Sit! Let's eat and discuss things," Viktor commanded. "Maxi has prepared quite the breakfast for you guys,"

"I hope you Americas like it. I prepare toast, the finest eggs of Germany, bake-on, sas-sage, pancakes and fresh squeezed orange juice," Maxi said in his broken English accent, pointing at each dish on the table as he named them.

"Thank you. We really appreciate this. Nothing like real cooked food," I responded. "Hey, wasn't there a nightclub here?" I looked around for familiar settings.

"Ah, yes! That's in the southern sector. We're in the northern at the moment. Anyway, I think you guys will find his cooking excellent. I personally think he is one of the best cooks in all of Germany," Viktor proclaimed. The ladies from last night came down and served and joined us for breakfast.

"As they say in Americas, dig in!" Maxi joked.

I had only been in Germany roughly a day, and after my first bite of the pancakes, I already agreed with Viktor and his thoughts on Maxi being one of Germany's best chefs. Even thought about him outdoing my grandmother in the kitchen but then a quick vision of my mom smacking me upside my head for such thoughts put that thought to rest. The eggs were from heaven or some place just like it. Definitely superior to the eggs we have at home. The OJ was amazing. It tasted so pure. The pancakes were so fluffed just right, and with the maple syrup, the 4th of July was in your mouth. The bacon and sausage I did not taste.

"Why no meat for you?" Maxi asked concern.

"Um, I just don't eat pork. Judging from the taste of everything and the way Vince hasn't said a word besides nom nom, I know it tastes great!" I explained in a friendly tone.

"You like?" Maxi asked Vince with his eyebrows touching his forehead, awaiting Vince's approval.

"Like? I LOVE! Can you come back home with me? I can sneak you in my suitcase," He said jokingly causing us all to erupt in laughter.

"Well more pancakes for you!" Maxi said, laying another 3 cakes on our plates.

With my eyes bright as stars, I'm sure they said feed me more and thanks. I could probably eat two more plates or maybe even three if my stomach would allow. Growing up, living with six people, there was never enough food to get seconds, so I was always hungry. Not to mention I always had a pretty fast metabolism. On top of my metabolism, I was preparing myself mentally for this eighteen-hour flight.

"This could be my last meal as a living man" I kept thinking with every other bite.

"Man, I'm stuffed! On the ride to the airport, I will be knocked-out," Vince said as he threw punches at the air like a retired fighter.

"I just may join you, my good man," I added. "Speaking of, hey Viktor, you going to inform us on what's next?" I asked.

"Right. Ladies excuse us please," The women excused themselves through a wooden sliding door to the left of us. My eyes followed Renee as she exited. She looked back giving me a seductive look. I cleared my throat and looked back at the table. "At the airport Maxi will give you an envelope with $50,000 dollars in it. I will email you the address where to take this package. My guys will be at that address. That is the purchase money for the garage we will be using. Now listen carefully," Both mine and Vince's eyes were glued to Viktor like a well-trained dog as he asked us to listen up. "Money is not to play with. Especially mine. Now, I have no reason to not trust you guys but make sure every last penny gets to its destination. Don't get any funny ideas. I like you guys, and if you knew me enough, you would know how rare that is for me. I wouldn't want anything to happen to you guys, understand? We are a team now. That is pretty much it. Any questions?"

"None from me," I said.

"Me either," Vince stated.

I didn't have any questions but I sure as hell had visuals. Mainly meat hooks swinging back and forth in a dark room with one light bulb on. Especially after that, 'I wouldn't want anything to happen to you guys' comment.

"Great. Maxi, bringrn Sie ihr Gepack. I'm going to take a nap. I will email you guys in a few hours. I'll be in the States to check on the progress of everything in about two weeks, as well as which we will go over the blacklist and which cars to get first," Vince and I both nodded.

After we shook hands, we were on our way. Maxi pulled around his white BMW, and we loaded up. I needed to take a quick second to skype my family back home to let them know everything was ok and I'd see them soon. Everything happened kind of fast, and I never got the chance to call them. They're probably worried sick I thought to myself. I gave myself a palm strike to the forehead and proceeded to making the calls. I prayed someone was online. I tried my Mom first, and to no surprise, she wasn't online, so I left her a voicemail.

"Hey, Mom! I was calling to just say 'Hey', and everything is ok. Sorry, I forgot to call you guys sooner, I kind of lost track of time. You know how Miami is right hehe, but hey I'm about to go out again. Tell Ms. Treaty I said hey and I love you all. See you in a day. Love you,"

Mom wasn't online, but my girlfriend has a smartphone. That means she's always online which meant I got some explaining to do. I dialed her skype number, and after the first ring I hung up. It just hit me upside the head that she thinks I'm in Florida, not Germany. If she would have seen the daylight in the background, boy I would have been screwed.

"Maxi, can I run inside to make this phone call really quick?" I asked.

"Sure, but please, make it quick. Flight leaves soon," He said, pointing at his watch.

"Ok, it'll be quick," I rang the doorbell, and Sasha opened the door.

"Heyyyyy. Back for more huh," She giggled.

"Uh not exactly, I just need to make an important phone call. Please, is there a quiet room?"

"Just go by the bar area, I'll keep quiet if you keep quiet," She said gently while rubbing my chest.

"No no no please, stop it. I have to make this call," I said irritably.

"Tisk, no funnnnn. Whatever," She said walking away.

Damn, what are they feeding this nympho? My thoughts ran. She just wasted like two minutes of my time. Before I can dial her number again, my phone started vibrating. TOYA, is what it read. She was calling me back. I hurried and threw on my tired act to seem as real as can be.

"Hello?"

"Boy! Where have you been? And why are you just now calling me at 2:45 in the morning?"

"Babe...I'm sorry. As soon as we touched down, we started drinking and partying, and I honestly lost track of time. I'm so out of it right now. I just wanted to hear your voice," I pleaded.

"Yeah...just be careful babe. Be safe and have fun. I love you," She said softly. I could tell from her voice she missed me and would rather have me locked in a cage with her than be in Daytona Beach having fun. If I was having fun without her, she borderline hated it. I could spend 23.5 hours of my day with her, and if I left for that last half of hour, she would be pissed.

"I will baby. Love you more. See you soon. Goodnight love," I told her. I shuffled quickly back outside so we can get out of dodge and catch our flight.

"Ready?!" Maxi shouted.

"Let's go!"

We made the flight just in time. The stewardess had just bought me a pillow, and I was just about to go to knockout land when Vince started talking to me.

"Bro, you woke?" He asked.

"Yeah what's up?"

"Man. I'm just thinking about all this, kind of taking it all in you know. Man, I was doing some math and can you imagine? We will get a lot of money doing this. I can see it now, taking trips to Cali and stuff, balling out! Trips to Miami, hanging with the finest of women. Driving the nicest cars man. It's almost unreal, you know," he whispered with excitement.

"Yeah bro, it's crazy. It's a lot of money, but truth be told, I plan to stay low key. That way it's less drama and less people trying to figure out what I do and trying to get in my business. I'm taking my money and finishing school. That's the only reason I'm going through with this in the first place, so I have to stick to the plan," I responded.

"I hear you. I just wanna have some fun man. I'm tired of struggling, and I'm tired of my household you know. It's depressing. I'm just tired of it all man,"

"No doubt. Get the money and have your fun man but don't play. Don't mess around and mess your money up for fun or mess up anything to do with this operation," I said.

"Why do you seem so uptight about this?" he asked.

"I don't mean to be uptight or anything, but I just want to be clear when I say it's not a game. We can end dead or in jail for a long time at the snap of a finger you know. So don't think I'm uptight, I just don't want this to be taken lightly and venture away from the game plan,"

"I hear you. I understand. I'm going to take a nap. We got a long flight,"

"True that. See you in a few hours," I replied.

My nervousness was setting in as the plane left the ground. I hated flying with a passion. It's not just the plane, it's the fact that someone is in control of my life. People always try to calm me down by telling me traveling by air is safer than traveling by car. But they never mention that survivor rate. More than likely, you can survive a car crash. Surviving a plane crash? Not likely in any way. Like sticking your hand in a garbage disposal and keeping your fingers, it just won't happen. My stomach started churning the more I thought about it. I asked the stewardess for a warm ginger ale to calm my stomach before I threw-up. Finally, 15 minutes later my stomach was calming, but I was starting to sweat. I took four sleeping pills to put me down like a wild animal.

I laid back, and I started to think about my current position in life. I started thinking about what and who I was becoming. The amounts of money that could come in and what that could do to a person. Vince already seems to be changing, and he hasn't seen a nickel yet, but I do understand his pain. Ever since his father passed away, he hasn't been the same. Vince used to be a good kid growing up. Even before I knew him. His picture was always in the grammar school hallways and being the only asian in an all afro-american school, it stood out. His name was always being called aloud for his excellent grades. Excelling in everything and his father was there every step of the way until things got bad. Vince's dad passed away when he was 17, and he stopped caring about life ever since, except for the next time he's getting high, sleep with the next woman or hit the next party. I felt bad for him, but I also felt deep down I could restore him. Who knows him better than his best friend.

He just misses his dad. Then again who am I to restore anybody, I thought to myself. I was becoming a criminal before my very eyes, and part of me liked it. Hell, part of me loved it. But I know it's wrong, yet I don't care anymore. I guess, otherwise, I wouldn't be here. My eyes were starting to get heavy. I don't know if I was scared, nervous, excited or what but my mind was racing at 156,974 thoughts per second. I started to think about whether this whole job was worth it again. I realized there are consequences for every action and one must be prepared to accept whatever the consequences may be. Otherwise, why do it if you are not able to accept the good and/or the bad outcome? I had dreams, big dreams, and going through with this scheme was putting my education within my arms reach. This was in my blood. I've seen crime my whole life. I'm surprised I didn't fully turn to it sooner. My mom and dad introduced me at an early age. I couldn't help but reminisce on my relationship with my parents, my childhood days, watching my mom and dad and their crews go to "work," I started to think about the small parts I played in it with them and how it changed me at an early age.

A Product of My Environment

My mom, dad and many of their friends composed a crew that would pull at least five to seven grand on a good night and some nights less. Some weeks they would be dry not pulling in a dime. I was the only kid in the neighborhood that was getting just about everything he asked for, especially at Christmas time. Imagine being a kid going to Toys-R-Us on Christmas Eve and picking your own toys out the day before Christmas. It was amazing. My mom and dad didn't believe in Santa Claus, but they believed in Christmas. Mom would always say,

"Ain't no white man in no red and white suit coming down no chimneys to bring you nothing! Your dad and mom are your Santa Claus."

I didn't really care as long as I was getting the toys I was asking for. I was the happiest and most spoiled kid ever but not the spoiled brat type of child. I knew my boundaries. There was one thing that started to bother me though as I got older and that was the simple question of how? How did mom and dad buy all those items because even as a kid, I knew what going to work looked like. I knew their working hours were not regular working hours. I also knew without going to work, you don't get paid. With this thought in mind, I told myself I would pay more attention the next time they took me to a store with them. While rare, the time came when my parents let me accompany them to work again. I grabbed some super soakers to terrorize other kids with, my favorite ninja turtle, Leonardo, and all the Power Rangers. My mom grabbed some VCR players and purses. We went to the register, and she pulled out a little booklet, wrote something down in there, ripped a piece of paper out and gave it to the lady. A few seconds later, we were on our way out with the goods.

"Mom how come you didn't give that lady no money?"

"Keep it quiet, boy!" my dad snapped quietly.

"We will talk in the car baby," my mom said.

Once we made it back to the car, she broke it down for me, but she didn't go in depth. I think she wanted to confuse me because I was a kid and would probably lose interest in the matter but once I'm intrigued, I am all ears until I understand everything.

In a nutshell, it was called the paper game. Mom and Dad were writing bad checks, using different identities to get what they wanted but what happens with the checks is what it's all about.

"Pay attention once we get in the store baby," Mom said.

My eyes and ears were fired up and ready to go. As we got out the car and she had everything she just bought minus my action figures in the bag. We walked into the same store in another location. Confused as ever I decided not to ask questions yet but to wait to see what happens. We approached the counter, and the transaction began.

"Hello there, how can I help you?" The cashier asked. The cashier was an old lady who looked to be in her early 70s.

"I would like to return these items," Mom said while using her professional voice.

"Is there anything wrong with them?"

"No. We just had an unexpected family emergency," Mom said while looking down, reaching in the bag.

"Ah, I hate when that happens. With my age, you know I've had my fair share of those unexpected awful surprises," The old cashier waved her index finger and rambled.

"Do you have the receipts please?" the cashier asked while popping her gum loud like it was going out of style.

"As a matter of fact, I do," Mom said while placing the items on the counter to hand them to the cashier.

"Hey, you know, you look familiar miss," She said to my Mom while gazing into her eyes.

My Dad was looking at watches about 5 feet away slowly made his way back over to us after hearing that comment. My mom was silent as she stared back. I could tell it was an uneasy moment for them both. The cashier starts to type in the numbers from the receipts into the cash register right before popping the question.

"You go to bingo nights on Tuesday?" The cashier asked.

Mom let out a laugh of relief.

"Oh no. You got the wrong lady ma'am," She said assuring her they were not previously acquainted. The drawer popped open, and the cashier took out a big wad of cash.

"Here you go. $657.67 back to you and you guys have a great evening ok. Handsome little guy you got there," the cashier uttered before winking at me.

"What do you say, son?" My dad reminded me. "Thank you, miss!" I uttered.

"Alright nah," Dad responded. Back in the car, I pieced it all together.

"Mom, dad, so you guys return all the stuff to make money?"

"Yep, that's pretty much it son," my Dad said.

"I wanna make money like you guys!"

"Ok, chill out boy, school is your only mission and priority right now. Do good in school, and you won't have to worry about money because it will come to you. Get a good education you can get a good job and make good money. Until you graduate, we take care of you, and we will give you anything you need and want as long as your grades are good," both dad my mom agreed. That flew in one ear and right out the other. From that day on my eyes turned into permanent dollar signs looking for ways to make fast money.

"Well I got good grades now, can you guys give a job? Pleaseeee. I won't mess up I promise!"

"You are funny, boy. We will work something out, ok son?" my dad said.

"Yes!"

The next day they called me in their bedroom after breakfast and broke down my new job. They explained the importance of going to school about 87,000 times before going into my new job. After I had weathered that school storm, they explained the only reason they allowed me to see this is because as my father said, nothing lasts forever, and if anything were to happen to them, they wanted to know I could survive in this world on the streets if necessary. But, they kept expressing the importance of education, and that must come first. Taking photos of my mom for her many identification cards was my new job. Simple enough, I would take her picture using a Polaroid camera, wait for the photo to dry then cut the photo out to fit the ID card and then laminate it over the original card and now you have Jennifer Simmons or whatever her new name was for the week. They had many IDs that would correspond with the checks they were using at that time and $30 per picture ID was my fee, and it was good.

In my childish mind, I was rich. All the snacks I could eat on any given day and all the toys I wanted. All the kids on the block wanted to be friends with me because I had the coolest toys. I was the envy of the neighborhood kids. Life was good. Then the unthinkable happened. My father took on a job alone one day and didn't come home that night. My mother sat me down and explained to me what the situation was. When a kid is in a certain fantasyland, it is hard for them to understand reality. That was the case with me for sure. It never dawned on me that they could be taken to jail for going to work. The state took my father away for 11 years of my life, and it tore me up on the inside. That was my best friend. Even after my mom explained the situation with my father to me, I was still in fantasyland. I rounded up all my weapons which consisted of a hockey stick, a plastic sword from my ninja Halloween costume and some rocks and then gathered some money up for bus fare in an attempt to bust my best friend out of that place. After a smack upside the head, followed by a few cuss words from my mother, those dreams quickly faded.

With my dad gone, times got a little hard. Mom rounded all her knowledge up and with a couple friends, started going to work all day, every day and excluded me from ever going again because of the dangers that existed now. Mom had to support the family by herself now. I would usually stay with my mom and dad at their apartment, but she moved me back in at my grandmother's house after dad got booked. The two-bedroom household had six people in it and with me added now, there were seven. With dad gone, she fended pretty well. She made sure grandma never had to worry about bills, and she made sure everyone in the house was taken care of. I can vividly remember this one night where my mom picked me up in a new, deep crimson red convertible I had never seen before. After going for a ride, she pulled out a stupid huge wad of hundred dollar bills.

"Look at all this money I made tonight, baby," she whispered to me.

Jack Williams

"Whoa, Mom! Where did you get all of that?" I asked her.

"I worked really hard today. Two, three, four, five..." she said counting the money out loud. "Take this. Put it in your pocket and don't spend it all at once ok?" She instructed me, giving 3 of the bills. I agreed while sloppily stuffing the money in my front pocket. "Come here baby, give me a hug," she said as she grabbed me.

I wrapped my hands around her tightly as if someone was taking her away. She ran into this apartment and came out with less money than she went in with. Then we made a stop at my grandmother on my father's side, place, and repeated the process. She would give her all to help others. That's just how she was. She was like a female Robin Hood. Mom drove to her mother's house to drop me back off. We hugged again and talked about my future for a little while which consisted of nothing but school. I told her how I wanted to play football or maybe even be a race car driver, but that was countered with school first. The bond between my mother and I was stronger than a lion's bite. Mmy heart was constantly hurt, as well as hers, because we were always apart. She was away at work or in the nightlife. We would only see each other once a week at night, or if we were really lucky, I would get to have her for some weekends. Those weekends were everything to me. I was constantly jealous of other kids in school because they had their complete families in their life. The mom and or the dad would come pick them up and me? I walked a mile and a half home to my grandmother every day, alone or sometimes with a friend or two but never with my parents.

The following weekend after mom picked me up, my mom decided to take a break from work and we took a quick drive to Indiana to buy some fireworks for the summer. They were so cheap, that we bought a trunk full of them and went to the beach for a little picnic and fireworks action. It was just me, her and nature. Some seagulls came around and circled us in. I instantly became frightened and was ready to stomp the first bird that came too close. My mom laughed hysterically at my defense.

"Ha! Baby, don't kick them. You crack me up son, they just want some food. They are just like you and me. They gotta eat, too right?" she said.

"But no, they only eat worms and stuff mom!" I replied confidently. I just knew they were waiting to peck my eyes out.

34

"HA! You silly turkey! Look," she said as she took a slice of bread and crumbled it up and threw the crumbs into the air. The seagulls went crazy! Flying around, making sure they got every last crumb. It was like they called their buddies over for a BBQ, I looked away and when I looked back, the numbers of the seagulls doubled!

"Baby, you give it a try. They won't harm you. You have a good heart," She told me.

"Alright!" I said excited and smiling. I took a slice of bread, broke it into fine little pieces and tossed them into the air using both hands. It was like magic the way they reacted to the bread crumbs. The whole day was magical. I was happy, my mom was happy not to mention the seagulls were happy too. God could have taken me that day, and I would have been ok with that.

"Alright nah baby, the trick is to leave while they are not looking because they'll never stop eating and you can't feed them all. So, come on!" she said. I hurried and gathered my belongings which were just my action figures really, and we headed out. Back to my grandmothers I went.

"See you next weekend love. I miss you already. Love you!" Mom said as I was getting out of the car.

"Can't wait! Love you too Mommy!" I responded while headed to the trunk to get my fireworks. "See ya Saturday!"

Once again...the impossible happened. Saturday came but no mom. I was sad, but I knew she would come on Sunday like she always does just to say hey and get a bite to eat if nothing else. Next thing I know, I'm walking home from school on a Tuesday, still haven't heard from my mother. At this point, I was furious but nervous at the same time.

"Where is my mom at!?" I kept asking myself. When I walked into the house, my grandmother had some lunch waiting on me.

"Baby. When you finish your sandwich and your little cartoons, come to my room okay?" She said.

"Ok, Grandma," The sandwich was consumed, Power Rangers and Dragon Ball Z was over with, and now it was time to meet with my grandma. I wasn't prepared at all. My ears started ringing, tears started flowing, and slob began to form.

"I want my mom! I want my Mom!" I ran and screamed.

"There is nothing I can do baby," my grandma said, as her tears started to flow too.

Mom had suffered the same fate as my father. She got caught just as he did. With no parents, my back was against the wall. With my parents gone we had no money, and my grandma was running short as well trying to feed a household full of people on a limited amount of food stamps. I didn't know what to do at first, and then it hit me. Grandma made me pack up my tub of fireworks and put them in the garage, after hearing they were illegal in Illinois. Grandma didn't always keep her eye on me or the fireworks. The next day after school, after I came home and finished my usual lunch, homework, and cartoons, I grabbed my book bag and slipped out the back door to the garage. I opened the tub of fireworks and stuffed my book bag with as many items as I could. Now I just had to get back in the house and hide them. I put them in the attic until I figured out a way to get outside with free time because grandma wasn't big on letting me go outside and play. They know I'm sad as hell and depressed giving my situation with my parents, so grandma has to tell me yes to anything with reason I thought to myself. I muscled up the confidence to put the act on. I rearranged my face as sad as possible and walked into her room "Grandma...would it be ok if I went outside for a little while. I just want to ride my bike and get some fresh air or something," I said.

"What you know about fresh air boy? Um-,"

"Please!" I interrupted her thought process.

"Alright, two hours and don't be late!" she told me and don't let those street lights catch you outside, I mean it!" Grandma warned me.

"Ok, thanks, love you!" I hurried to the attic and grabbed my book-bag, a few packs of matches, and out the back door, I left to avoid my bulky backpack being sighted.

I hopped on my Huffy bike and hit the next block where I heard most the kids playing at. I took out a pack of Blackcat Firecrackers, struck a match, lit the fuse and threw them in the middle of the street. I knew I had to attract a crowd and this would do the trick. Sure enough, a flock of kids ran over asking me if I had any more firecrackers and if they could have some but this wasn't a charity case, and I didn't have anything for free.

"Hey! You got any more fireworks man?" One kid asked.

"Ooh yeah! we want some! What's in the bag?" The other kids around chimed in.

"Yeah, I do! And I got bottle rockets, firecrackers, jumping jacks and a bunch of other stuff. What you want?"

"Let me have some bottle rockets and a roman candle!" One kid begged while sticking his hand out.

"This stuff isn't free dude, its costs money man. I gotta make money," I told him, looking down while pushing his hand away. I really wanted to just have fun and give it all away for free but I just couldn't.

"Shoot. I only have enough money to get ice cream when the ice cream truck comes around," he responded with a sad face.

"Well, this is way cooler than ice cream. You can get ice cream any day dude," I told him while throwing a loose firecracker in the air. I looked at him after the firecracker exploded with a face that said what are you waiting for.

"Ahhh ok, you're right. What can we get for a dollar?" The kid asked.

"Well, you can get four bottle rockets, four packs of firecrackers or four packs of jumping jacks. Anything else costs more. Roman candles are $1.50, and these rocket shooters are $8 each, and in case you don't know what a rocket shooter is, just buy one. Light it, stand back and enjoy the show. I also have M80s for $3 each, too. If you don't know what a M80 is, listen for a loud noise later tonight. I'm sure you'll buy one tomorrow," I explained to the crowd.

"Uhh ok. Umm let me have four packs of firecrackers," One kid said while flashing a dollar in my face.

"Coming right up!" I responded while digging in my book-bag for the firecrackers.

The kids were monkey see, monkey do. I knew if I could get one buyer, the rest of the kids would fall in place. Right after that kid handed me that dollar and received his product, all the kids placed orders. Firecrackers here, jumping jacks and roman candles there and even managed to sell a rocket shooter to an older kid around 14 years old. I made one final announcement as I zipped my once bulky but now empty book-bag back up and got back on my bike.

"If your parents catch you with these, you don't know me. Don't ruin the fun for everybody," I told the crowd of kids aloud. I managed to sell 43 packs of firecrackers, 47 packs of jumping jacks, 32 bottle rockets, a rocket shooter and 17 roman candles.

I made $64 in one hour and a half and on top of that, I still made it home in time to kiss my grandmother's cheek, which confirmed the fact that I could make it home before the street lights came on. That let my grandmother know she could trust me because, without her trust and permission to come out the house, I couldn't make any money. With my book bag empty, I filled it back up with my books and folders for school and placed it by the front door for the next day. I ran up to my room to recount my earnings again before my older cousins came up for sleep because if they caught me with a dime or anything they wanted for that matter, they'd rough me up and take it.

"Sixty-two, sixty-three, sixty-four!" Counting aloud, my profit for the day, again. I was happy I could make money but disappointed because I knew I could make way more than $64. I figured the next day, I'd widen my horizon and step out of my territory. My bedtime was closing in fast. I had to deliver on my promise. I grabbed a M80 out of my book-bag side pocket and checked for my grandmother's location. She was laying in her bed, so the coast was clear for me. I grabbed some matches and once again slipped out the back door and ran into the middle of the street. I lit the M80 and ran away back towards the house as fast as I could without looking back. As soon as I slipped back in the house, the house shook from a defining explosion sound as if it was the first bomb dropping of a new war.

"What the hell was that!?" My grandma screamed.

"I don't know grandma! Kids probably just let off some fireworks or something," I responded with a smirk on my face.

The next day, I returned home from school to my usual routine. Lunch, homework, cartoons in that order. I figured if I could cut my cartoon time down I could possibly make more money. Then I watched Spiderman web-sling from a building, and those thoughts quickly faded as I pretended to be him for a little while, sliding on the hardwood floor and jumping on the couch. Cartoons went off, and my priorities started to set in. Grandma rewarded me with four hours of freedom this time. I filled my backpack as much as possible, slipped out the back door and jumped on my Huffy for another day of hustling. I hit the same block I hit yesterday first, and it was like the kids were anticipating my arrival. I was the new ice cream man in town. I just didn't have any ice cream music to go with my bike.

Thanks to my M80 stunt, I instantly sold double of what I sold the day before, and kids were telling me other kids on other blocks wanted to buy some too. Before I knew it, I headed back home to re-up. I re-stuffed my backpack as best possible with mostly Roman candles since they were $1.50, everyone was buying them. A few blocks over, I saw all the kids outside playing, and I followed the same routine to get attention. I lit and dropped a pack of firecrackers in the street and watched the kids flock.

"Cool man! You got any more firecrackers?" a kid asked.

"Yeahhh?" all the other kids chimed in.

"As a matter of fact, I do. Actually, I got everything you need. Firecrackers for 25 cents each, candles for a buck-fifty each. M80s for $3 each, too. I also got jumping jacks and bottle rockets for 25 cents each. too," I explained once again.

"What's a M80?" A kid asked.

"Did you hear a loud boom noise last night?"

"That, was you?" They all gasped.

"Yeah. That was me and my M80," I responded.

"Let me have five of those M80s," A kid ordered.

"You got it. 15 bucks man." I sold everything except five packs of jumping jacks which I could probably sell on my way back home. I stopped and put a wad of cash in my sock, all the way at the bottom of my shoe so I walked on it, ensuring its safety and put a smaller wad in my pocket so I could buy a large of amount of junk food from the candy store on my route home because I felt so accomplished.

Riding my bike towards the candy store, I saw two older kids coming my way. The closer they got, I recognized their faces because they went to school with me. They were a lot older, though.

"Aye, shorty! You that kid with them fireworks, right?"

"Yeah," I said. I could feel the negative energy just radiating from them like a heat wave.

"Let me hold something. What you got?" He asked.

"Man, I sold everything. All I got is a few packs of jumping jacks left. I can sell you some other stuff tomorrow, though."

"Naw, let me get those jumping jacks from you," He demanded.

"Ok cool. You know what...they 4 for a dollar but I got 5, so I'll give you an extra pack for the free. It's cool," I explained. I tried to solidify my placement with them by giving a free pack. Maybe they would think I was cool or something, but I forgot there is no church in the wild.

"I'm taking all that for the free little homie. Give it up," He ordered.

I turned to run, leaving my precious bike behind but before I could get my footing right, his partner grabbed me.

"Rob, rough this little nigga up," The partner ordered.

Scared as ever but not defenseless, I knew I couldn't beat these guys up by myself, but I wasn't going to let them just take from me without a fight either. As Rob was approaching me, I wrapped my foot around his partner holding me and pushed backward, tripping us both to the ground. As soon as we hit the ground, I turned over on top of him and started throwing a barrage of punches at his face. Before I could really get loose, Rob tackled me off of him. I curled up like an armadillo as they both proceeded to stomp on me. Flustered and confused after the attack, I got back up to my feet. My vision was a bit blurry, but I could see them walking off. I grabbed my book-bag that was now really empty and picked up my bike. Too sore to ride, I just walked home with the bike by my side. I checked my face in a nearby car mirror to see if I had any cuts or marks. I smiled as I didn't see any which meant my grandma and the family wouldn't find out I just got pounded on like a bass drum. I parked my bike in the backyard and gave myself a final brush off of any dirt left on me and walked in the house.

Upon walking in the house, I smelled my favorite meal in the air. Grandma was cooking her family famous cheeseburgers and fries. I wasn't in the mood to eat at all.

"Hey baby, got your favorite today. Be ready in 10 minutes. Go wash your hands nah," She said.

"Hey grandma, I got a headache. I think I'm going to just lay down for a little while. Can you put me a plate aside please?" I asked of her.

"Sure, thing dear. I also left some mail on your bed."

I was pissed. Those punks messed my favorite dinner up. I stepped into my room and gave my pockets a pat down, and I came to the realization that they were just as empty as my book bag.

"Those punks took my money?!" I angrily asked myself. "I wish I was back there with them now. I'd knock them the hell out!" I told myself while throwing shadow punches.

I didn't even know how much they took. I still could feel a knot in my shoe, so they didn't get the big wad. I took my shoes off, sat on my bed and counted the money I made.

"$203, $204, $205!" I counted. I smiled at the amount I made then frowned because I know at least 50 to 100 more dollars were stolen from me. I punched the bed as my breathing elevated.

"They better pray I don't see them at school tomorrow," I told myself. I grabbed the mail on the bed and laid down to rest my angry volcanic mind. I quickly sat back up as I looked at the mail in my hand. It was mail from my mom and one from dad.

Dad's Letter,
US Prison Bureau
71 W. Van Buren St.
Chicago, IL 60605

What's up daddy little man! I hope all is ok. I know this is a lot for you but trust me when I say I'm sorry this has happened. I did what I had to do in order to provide for you and your mother. I'll be here for a while man, so you're going to be the man around the house for me. I know you can do that. I need you to stay focused and dedicated to your goals and your schoolwork. I need you to be strong, son. Don't take no bull from anyone. It's a cruel world out there...but I know you'll be fine. You are my son. I love you.

PS: Write back. See you before you know it.

Mom's Letter,
Genesee County Jail
1002 South Saginaw
Flint, MI 48502

Baby, I am so sorry. I never meant for anything like this to happen to us. I know you know I love you unconditionally and I'll never forgive myself for this. But I need you to forgive me. We only wanted to provide for you and the family you know...I'll never leave you again. I promise you that. I miss you so much. Please write me back baby. Know that you are a strong young Black Man and that you will go far in life if you keep the faith in God and yourself. Let nobody stop you from going after your dreams because they are yours and yours alone. It's up to you to follow them and move the obstacles out of your way to reach them, and there will be many. Remember, school is your priority, and that is what you are to focus on, that and nothing else. Get and keep your grades up, and I mean this! Do not get behind in your grades because it will be even harder to catch up. You are smart, and you can do this. Keep reaching for the Sun, son, and you will land among the Stars where you do belong. I need you to know and trust and believe that your dad and I love you with all our hearts and souls and without you, I am nothing! This will be over before you know it...and I will be home to be with you. So be good and take care of yourself and Grandma.

Love you dearly,

- Mom

I folded the now wet letters back in their envelope, turned over and cried myself to sleep. The next day at school was just like any other day. Only change was my ability to focus. I didn't even talk much. I couldn't think about anything but revenge. The only thing I could see was Rob and a shadow next to him in my mind because I didn't know his partner's name. Before I knew it, the last bell of class was ringing. I grabbed my book-bag and left. No homework, no books, no nothing.

Walking towards the main intersection, my eyes lit up like a solar flare. I saw Rob and his little friend across the intersection. I sped my walk up to catch up to the next wave of people to cross the intersection. Crossing the intersection and closing in on my prey like a beast, my adrenaline was pumping like someone had just given me a shot of epinephrine to the heart. I know the day before, I said if they were in front of me I would knock them the hell out, but I started to second guess my actions. About 15 yards in front of me, I could hear them talking. They shook hands and split directions.

"Alright Rick, see you tomorrow G!" Rob shouted.

"Rick, huh?" I whispered to myself.

I shook off the thoughts and continued to follow Rob. He stalled for a second removing something from his back pocket. I kneeled down and pretended to tie my shoe so he wouldn't make me out. He continued to walk forward. As I got up, I grabbed a piece of broken concrete from the ground and continued to follow him. I picked my pace up to close in on him. His head was down at whatever he removed from his back pocket. It was the new Game Boy Color. I could only think that he spent the money he stole from me to buy it.

That's my Gameboy now nigga. My angry thoughts said. He stalled again while in front of me, about five yards now and I proceeded to strike like a cobra. I clinched the small block of concrete about the size of my hand as tight as I could and then struck him in the back of his head. He fell to the ground instantly. I didn't mean to keep striking him, I swear but when I regained consciousness people were screaming and pointing in my direction.

I grabbed the Gameboy he dropped and ran as fast as I could. I didn't stop until I got home. Out of breath, I ran up to my room and just laid on my bed.

"You didn't do anything wrong man," I told myself. "He robbed you, you only paid him back," I tried justifying it all while gasping for air. I finally calmed down after a plethora of breaths and went to my grandma room.

"Hey, Grandma! What's up?" I asked.

"Oh, nothing baby, just playing a little solitaire," she said while turning over a few cards. "Hey, we short on money this month baby, so the food may be a little tight ok. It's gonna get greater later, though. I know God will deliver," Grandma explained.

"Yeah. He will. I got a surprise for you. It's not much, but it can maybe get us through the month. Don't worry, my dad put away a little money for me. You can have it, though. We need food. Plus, your cooking is the best!" I said, while handing her $250 in cash.

Shocked, she instantly teared up. "You are a wonderful grandson baby. Heaven sent," She said.

"You are a wonderful grandma, grandma!" I said while smiling.

I was smiling but couldn't help but feel a bit hell sent. My grandma tells me how good I am and I just beat a kid to a pulp, and I just lied to her about where the money came from. I just had to escape what I did to that Rob boy. I just wanted to be a kid again. Free again. The truth couldn't do it for me, so I had to tell a lie to set myself free. I even lied to myself as I told myself I wanted to be away from this evil feeling. I told myself that the day I see Rick, he was my next victim. There would be consequences for anyone that wronged me.

Back on Home Turf

Driving like a bat out of hell, I pulled up at Vince's house at 8:30am sharp and I just knew he was going to still be sleep or something wild like that, but he was actually, sitting on his porch eating a sandwich.

"Uh Oh. You sick or something? Where is Vince and what did you do to him?" I said jokingly.

"Ha! Real funny Richard Pryor! I'm just motivated man,"

"I see! Good to know. With both of us motivated, we can't be stopped, baby!" I said.

"True that! So, where we headed?" Vince asked.

"Let's see," I said while checking my email via my phone for the address Viktor was providing. The warehouse was at 3310 W. Columbo Ave. Viktor said they were expecting us and to give the package to a guy named Duwane.

The drive was a 25-minutes, but I got us there in 17 minutes which was good because we had time to compose ourselves and get our game faces and game voices together. Although we were expected, I still parked about a half block away, so we didn't seem frantic or suspicious.

"Three, three, one...zero," I said to myself confirming the address. Vince and I crossed the street headed towards the building. It was in a deserted looking area. One of those areas that looks like everything is out of business but it's anything but that.

"Who's this fat dude they got guarding the door, man? What's he gonna do? I'll smack him and run," Our faces swell up like blowfishes as we attempted to hold our laughter in.

"Alright, chill, chill. We are here, game faces on, baby," I said, putting us back into business mode.

Although we clowned about his size, this Russian guy guarding the door was massive in size. I was guessing 350 pounds 6 feet 6 inches tall but just plain scary. But despite what we were feeling, Vince and I did not have time to show any fear.

"Alright, let me do the talking, bro," I told Vince.

"What's up, how you doing? My name is-"

"What the hell do you kids want? I'm not buying any Girl Scout Cookies so you both-"

"Girl Scout Cookies, huh? Listen to me, you big asshole, if you don't want this package from Viktor, I'll be more than happy to let him know his caveman, henchman or whatever you are at the door, wouldn't let us in. He doesn't look like the type of guy you'd want to piss off so I suggest you get Duwane and tell him the package is here. Understand me?" I ordered while staring him down. The silence was long, but he came to his senses.

"Duwane...the package is here. Come quick before I lose my patience," He responded.

"You're crazy man. Crazy," Vince said.

"Yeah maybe so. But you have to take charge sometimes. We on a mission and we're the head of this operation right now, and it will go unnoticed if disrespected."

"Yeah, yeah, you're right," Vince agreed.

The big guy lets us in the garage shortly after radioing Duwane. The garage was pretty big. I thought it would be a basic auto garage size, but it was more of a huge warehouse, which made sense considering they were using it as a front for a transportation company.

"What's up? Viktor sent you guys? Got the package?" Duwane asked.

"You Duwane? Let me see some ID man," I ordered.

"ID? Who do you think you are?"

"I'm the guy holding the package we all need, to make this deal happen. I'm the guy with his life on the line if this package doesn't get to where it needs to be. Now please, show me confirmation of you being Duwane," I demanded.

"I can respect that. See. Duwane. Now package, please," He said, showing his credentials. "And just call me D," He asked.

Emailing Viktor that the package has been delivered, I reached down in my book bag, unzipping the inside pocket where the package was. Before finally handing it over, I took a still picture with my phone for proof.

"I like this kid...come meet the rest of us."

Vince and I walked in, both of our heads spinning around as if we were possessed by evil spirits as we looked around the warehouse, analyzing everything. After meeting everyone, we got an understanding of what everyone's roles were, and expectations of everyone were laid out. The big guy at the door was just that, the big guy at the door. There for intimidation, fear, irritation even. D was Viktor's dog. Anything Viktor needs, D will do. D was also the finance guy and overseer of the operation to make sure everyone was doing their job and ensuring the money flowed in the right directions. We had Moe who seemed to be posing as a displaced Muslim who was mad at the world for whatever reason. He was a short and stocky man and looked like he was in need of a shave and a haircut. Moe was fronting as the business manager running a transportation Company. He actually ordered a crazy number of T-shirts at wholesale prices to mask the whole operation just in case we ran into the police or other legal issues. He even had a couple of printing presses in the warehouse to make the business look legit, and it did cover-up our other business pretty well.

Next, we met Big G and Guido. They were brothers but extremely opposite in personality and appearances. Big G was seemingly a gentleman. Tall, with reddish hair and a long, pointed nose that made him look quite comical. He was the quiet one of the two...but quick tempered when things didn't go right. Guido was the younger of the two. He was shorter, and his nose was flat like he had been in a major fight somewhere in life and got his nose smashed. I refused to believe he was born like that. He was the more even tempered of the two. He never got upset or excited about anything. You could sense the un-inviting aura around him which sucked because the two of them would be working with Vince and I on this job. They were the extra drivers.

Lastly, you had the beautiful Jean. Jean was Duwane's wife and his assistant. She was smart, brilliant actually, and the biggest distraction of all because she was drop dead gorgeous. She had these sexy lips with the same pink shade of lipstick that her dress was. When she smiled she lit up the entire room. She was about 5 feet 7 inches tall and weighed about 140 pounds. Jean had that hourglass shape that most women wanted and it was covered by an orange dress that was just the right length so as not to be obscene. It fitted her to a tee. Any man watching her walk by would have to do a double take.

"D," she called out to him in such a sweet and soft voice that it made you almost strain to hear her, but you could hear her. "Can I have that package? We got bills to pay baby, and I mean today!"

"Ok, I hear you," D replied, "I got you."

There it was. The team. Together we were going to pull this off without a hitch, and all of us were going to make an insane amount of money in the process. I smiled to myself, almost laughed out loud. My phone buzzed, and I looked down to see it was Viktor.

> *Well done. You two are done for the day so prepare for tomorrow. Take as many pictures as you can of the vehicles. Tomorrow night, we will chat and discuss the plan you have developed and go over it with the rest of the team.*

I showed Vince, and he nodded.

"Hey D, it was good meeting you guys. We're done here for the day. Viktor says we will all chat tomorrow to go over everything,"

"Cool, talk to you guys tomorrow," he said while reaching out to shake our hands.

"See ya big guy!" Vince said walking out the door, poking fun at the big Russian guard.

"You better not make Hulk angry bro!" I said laughing.

"Listen bro, I got to come up with a way to get these key-plugs for the cars so everything can go as smoothly as possible because, if I go down, we all go down. I need your help, though. I need you to be our tourist guide. In other words, our navigator. I need you to map out the best inconspicuous route possible. I can't stress it enough, that we cannot be caught,"

"No worries, I got you. I got us. I'm going to get all the information tonight and map everything out. I will map it out 100 ways before I even show you. Then we can test out the best route before making the final move. Cool?"

"That's why you are my brother!" I responded.

I dropped Vince off at home and headed to the gym to clear my mind and take everything in. After the gym, I got something to eat and paid a visit to my girlfriend who I'm sure was going to kill me since I've been gone almost all day and I'm just now seeing her.

"Oh my God. Where have you been all day?" She asked.

I said the first thing to come to my mind without thinking.

"I have been working! I got a new job today!"

"It is Sunday!" She yelled.

"I know! It's a private corporation baby! I met this German guy at work who wants me to work in his building and be his assistant. A lot more money, he's a millionaire!" I told her, but I wasn't totally lying. If she only knew what kind of weekend I just had.

"Whatever!"

"Give me some love woman, I've missed you!" After spending the night with Toya, the next morning, I headed home and went back to bed. I had an important day tomorrow, and I needed every bit of rest.

Monday finally arrived. I woke up an hour early to prepare myself mentally for what would be the start of the hardest, yet easiest, most risky illegal task I've ever attempted to accomplish. I'd acted out exactly what I was going to say with my movements to make sure everything could go smoothly on my part. It has to go smoothly. This whole operation is in my hands now.

"ONE, TWO, THREE, FOUR, FIVE," I yelled my pushups count aloud to calm my mind, as I prepared to act out my actions. I might have yelled too loud because now I had some minor explaining to do.

"BOY! What the hell are you doing in there? I'm trying to sleep!" My mom yelled outside my door. "Get ready for work and get out!"

"Jeez, mom! I'm doing some pushups, trying to pack on some muscle to protect you," I responded with a smirk.

"Yeah, yeah, whatever, take your muscles on somewhere else!"

"Okayyy!" I was leaving but not before I got my practice rounds of acting in.

I just had to keep it down while the dragon was sleeping. Whispering to myself,

"Hey Martin, you got that bucket of key-plugs? I need to gas some cars and reorganize the lot,"

"Sure kid. Make sure they are spotless too," I imagined him saying. I acted as if I took one plug, but I stuffed five or seven in my pocket.

"Shit!" I said as I looked at my clock, 8:40? "Where the hell does time be going?" I uttered. I had twenty minutes to get to work.

"Bye, mom!" I yelled running out my room. I grabbed my work shirt, lunch, keys and headed for the car. "9:05...not too bad I guess," I said to myself. I snuck in through the back so the bosses upfront wouldn't see that I was running late.

"What's up, Carlos, Art, Lee," I greeted my co-workers while walking to my porter station.

"That blue Chevy needs to be gassed and detailed if you want to knock that out," Lee told me. "Quick, look busy. Here comes one of the GMs," He whispered.

"You people kill me!" Mike said.

"You people?" I asked abruptly.

"Yes. You people! Black people. Always late. Always up to no good. Always something. I cannot stand you all. That's why you stay in the back. Like dogs. Black dogs. Ha-ha."

I was stunned into disbelief from what I was hearing at the moment. I knew he had a distaste for African-Americans but not to this degree and never had he verbalized it so maliciously. I balled my fist, and I felt the anger starting to rise inside me like smoke coming from a chimney, and I clenched my fists tighter.

"You know what?" I said while approaching him. "Your day is coming." I then cracked a smile and walked back to my station. I wanted to hit him in his face harder than that arcade game with the little groundhogs that pops in and out. I turned and looked at my coworkers who were just too sorry and scared to say anything.

"One day you guys will stand up for yourselves," I said and headed to the main car lot.

Pacing up and down the lots, still pissed at what Mike had said, I found the car that needed to be gassed up. A beautiful baby blue, 1973 Chevy Chevelle. I smiled and said, "Well hello there my love," as I walked up to her. I thought about the best way to get even with Mike was to hit him where it counted the most, in his pockets. I knew that our plan was going be my ace in the hole that would do this very thing. Mike

49

would be close to broke when all of these cars come up missing. The embarrassment alone would be worth its weight in gold. My smile broke into laughter like I had heard the funniest joke, but the joke would be on Mike, the bastard! I went to the main plug board to retrieve the keys only to be stopped by this fool, Mike again!

"Hey. What are you doing, black dog?" He had a smirk on his face.

"Nothing much. Just my job Mike," I answered like a good employee.

"Good dog," he said handing me the slip for the gas station and walking away.

"Oh yeah, you keep thinking good black dog, I got your black dog alright. I will have the last laugh!" I thought to myself while I heading to the car.

"HEY!" Somebody shouted. Startled, I checked my surroundings abruptly. "What are you doing, man?" It was Carlos, one of the porters from the back.

"Man, what's wrong with you? You scared the Jesus out of me! Yelling and whatnot," I said.

"Sorry man, I saw you leaving. Take me with you? I'm starving! I wanna get something from the gas station," he asked.

"Man, hell no. If one of those managers sees us together, you know they are going to assume we are joy riding, and fire both of us!" I told him.

"Don't trip, if they say anything I'll get us out of trouble."

I sighed heavily. "Alright man, come on." We got to the gas station, and everything went smoothly until Carlos got a text from one of the managers.

"Oh hell. They are looking for us man," Carlos said.

"Oooh shit, see man, I told you!" I said irritated. "You gonna pay my bills?" I asked.

"I got an idea. Don't trip. The only manager that is looking is Mike. Mike is a fatty patty. You ever seen him eat before? Food is his crutch, his addiction. Watch this." He ran back into the gas station and came out with donuts.

"Donuts? He's not the cops!" I said.

"Trust me, bro," He responded. "Thanks to my sweet talking, the cashier didn't charge me anything. Life just isn't fair," Carlos said laughing.

"Whatever pretty boy. Let's go!" I responded.

We headed back. Carlos said to trust him, but I refused to. On the way back, I took the back route, just in case I got fired. I can see the back lot of cars even if it's just a glimpse, I can still get an idea of what's on the lot. Good thing too because what I saw was an issue. The reserve lot was full of surveillance cameras. I slowed the car down to the side of the road.

Everything is messed up now I thought to myself. I was on my way to entering a long tunnel of depression like I lost my dog. I couldn't believe my eyes.

"What you doing man? You want us to get fired or nah?" Carlos said.

"My bad," I just never noticed this lot before. Why they got so many cameras, though?" I asked.

"Ha! Those cameras don't work! They just there to scare people. Some little punks stole some parts a couple of years ago from one of the cars, and they put those cameras up for fear tactics. The cheap bastards. They make crazy cash and won't even buy a real security system," Carlos explained.

"Yeah man. They are stupid!" I laughed and stepped on the gas for the whole stretch down the block to the dealership. What Carlos just explained was music to my ears. I just found my lost dog, and my happiness returned just like that.

"Alright, there is Mike. Let me do the talking. You just cosign alright," Carlos said.

"What choice do I have? Do your thang," I responded.

"Hey stop!" Mike demanded. "What the hell you two idiots doing?"

"Mike my main man, I tagged along to gas a car simply because my wallet fell out my pocket the last time I went up there to gas a car…and guess what? It was right there at pump four where it happened. I know the rules, but you have to understand that my life is in my wallet. My cards, my social security card, my ID. I don't need to go into identity theft statistics, do I?" Carlos explained.

Jack Williams

"I don't give a rat's ass! I need you both in my office for write-ups."

"Wait man, wait! You didn't let me finish. Be fair man," Carlos said. "The best part is that I was so happy to have found my wallet, you crossed my mind. I'm allergic to chocolate but not you. I got a half dozen of those double chocolate donuts you adore so much. I thought we were doing good by you, but now you want to write us up. That hurts us, bro."

"Yeah, Mike. I even suggested the half dozen," I chimed in. "But I guess if you must write us up…"

"Just give me the stupid donuts and get back to work!" Mike snapped back.

I sped off to the back of the lot. "Ha, you're crazy man!"

"I knew it would work. His fat-ass couldn't resist. I bet he's sitting in his truck right now demolishing those poor donuts." We laughed as we headed to our different work bays.

Now that I still had a job, I had to figure out to get more key-plugs. Key-plugs were these little-colored key shaped tools that were used to unlock car keys at the keyboard. They actually looked like safe keys. The issue at hand was I had to get at least five of them. Now when I first got hired they gave me three red ones with my name on the tag. That way, if anyone has a car out, they know who has it. I needed to find five unmarked key-plugs. I could steal my co-worker's plugs, but I don't want them to catch trouble for this job. I don't really care if they do or don't but I've never been that kind of a person. There has to be another way. I went to my only hideout which was the dealership bathroom to think of a plan. It took me about 15 minutes, but my eyes lit up like the Massachusetts Christmas tree when I figured it out. The body shop keeps a bucket of plugs that are unmarked and different colors too. The dealership had their own in-house body shop, and they used key plugs to signify they were working on a car. This was great because I no longer had to try and steal plugs out of the manager's office and risk the whole operation. I hurried and headed to the body shop. Now how will I get Francisco out of the shop? I only need five minutes. I did the first thing that came to mind.

"Yo! Francisco! Carlos needs your help with something in the wash bay."

"OK coming!"

"When you gon fix up my Camaro man?"

"Ha! Never kid. That thing needs Jesus!"

"Ha. Got jokes I see," I said while laughing. As soon as he left to go see Carlos, I slid right in the shop and walked over to the plugs. They were in a Halloween pumpkin bucket.

Weird, I thought. I grabbed a handful of plugs and stuffed them into my baggy pants. I proceeded to walk out, as soon as I turned the corner from the entrance I bumped right into Francisco.

"What the hell are you doing man? And Carlos said he never said he needed me. You going loco essy?" He said in his Spanish accent.

I was instantly flustered and lost for words. My mind went on auto-pilot.

"Uhhh Carlos tripping. I could have sworn he asked for you. You know you can't really hear with those mechanics using those loud tools and stuff. Sorry about that." Lucky for me, he just shook his head and proceeded back to work. I had roughly two hours left before my shift ended and I had to hit the reserve lot for pictures. Instead of taking a car to gas and cruise the reserve lot, I walked down to the lot since it was just a five-minute walk. I doubted the managers would write me a gas ticket anyway because of my donut incident. I got to the lot, and I took detailed pictures of the lot and every car. Sides, fronts, back, and the VIN numbers.

My phone vibrated; it's a text from Vince confirming he has the perfect escape route.

Awesome, I just finished with the photos myself. Meet me at the coffee shop by my place in about an hour in a half so we can go over everything before our conference.

I responded. I headed back to the main lot to hang out until my last few minutes were up before clocking out for the day. I gave my gas pedal a few pumps, started her up and shot over to the coffee shop to meet with Vince before doing the video conference with Viktor and the rest of the crew.

"What up baby?!" I said, reaching out for a handshake.

"Everything is love, let's exchange that info, but let's go outside. Too many people in here you know," Vince responded. "Alright look at this," He said pulling out some papers.

Vince had a great plan of gathering the cars and hitting the back roads all the way to the shop. I originally objected because there was a police station about a mile away from the dealership and a block away from those back roads we would be taking. His pitch was it would be best to blend in. It made sense. I guess they wouldn't suspect anything like this if we happen to run into any cops. It's not like they were alerted or something and would more than likely view us as nothing more than a mere car club. The thrill was becoming real. I couldn't wait to have the conference with Viktor and his crew to actually do this, now that it was becoming more realistic by the day. I wasn't even thinking about the money. My mind and body were solely running on pure adrenaline at this point as if I were being forced to enter a cage to battle a lion. I was shaking and trembling at the very thought of pulling this off.

"I can't believe we were about to do this man," I repeated over and over to Vince.

"I know man. I can't wait to get paid. I can't wait to fly," Vince responded. "Let's go. Let's get this conference thing done,"

I emailed the pictures of the lots and cars to Viktor and informed him we are on our way to his warehouse to meet. We pulled up the warehouse around 9:30 at night. The block was quiet as a Buddhist temple and dark as a cave. There were only a few street lights that were working, and the warehouse had its lights off. BOOM, BOOM! Vince knocked on the door. One of the lights turned on, and the big bodyguard let us in.

"Hello, children," He said.

"Don't start King Kong," I replied back rather smartly. "Where's D and the rest of the guys?" I asked.

"Upstairs. D, your guys are coming up," He said through his earpiece. We went upstairs, and Jean let us in.

"What's up everyone," Vince and I said.

"Just waiting on that call from the boss man," D said. He started hooking his laptop up to a projector. Five minutes went past, then a ringtone and video chat icon popped up on the projector screen that read Viktor. D pressed the answer button with two rings in, and Viktor's face popped up.

"Ah! Nice to see that everyone is here. I will be in town next week, so we can get this thing moving. I have uploaded the list of the cars that was sent to me earlier so you can see for yourselves. In a week's time, everything will be finalized from our buyers for the shipment as well as the containers to ship the vehicles off. It should take a full two to three weeks for each buyer to receive their shipment in which they will pay half up front and half when they receive the shipment. Now, as for the cars, we need keys for all the cars since we do not know what we will be taking orders for just yet-"

"How am I supposed to do that?" I butted in.

"My little mastermind, I was doing some thinking and do you know what the best part about these cars is? I'll tell you, the keys don't take computer chips so essentially this plays in our favor because now you can get those keys and make copies of them and return them along with the key plugs. That way, you were never there! Catch my drift? I need you to do that tomorrow. Brilliant idea I know, thank me later," Viktor said chuckling. "D. You're in charge of getting the VIN together. I don't care if you have to go one state over to a specific junkyard to get a car, those VINs are a must, and they must each match the vehicles. So, you, Big G and Guido split up. You'll have that VIN list shortly. Moe, I need you to get the tools together, so we get those paint jobs done quickly. The dealerships are closed on Sundays. so, Sunday we will strike. Jean, get our two newbies their trust fund account, so everything runs smoothly. And no worries, I will be in later this week to set everything up else for Sunday. Tschuss," Viktor said before the screen went black.

Jean pulled out a notebook for Vince and me and started explaining the whole trust fund account and how we get paid. It was simple enough. I would be provided a fake ID, and the trust would be set up in the fake name of Temar Jordan with the Trust of Florida Bank & Holdings. Viktor had someone on his payroll to handle the wire transfers that would come in. He would disguise the wire transfers as online gambling winnings so officials wouldn't raise their eyebrows too much. Once the money comes in, I show my paperwork, fill out a withdrawal slip and walk out with my briefcase.

"So how do we know we will get paid? What's to stop Viktor from screwing us over once he gets paid from the transaction?" I asked.

"You'll have to walk by faith. He is a man of his word," Jean said.

I sighed heavy. I've been let down after being promised the world before so it weighed heavy on my mind. It was risky to walk on blind trust.

"Well, it's not like we have any other choice at this point, right?" Vince asked.

"That is true. So, going forward, take this. In the folder ia the account information and the fake identification. That is pretty much it. Do you two understand?"

"I think we got it," I told Jean, looking at Vince for confirmation.

"Good. Now, all we have to do is wait. We will be in touch," Jean said.

"Now that the meeting is over. I have to find a way to get all those keys and make copies and return them."

"Got anything in mind?" Vince asked.

"Actually, I do, but I need your help."

I could get the key plugs that's a no brainer, but I knew I wouldn't be able to make copies of all the keys at once and return them in a timely manner without being questioned or interrogated to death. I needed Vince to cause a scene and disrupt their time management. We both had disguises ready. Mine for the key store, his for the academy award winning scene to be caused.

Back at the car lot, Vince sent me a text, while I hid out in the bathroom closest to the showroom floor,

Ready when you are.

My pockets were stuffed with key-plugs, and my heart rate was elevated, palms sweating and stomach feeling sick. This was the moment.

Action!

I replied back to my best friend. Vince came inside the showroom looking pretty dapper which caught my eye and stalled me a second. He was usually raggedy but he had on a maroon button up, nice jeans and dress shoes.

"Where all the fricken cars at?! I got big money! I am ready to spend some! Where the damn managers at? Where the head honchos?!" Vince roared.

I saw all the managers look up and head out of their offices to the showroom floor to see what all this commotion was about. I shifted right past them like the character in Galactica, heading to the key plug board. I was moving faster than the speed of sound, plugging the key plugs into the corresponding key number, releasing the keys of choice. Nin, ten, eleven, I quickly counted the number of keys. I gave Vince a quick head nod as I headed out the side door to my car. Keep them busy.

`Talk numbers for as long as you can.`

"Hey! Where are you going?!" I heard from behind me. I quickly threw the keys on the floor before looking in the mirror. It was Carlos. I hurried and started my car like a masked serial killer was chasing me.

"Going on break! Got to go!" I yelled out the window, leaving Carlos in the dust.

I pulled up to the key store and checked my surroundings before putting on my costume. I had a Chicago Bulls cap, reading glasses, some dirt I rubbed on my face and hands and came up with a horrible Jamaican accent.

"Aye man. I need some help here. I'm working on some cars for the dealership by contract, and they sent me here to make some copies of some keys. Can you do for me miste, ehhh?" I was going for a Jamaican accent but probably sounded British.

"Whiteside, Mister Whiteside. Sure, how many keys you got there?" Mr. Whiteside asked.

"Uhhh about uhhh let's see here. Eight, ten, eleven. I got eleven keys for you."

"Ok. That will be $27.34. Cash or card?"

"Uhhh, let's do cash. Cash is good, right?" I said flashing two twenties.

"Ok, keys please. It'll be about ten minutes," The old man said.

"Sure. Sure. Hurry if you can. I got to get back to those cars you dig," I explained while looking at my watch.

Twenty-five minutes had gone past, and I was finally on my way back to the dealership. I drove past the front to see the scene. Vince was still in there, and there was a crowd surrounding him. I couldn't wait to see what he had come up with. I parked my car in the back and removed my costume as well as my accent. I grabbed my book-bag from the backseat and stuffed the spare keys in the bottom then folded the book bag and placed it under my driver's seat. With my pockets stuffed with keys, I headed back to the showroom floor. To my surprise and I literally mean surprise, Vince started a dance battle with everyone. "Beat me in a dance-off, and I will buy a car!" I heard him saying. I hurried and returned the keys to the board and retrieved the key plugs. I gave Vince another head nod and a concealed thumb up to let him know the job is done. I had one more thing to do before I could give my nerves a rest.

"Yo Francisco?" I said walking into his garage. "Man, this crazy dude got everyone in a dance battle on the showroom floor! You have to see it, man! If you can beat him, he will buy you a car!" I persuaded him.

"What! Right now? I can take him!" Francisco said while rushing to the front.

I slithered my way to the bucket of key plugs as soon as he ran to the front and deposited the key plugs right back where I found them. I texted Vince.

Mission accomplished. Academy award.

I headed to my bay to clean up some cars as I saw Francisco walking my way.

"They said I just missed him, bro. But he was full of BS anyway the managers were saying. He was just some silly character," Francisco said.

"Damn. That sucks. I hate when those clowns come in," I responded. My shift had ended, and I couldn't wait to go home to get some sleep. This week was going to be a non-stop ride. I sent a text to Viktor on the walk to my car to let him know it was done.

Wednesday

Wednesday was my day off, so it was perfect for me to visit the yard to see what was going on and how things were shaping up for Sunday. When I got to the door, I was surprised to see Viktor open the door.

"Oh Viktor, didn't expect to see you so early," I said.

"Yes, I caught an earlier flight, so I'm here now," He responded.

"Cool, gave the big guy the day off, huh?" I asked.

"Money never takes a day off so no. He is in the back where we are going, actually. Follow me," He said.

"Alright. How was the flight?" I asked.

"Not bad. I had a small layover in Greece to fuel the jet but nothing out of the ordinary. I can't complain about flying private you know?" He answered with a smirk on his face. "Paul! How is the construction coming along?" He stretched his left arm out under his black suit jacket to look at his watch.

"Good sir," An echoed responded.

Viktor had three trailers in the back ready to host the cars and ship out. Paul, or Kong as Vince and I called him, was constructing the ramps and dividers to get the cars inside the trailers. Viktor handed a small laptop with a list of the cars with the color wanted and prices next to them. I couldn't believe my eyes. I was looking at over $1,000,000 in total.

"Dude," I uttered.

The list reads

```
11. 1971 Plymouth Cuda - Purple - $102,000
10. 1970 Buick GSX - White - $83,000
9. 1968 Pontiac Firebird Coupe - Black - $50,000
8. 1969 Dodge Charger - Black - $72,000
7. 1970 Boss 302 Mustang - Dark Green - $85,000
6. 1965 Pontiac GTO - Gray - $67,000
5. 1970 Plymouth Cuda - Lime Green - $95,000
4. 1970 Chevy Nova - Green - $62,000
```

```
3. 1969 Z28 Chevy Camaro - Red - $85,000
2. 1966 Shelby Cobra 427 - Black - $271,000
1. 1966 Lincoln Continental - Black - $47,000
```

"Dude? That's at least $350,000 for you, and that's all you have to say?" Viktor asked.

"I don't know what to say right now. I just can't wait to get this done."

"Agreed. Now you see why I needed all of the keys, and yes, I know we only have six drivers and eleven cars. We will have to make two trips. It's the only way. It's all the difference between getting paid and just making a little money," Viktor explained.

"Understood. So, what is the plan on making two trips?" I asked.

"Really simple actually, Jean will transport you guys there, you bring back six cars, and she will transport five of you back there again to get the remaining five. Easy."

I responded with a nod.

"Inform your partner Vince, so he understands everything. We will meet again this Sunday before executing everything."

Sunday

Tonight, was the night. We all met at the warehouse for one last powwow before heading out.

"Everyone know their positions, right?" Viktor asked.

"Yep," Everyone responded.

Viktor started going over our route again, and for the life of me I couldn't figure out this uncomfortable feeling. Then it hit me like a ton of bricks.

"Wait!" I shouted. All eyes were on me. "Plates. We need plates! This route might not work. Our plan was to blend in, but we can't do that without plates. I can't take the plates. Plus, they don't have that many. One look at us without plates and we will be stopped. It's happened to me numerous times just going to gas cars. We're going to have to go to plan B."

"What's plan B?" Everyone asked. I literally made plan B as I was speaking.

"The expressway. It's still risky but less risky if you ask me. It's about 10 miles between the dealer and us and pretty much a straight shot off exit 57."

"Yeah but what about gas?" Vince shot.

"That's a chance we have to take. Cars get better mileage on the expressway anyway. Everyone, just follow me. It's all we got at this point," I explained.

"The kid is right," D said.

"Alright. This what we will do then. I'll be here waiting. Remember two quick beeps when you're outside. This shouldn't take more than 45 minutes. When you get here, we have to strip the VINs and sand the paint off very quickly and repaint them. No sleep tonight guys so grab a red bull or some cocaine or something. Everybody grab a two-way. Our communication channel is 4. Let's go," Viktor said.

"Everybody grab a key," I said putting all the keys on the table.

"Mustang baby!" Vince said excitingly.

"You going to be ok driving something with that kind of power?" I asked Vince while heading downstairs.

"I'm a fast learner. We good."

Jean was waiting outside with a smoky gray minivan. We all piled in like kids in route to a soccer game. She put on Steely Dan's "Do It Again," and it felt like we were on our way to Vietnam to do the nation's dirty work. We pulled up about 1/4th of a mile away from the dealership on this long stretch road.

"Look, the back lot is right down there," I said pointing in that direction. "Wait here. I'm going to take a look at the mechanic's bay to see if anyone is there. Sometimes they get cars from the back lot to tune up over the weekend," I explained. I snuck up just enough to see through the window. No mechanics were around. No Randy, Lee, Butch, or Martin.

"Green light baby," I whispered to myself. "Proceed to the lot, I'll catch up," I told the team over the 2-way. We all reached the lot, and it looked like pirate treasure as we all marveled at the collection of automobiles.

"We are live on channel 4," We heard Viktor's voice come in.

"Roger. We are about to perform now," D responded.

"Okay. Remember the plan everyone. We are taking the e-way and stay close. For whatever reason, if anyone gets separated, remember our exit is 159th EAST! Not west. Right off the exit, turn right, and that takes you right to the finish line. Any questions?" I asked.

"No. Nope. We're good," Everyone responded.

We all entered our assigned cars. Our engines started one right after another. It was a beautiful melody. One of the best I've ever heard. The sound of the chain gurgling noise mixed with the smell of sweet gasoline was an instant pleasure. The rumble that goes through your body while you're behind the wheel is indescribable. You could feel its power just waiting to be released, like a tamed beast waiting for the command to attack. The slightest touch of the pedal could do things like making a baby if given the chance with a woman because she would be so turned on by the power of the engine.

"Sweet Chevy Nova. Gentlemen, let's get this money," I whispered.

Everything went as planned and as smooth as possible. We all shared the experience of pure thrill and adrenaline fueled by automotive joy, especially on the expressway. The tap of the pedal just threw you in the back of the car with its power. We didn't get too crazy though because we couldn't risk it. We stayed true to the 60MPH speed limit. Everything ran smoothly, pulling car after car in. Jean piled us in the van once more to retrieve the final five vehicles. Moe stayed behind to start work on the captured beasts.

"The Cobra, Camaro, two Cudas, and the GSX," I said aloud, reading the final list of cars. "D…you take the Cobra. Vince, you man the Camaro, Big G and Guido, take the Cudas, and I'll man the GSX," I ordered.

"Sounds like a plan," D said.

"The Cobra is the most expensive vehicle we have. D, be gentle," I reminded him.

"Ha. No worries kid."

"Alright. It's time. Let's bring them home," Vince said.

It was déjà vu as we all entered our designated machines and sat there with the beautiful melody of the muscle once again pleasured us. Everything was smooth until Murphy's Law ran its course. Right off the exit, I started to feel the steering wheel uneasy and unstable and then a rapid rumble from the bottom of the car.

"I'll be damned," I said to myself.

"You are running a flat kid," I heard D's voice come in on the two-way.

"Yeah. You guys just go ahead. I'm going to put the spare on really quick. We shouldn't risk everyone being out here at the same time."

I pulled over in a shady looking area. There was an old gas station, some factories, and open field. Occasionally a car would drive by as well. It looked like a setup for a stick-up, and I didn't feel comfortable but what could I do at a time like this. I got to work and quick. Luckily my mother taught me how to change a tire when I was younger, or I might have been in some trouble. I got the tire on pretty quick, got the tools back in the trunk with the busted tire and hopped back in the driver seat. As soon as I cranked the engine, I see public enemy number one ride up right behind me, blue lights blazing. Damn. Damn. Damn! The Cops. 5-0. The boys in blue. The Pigs. The damn Police. I couldn't believe my eyes but this was reality, and it was happening. We both had our windows down and yep, they were getting out of the police car, one on each side. I knew at this moment; my demise was near and then

"Where you at man?!" blared over my two-way. I quickly but calmly turned the knob to off and continued to look straight as if nothing happened.

"Hey!" One of them said. I took a big gulp as I slowly turned my head and put on my best cool act.

"Yeah?" I answered. I just knew the license and registration question was coming.

"What you got under that hood buddy?" One of the cops asked.

"Man, you know the V8 block is the only way to go. Nothing less than 7 liters! Want to race?" I asked jokingly.

"You not ready, pal. You're lucky I'm on duty. I got a '67 Dodge Charger that's just waiting on new prey."

"That's it?" I said while laughing and revving the engine a little bit. "But no man, you'd probably destroy me. I don't want the L on my record, but perhaps some other time I'll catch you in the streets," I told him.

"Glad you know your place," He responded while laughing as well. "We just wanted to make sure you were ok and safe," the one at my window said, smiling and actually being nice about it. "Take care and be safe."

I couldn't believe they were letting me go! As soon as they turned around, I shot straight to the finish line.

"Hurry and let me in!" I said over the two-way. Everyone at once was asking what took so long and where was I.

"I think I am about to throw up," I uttered while panting. "Dude, the cops came out of literally nowhere. It was like they just manifested out of the concrete."

"So, what happened?" Viktor asked.

"I kept my cool. They wanted to race! I couldn't turn it down. So, I dusted that ass!" I explained with a smile on my face.

"No way! C'monnn" everyone said.

"Okay that didn't happen, but it was close! The cop was talking about he had some Charger that would leave me in the wind, but I just let him keep talking and got myself to safety quick as possible. I thought it was over for me!" I explained.

"Well, glad you kept your composure. Everyone clap for this kid and a successful run so far," Viktor said, clapping his hands and looking around to make sure everyone was clapping. "Well okay! Back to work! D, Big G, Guido and Jean start getting those VINs together so we can stamp them!" Viktor ordered.

After all the commotion died down, the real work began. Moe was on the paint jobs. Vince, Viktor and I were on the tree-house duty, assisting King Kong with constructing the wooden ramps and dividers to fit four cars in each trailer evenly, and safely. Everyone was doing something, and we had been at it for hours. Viktor and his men were all coked out on coffee and possibly something else. As for Vince and myself, we were using energy shots to keep our output going. Viktor put a record over these nice speakers he had. It was Lenny Kravitz's "Bring it On." He called it motivational music. The way Viktor was moving to the beat of the drums and guitar, I supposed it was his favorite song. After about thirty seconds, it became infectious. I looked over at Vince, and I couldn't fight the feeling any longer. I started moving my arms and hands like I was Lenny in the flesh using a wooden plank as guitar. Vince caught the bug next, rocking his head back and forth. When one task was done, we helped the next man finish their task and learning while helping. Before we knew it, the sun was out. We literally worked for seven hours straight not including the hour it took to steal all the cars. Vince and I went to see Jean for our final instructions.

"So, we just wait four weeks? Don't leave us hanging," I said, displaying my level of trust to Jean.

"Viktor should be in touch in four weeks. Take these burner phones and await the call."

IV Weeks

I got to work the next day, and just as I expected, the boys in blue were swarming the place.

"Hey bro!" I heard Carlos say as I entered the back. "You heard what happened? It's crazy!" he asked.

"I haven't heard anything, but it looks like a homicide," I said, pretending to be clueless.

"Might as well be a homicide the way whoever did this just killed the company. Man, the top dogs will have to take pay cuts and everything. I applaud the culprits," Carlos explained.

"So, what happened?" I asked.

"Man. Somebody or something hijacked the whole reserve lot! Did not leave a trace or a blue's clue to be found."

"That's crazy! So, they can't a trace or anything?" I asked to make sure we did not make any mistakes.

"Nothing bro," he responded.

"But check it out, the investigators are interviewing everyone that works here. Employees here are the first suspects of course. I was at my grandma house all weekend, but they still going try to dig deep and whatnot. Oh well. Where were you this weekend?" He asked me.

"Man, I actually went out of town this weekend with my mom and best friend. Yeah, we went to ummm Detroit to visit some family you know," I said convincingly.

"You should be good then. In fact, here they come now. Put your game face on," Carlos said jokingly.

Carlos was joking, but I really did have to put my game face on. I couldn't have any holes in whatever story I was about to tell, or I would be sent away to the pits of hell instantly. I was worried to death as I saw the investigators walking in my direction. I wanted to throw up. It seemed like a dream, but it was very real.

"Hello. My name is Detective Julius Dunn. I would like to ask you some questions regarding last night's incident. That okay?" He asked.

"Sure."

"So. Where were you last night?" He asked with the sternest face imaginable.

"With my mother. On a road trip," I responded.

Detective Dunn was writing my every word down on a notepad. The more he wrote, the less I wanted to talk. The less I spoke, the lesser the chance I had of screwing up my story. The more I thought about it, though, the more I spoke.

"Where did you guys go?"

"Detroit. Before you ask, visiting family. We're from Detroit,"

"Okay. So, I assume you know what has happened here?" Detective Dunn asked while tapping his pen on the notepad, awaiting my answer.

"Yeah. A coworker just told me. A whole lot of cars are missing,"

"Right. A whole lot of cars are missing. Do you think there is anything you think I need to know or you need to tell me?"

I figure I would take a different approach to the situation altogether. Make it real hard for the detective to get anything out of me. I wanted to make him tired of me so he would just let me go. Maybe we would think I didn't have anything to give him.

"Besides me being hungry? Nope. I'm answering all your questions."

"Hm. Well, this interview is just about over kid. You'll have your pop-tart soon. Just know the bad guy never wins. I don't know what that means to you. But know it and understand it. Enjoy the rest of your day," he said, reaching for a handshake.

"I already know that. That's why I'm not a bad guy," I responded while meeting his hand with mines.

I left the interrogation confident but nervous. I texted Vince what was going as far as the interrogation but not too much information just in case the boys grabbed hold of my phone. He texted back with paranoia, and I was not going to respond until after work. At this point, I decided to use the burner phone from now on for communication. I didn't want to risk anything if I didn't have to.

As the day went forward, my patience started to run lower than expected. I started to get a bit more disrespected than usual. Since the incident happened, touching cars was off limits. Unless they had buyers and even then, we were only to wash them. Carlos and the other porters left early because business was slow, so I covered for them. It was about 6pm when I was cleaning up the bay area, and Mike came in the back looking for a victim.

"Follow me" he ordered.

"Since cars are off limits to you idiots, you'll be picking up all these cigarette buds around the building. Before that, you need to chop the weeds growing around the building as well. Here is a razor blade.

"What's the blade for?" I asked confusingly.

"To cut the weeds stupid!" I had the most confused and disgusted look on my face as I looked at the razor blade in my hand.

"Oh, and we just sold four cars. They should be in the back waiting for you by now. So, take care of the deliveries first. The customers are waiting. Chop! Chop!"

"Four deliveries huh. Ok, sure. I'm going to do this in record speed for you guys. Coming right up massa."

I turned and angrily walked to the back where the deliveries were. I couldn't believe they would try and treat me like I was some sort of slave. But I was about to remove myself from the situation. I grabbed a bottle of wax in one hand and a bottle of paint in the other hand and poured it all over the deliveries. I started knocking everything off the shelves, flipping chairs and tables, making a racket like a madman. That is exactly what I was in this moment, a mad man. All the mechanics were looking at me like I had two heads but I didn't care. I had finally reached my breaking point, and I broke big time! I stormed outside to my car and got ready to ride off but then I was thinking, that's not enough.

I didn't do enough damage yet. I got in my car, and it was like the car knew I was upset because I did not have to pump the gas or anything. It started right up like a car right off the showroom floor. I drove around to the front and found exactly what and who I was looking for. I was laser focused on my target. I was the Terminator and he was Jon Connor.

I got out the car, with the engine still running and the door wide open. I trotted towards my enemy and his partners, and the battle began.

"What the hell are you doing boy?" I know those cars are not finished! Get back in there now! Mike ordered. "Consider your pay and hours docked!"

I continued walking through his rain of verbal attacks, each word coming from his mouth making me stronger. The closer I got, his associates started to back away as they could more than likely see the fury in my eyes.

"Are you deaf or something? One more step and you are toast!" He threatened.

I was directly in his face.

"You can't toast someone who already quit," I whispered. I balled my fist, gathered as much strength as possible and threw the meanest right hook straight across his chin and knocked him smooth out. "Don't ever disrespect me!" I screamed at his limp body.

I regained my composure as I walked back to my car and drove to the nearest gas station. All the adrenaline had made my mouth dry, and I needed a bottle of cold water. I called Vince to see if he was home and filled him in on everything that was happening and what had just happened.

"You alright?"

"Yeah, I'm good bro. Wanna smoke a joint?" I asked. He hesitated before answering, like he needed to think about it.

"You know I do! Come on by the crib brother," he said. I could see his smile through the phone. Vince was waiting on his porch when I pulled up to his house. As we smoked and talked, we discussed what we would do with our cut of the money we were receiving. We both wanted the same thing which was to make sure our mothers were going to be okay when everything was all said and done. In addition to that, I wanted my slate to be clean more than anything. I wanted to be debt free.

"I'm tired of being a slave, brother," I said as I blew some smoke from my lungs. "Debt makes you a slave. The man never wants to see you succeed but we going to do just that regardless. You feel me. I cut one shackle today. The biggest one is still on my ankle though."

"Yeah but not for long brother. Not for long. Soon our lives are going to change. We are going to get what we deserve. I was shaking my head up and down like a seesaw while Vince talked, confirming everything. "I know you want to go back to school but we going to have some fun, too right?" Vince asked. "Fast cars, right? Versace shirts, right?! New girls every night right!?" I smiled as I looked at him, I was happy he was excited.

"We going to do all of that! I might have to pass on the women, though. You know my situation man. I'll live through you, though."

"You weren't saying all that jazz that night in Germany!" Vince said while laughing. I gave Vince a serious look and pointed at him.

"Aye man. Don't ever say that aloud again. I was under the influence! That never happened!" We both laughed.

"Yeah. Yeah. Anyway, let's clear this smoke out. Mom will flip out if this smell gets in her front room."

Vince opened his room windows and turned on his fans and waving towels to help air out the room.

"I'm about to run to the crib and tell mom this news about me quitting. She's going to wonder why I won't be working tomorrow. You getting online tonight? I need to smack you around in Call of Duty. It's been a minute." Vince gave me the serious look.

"Now you know I will be online. You also know nobody is smacking me around! Now go home before your Mom smacks you!"

"Whatever fool! Be on at 7. Peace."

I finally got home, and the first thing I get when I walk through the door is a ton of questions about nothing, and a bunch of yelling about nothing. Not only is my mom home but Toya, my girl, is here with her. Now I got to explain my actions to two difficult women.

"Why the blue face?" Toya asked me.

"I quit my job today,"

"What?! Why?!" They both asked, sounding like they were singing a song together. I let out the deepest sigh as I was tired of thinking about this whole work situation.

"Because I am tired. I am tired of being low-balled. Tired of being treated like a slave, like I am less of a man than the next person. Tired of being treated like the dirt on the bottom of someone's shoe. Tired of being disrespected. That is why!" I raised my voice.

"Well, sometimes that is what it takes to advance in-"

"Advance?! Advance in what? That company? Is that a joke?" You don't know what it is like to work there. You cannot imagine the things they say to me or have me doing. Today was the break, and I broke! Everything is good where you work. People can advance there, they treat you nice with respect. Not where I work." I was starting to get hot as I shouted. My breathing was starting to elevate. I looked at my mother and Toya, who was staring at me with a sad expression, I started to calm down.

"I'm just saying, babe,"

"Well, I am just saying as well. I quit the damn job, and it is done. I even punched my manager in the face. Why are we even wasting time talking about it?"

"Baby! You have to control yourself and your attitude. You can't go around punching people out. What if he decides to press charges? Then what? What are you going to do now?" My mom asked me.

I looked down before responding and headed to my room. I was growing tired of the questions. I was food deprived and energy deprived. My mind and my body were burned out.

"Right now, I am going to go to my room, and play Call of Duty, Black Ops, zombies online. I am tired. And like I told both of you, I have another job already. Don't worry, goodnight,"

Days went past until the fourth week came. No contact from Viktor or Jean or anybody. Vince and I were starting to feel like we got took for our services. Like we got beat! I thought maybe it'll be a few days but some things can take longer than expected I figured. It had been four weeks since I quit my job at the dealership, so I had no income. Not a dime. I had one hundred and seventy-five dollars to my name. Not to mention I had bills to pay. Vince was telling me to ask my mom for money to get me through the month but I couldn't. Besides hating to ask anyone for anything, mom didn't have any money. Mom got $700 a month from Social Security, and rent and medical bills were killing her pockets. Not to mention her condition was getting worse. Every time she would come from the doctors it would be something else she needed to pay for and what-not. I needed to be helping her, not asking her for money. I also couldn't ask because I raved on and on about the new job I got. I would be the laughing stock if I asked for some money. Even though I knew mom would understand, I just couldn't do it. This weighed heavy on my conscience for a while. Then I figured there is someone I could call, that person being my dad.

I gave my dad a ring, and as soon as I did, I wished I hadn't. My father and I had a weird relationship. He was incarcerated off and on during my transition from kid to teenager to becoming a man. All my memories were from my childhood days which was kind of a good thing because they were good memories. He was an awesome father to me, but because of that gap, we didn't talk much. We had an understanding. We both know what this unspoken agreement was. Although it was never verbalized, it defined out relationship. Every time I asked him for anything, I had to endure a story and arrange a schedule to pay him back. This time was no different, but it rubbed me a certain type of way. I figured he owed me this.

"Hey dude, what's up, Jack? How's it going? Everything good?" I had to make something up to get through the fences, if not then I wasn't going to get anything.

"Yeah, everything is good. School and work trying to kill me you know?" I responded with minimum excitement.

"Yeah well, what else is new right?"

"Hey, I know you wouldn't want me to beat around the bush, so I won't. I made a poor decision, and I messed my money up. I got some bills coming up, and I need help. I need a hundred dollars. Can you help me?" There were about seven seconds of silence before any sound was made.

"Hmm, son, I will do anything for you. If I got it, you got it. You know that, right?" he asked.

"Yeah dad, of course. You know I don't like to ask for anything so I wouldn't if I didn't need it," I was starting to feel good as he was opening up to giving me the money.

"Um, okay, well I just wanted you to know that. I don't feel comfortable giving you the money," My eyebrows instantly went down as he continued to talk. "You have a job. You are a man now, and you should find your way and figure it out," I clinched my phone tight as I wanted to throw it across my room out of anger.

"Dad I need it. I will give it back to you. Come on."

"You should look into going into the military, son. You will get to travel, all expenses paid for, including school. You will have money in your pocket. Life is different than when I was growing up. And you need to do something because I don't want you following in my footsteps. You wouldn't make it anyway…"

I held the phone away from my ear as he continued to babble on and on. When I put the phone back to my ear, the energizer bunny was still going.

"You see, back in my day, I was brought up with the pimps, the players, the hustlers and the radicals. I wasn't about anything but my money, so I chose to be a hustler. You can't do any of those things. You would be stopped in your tracks."

I didn't know how to tell him or in what way. While he was still talking, I thought, if he only knew. If he did know, would he be proud of me?

The fact that he kept writing me off was making me so angry. It was like he thought of me to be some little girl or something. Like I can't hold my own or something. I guess he forgot who I grew up with. I guess he forgot I watched him and mom growing up. I was just as much of a hustler as he was, if not better and smarter. I guess he forgot the phrase "Like Father, Like Son". I was angry, but I calmed myself down as I thought to myself, I don't need to prove anything to him. He forgot those things, and I forgot he didn't know me. He used to.

I also thought about who I was talking to. My dad was borderline genius. He looked at the world and everything in it differently than most people. He was in a lane all his own, and most people didn't or couldn't understand it or him.

"I just want the best for you son. I will send you the money. You have two weeks to get me my money back. If it is not returned to me, I will break your legs, your hands, and your fingers. Understood?"

"Sure pops. Thanks, I appreciate it. I wouldn't want you to do those things, so I will return your money to you in two weeks. Love you, bye," I hung up the phone confused.

I didn't understand how he could say those things to me. I think that was his way of saying "I love you, so I will help you". Then I wondered to myself if he really knew what we had just pulled off and the kind of money I was about to come into. Would he be proud of me then? Who knew and I would never know because I would never tell him. Then I thought, he couldn't be serious about what he said because I would really mess him up if he tried anything close to that level.

"Shit. Now how will I get him his money back?" I whispered to myself. "I'll figure that out later. Don't want my fingers and legs broken!" I said, mocking my dad.

Even after the call to my dad, and the fact that I got the money from him, the thought of my mom going from thousands every night, to merely $700.00 a month from Social Security was mind boggling. I paid for everything else with my measly minimum wage check. The money I had plus the money dad gave was practically gone already. I needed to take care of our phone bills and the groceries. Beans, rice, and noodles were getting old. I missed the old days when mom could buy anything. I wish she was smarter during those times. Smart enough to put up a portion of her earnings for rainy days. We wouldn't be caught in a thunderstorm now. I wish I was older when her and dad were double breasted. Maybe I could have saved them, maybe school them on saving money perhaps. But there is no going back, and it is what it is in the present.

I called Vince, and he was almost in the same situation. We put our heads together for extra brain power and started to do little odd jobs here and there. Usually yard or house construction work with Hispanics. That put the tiniest bit of money in our pockets usually just enough to put a little a half tank of gas in the car and a little bite to eat or maybe a few groceries to hold us till the next call from contractors. I was growing increasingly tired of this life.

"We need something more man," I told Vince after our last job of the day.

"I know. I got an idea. It's been on my mind for a minute. Let's go to my house," he said. We pulled up to Vince's house to discuss this idea he had on his mind. I was just hoping it was promising because I was all out of options and exhausted. "Mom is probably sleeping. Which is a good thing," he said as he opened the front door.

"Hey, mom," He said dryly.

"Hey, Ms. Owens!" I said with excitement following his greeting.

"Hey, baby. How's your mom?"

"Oh, she's fine. Driving me crazy as usual of course," I joked.

"That's what we do right. I'm sure Vince thinks the same thing," she said giving Vince a dirty look. "Tell her I said hey." It was clear she wasn't well.

As soon as we entered Vince's room, he started pacing back and forth, mumbling to himself like a crazy person. All the antics were starting to make me nervous because without a hint of what he had in mind, my mind was able to roam and make up whatever. Like what if his mom had an insurance policy and he wanted to take her out for the money? He had me shook.

"So, you going to tell me what's up or what?"

He went to his closet and came back with a shoebox.

"Look," he said as he opened it. "It's a .22 pistol. I just don't want to hurt my mother." My heart dropped into the lower region of my abdomen once I figured it out. I was speechless as he stared at me.

"Bro. There has to be another way. I can't believe you would even consider this," I said softly.

"What are you talking about?" He asked.

"You want to take your mom out for insurance money, don't you?"

"Again. What the hell are you talking about?!" Vince yelled sternly.

"I don't know anymore! You flashing the heat and you said you didn't want to hurt your mom and you pacing back and forth. Maybe I got the wrong idea!" I explained. He stared at me in silence for about three seconds before speaking.

"You are retarded. I want to see if we can hit that cash advance on 95th street."

"Oh. Okay," I uttered in confusion. "And I'm the retarded one?" I didn't know where he got this plan from, but I wasn't down for it.

"I don't want to hurt my mom by getting caught. She would be alone you know. What do you think? I mean we heisted a whole lot. This should be child's play," He explained.

I stayed quiet as I thought this through for a few minutes. I wasn't sure if this was a smart plan. If we pulled it off it would be great. But if we failed, what would we be up against? We needed to weigh out what we could lose by losing vs. what we had to gain.

"I don't know brother. I don't know if this is a good idea. I mean we had an inside person to pull off the dealership job. That took me working there for years to know everything in and out," I explained.

"Yeah but I figured it would be quick. In and out."

"I hear you. But you don't even have a plan. And besides that, I don't want to hurt nor kill anyone. That's not me. That's not us."

Vince looked sad for a second.

"Look. I do have a plan, and I don't want to hurt anyone either. We won't hurt anyone. We won't even load the gun. We will just scare them. This one job should give us a few grand each to hold us. You asked me to follow you on your job, and I did. I'm asking for the same. I wouldn't even consider this if we didn't need it," He told me. "Did you not just have an episode with your mom? If you had a better car or even had your car fixed, wouldn't you have been able to get her to the hospital sooner? You almost lost her. What if it happens again? We not going to be rich but hell if you can't afford the constant medical bills, at least you can get your car fixed to make the hospital trip," He reminded me. Even though I thought that was a low blow, Vince had a point.

"Yeah, but this is different. A whole different beast. But okay. Okay. Nobody gets hurt. I'm doing this for my mom. And for you too I guess. Shit. And if we not in and out in seven minutes tops, we walk away. You hear me? We walk away. So, what's the plan?" I asked.

Buried Surprise

Vince devised the best plan he could to pull this job off. I couldn't believe I was even involved in this, but I had to have his back like he had mine. Vince spent about two weeks planning. Time inside and time outside, observing the cash advance place. Taking notes on how many people were working, the times they worked and when the armored truck would come to pick up cash. He had it all mapped out. Friday was his preferred day to attack because Friday is usually when people get lazy. I remembered him saying this.

The day had come, and it was time to strike. Vince and I were chilling at his house going over the drawn-out map he had prepared before we headed to the cash advance. Vince wanted us to get there at 7:45pm to observe whether the cash truck was coming or not.

"If the truck comes at 8:30, then we call it off. If it misses 8:30, then we hit. We have to get them before the truck picks up all the cash. Through all my observing, the truck comes at 8:30 or 9:00, and it is never late," Vince explained. "Ok. Let's catch this bus. It's time," he continued.

We were going to do this job on foot because Vince says that's how people get caught. They rely on the getaway car which is often caught on camera and is a big target. On foot, we can change our appearances and blend in with our environment. It made sense to me, I was impressed.

"You got the hats? And the hoodies?" Vince asked.

Vince had gotten two custom hats with the word GUARD embroidered on them to get the cash advance workers to open the door when they look through the peephole.

"Yeah. It's in my bag. It's actually the same bag I used during the dealership job. I feel like it's my lucky bag," I said holding the rucksack up like a prized possession. "But yes. Hats, hoodies, and gun. Check."

"Lucky bag huh? Whatever, just come on," Vince responded while shaking his head. We got off the bus at 7:20pm to walk a half mile to the cash advance which took about ten minutes and gave us time to spare. We staked out at the subway directly across the street, quiet and patiently awaiting the arrival of the armored truck harder than believers awaiting the rapture.

"What time you got?" Vince asked.

"7:45," I answered.

"Ok. Keep an eye out. I'm going to grab some cookies from Subway. Kill some time. You want anything?"

"Yeah. Grab me three chocolate chip cookies," I said as I shook my head. I usually kept a pretty clean diet free of sweets but this night could potentially be my last night as a free man. Vince and I ate our cookies and continued our focused silence as we killed time and awaited the armored truck's arrival.

"Alright moment of truth," Vince said alarmingly. "Get ready because we move at 8:31 and It's 8:30 and dammit! There it is. Hold on bro. That looks red. They truck that usually comes in gray," Vince said while we both stood up to see. Our eyes were locked on the red truck like a homing missile. Vince's eyes light up as the red kept driving by. "Okay. Okay, it's now or never. Grab the bag we're up."

I scooped rucksack up, and we both headed across the street urgently. Lucky for us, the way the building was positioned, the workers couldn't see us go around the back. We got to the alley at the back of the building and froze, like a game of Mr. Freeze.

"What now?" I asked. "We don't have too much time to be standing here."

"I know, I know. Ok. Let's put the hats on," Vince said. "Ok. I'm gonna fricken knock man. Here we go."

I had the rucksack on my back and was ready to go. Vince had the gun and was about to knock. He raised the gun to knock on the door then stopped.

"What the hell are you doing man!? Knock on that door!" I ordered.

"I'm trying! I'm nervous! You knock!"

"Ok. Give me the gun. Since you are so nervous at the wrong time. Watch my back," I stepped up to the door like a batter at home plate, ready to order and demand all the money in this place. I got ready to knock on the door, and suddenly my rucksack started ringing crazy, startling the both of us.

"What the hell is that?" Vince asked.

"I don't know!" I said while shaking the rucksack to inspect it. "My phone is in my pocket. Did you put your phone in here?"

"Naw man. Hurry up. Someone is going to hear that!"

"What you think I'm doing?" I snapped back.

As I was inspecting the bag to find this mysterious ringing device, the devil decided to show itself. We heard heavy unlocking sounds coming from the door. It sounded like it took three codes to unlock and then it opened. Emerging from the darkness behind the door may as well been the devil himself with the terror of fear we were facing. In actuality, it was a young Caucasian kid, no older than twenty-one, small in size and holding a bag of trash.

"Who are you guys?" The kid asked. The ringing from the phone stopped as I looked up.

"We are the Garda guards. We are here to collect the money," I said. "Who are you?"

"Jacob. I'm a new employee here."

The fear turned into raw strength as I nodded to Vince to continue. The ringing started again and was driving me crazy. I tossed the gun to Vince so I could focus on this annoyance.

"Sorry, Jacob. We are truly nice guys, but tonight we can't be," Vince rushed Jacob against the wall with the gun in his face.

"Look! You're going to take us in there and keep everyone calm and help us get the money. Okay? Nod if you understand!" Vince said quietly but forcefully.

Jacob nodded quickly as he did not want any trouble. Jacob started to try to talk and explain, but Vince wanted none of it. I wanted to slam my rucksack on the ground to crush whatever was making this ringing noise and then it hit me like a ton of bricks. The bag had a zipper inside of it.

"It's that phone from the job!" I said excitingly.

"Who is it? Tell them we busy!" Vince said.

I flipped it open to see who it was. It read two missed calls from Jean.

"It's Jean!" I tried to call it back immediately, but it went straight to a non-serviced message. It rang again, but this time it was a different tone. It was a text message from her. Before I could read it, a loud monster truck engine noise was approaching us from down the street. I was expecting to see Grave Digger, but it was much worse.

"We have trouble approaching very fast! It's the Garda truck man, what do we do?" Vince asked panicking.

"Shit. Ok, grab Jacob. We are going inside," I told him. "Jacob lock this door!"

"Ok now what?" Vince said.

"Hold on and calm down. I will figure something out," I assured him. I flipped open the phone again to read the text from Jean.

"Are you serious right now? You're texting?"

"Relax!" I yelled. The text from Jean read

    Meet me at the Florida Holdings and
    Bank tomorrow at noon. Text back the number
    1 to confirm.

I texted back the number 1 faster than the speed of light.

"Hey, Vince we have to get out of here," I told Vince. "Jacob, you are going to help us right?"

"The truck is here, I can hear the engine" Vince said.

"Jacob do not even think about making a sound. Vince, give me your hat, he's going to see our faces," I repeated it again. "Give me your hat. We don't have time for explanations right now,"

I put our hats back in the rucksack. "Ok, now Jacob. Give me your ID," He handed it over with no fight at all. I handed it to Vince. "Remember that address. Now Jacob, do not make us visit you and your family. I do not want to see your face ever again just as you do not want to see ours. Now when we open this door. You say hey and act normal. We are new employees, and we just got off okay?"

I looked him in his eyes to let him know I was serious. Only if Jacob knew, had he put up a little fight, we would be in serious trouble. We just wanted to get out of this situation, we were just as scared as he was. Boom! Boom! Two heavy knocks came at the door.

"Garda!" one of the guards announced.

"Okay. Open the door and stick to the plan," I uttered as I whipped my rucksack on my back. Jacob cranked the heavy door open. Vince and I proceeded to exit out the door first.

"What took you guys so long?" The Garda guard asked.

"They just got hired so I was just giving them kind of crash course on what to do when you guys get here. They are leaving now though so the rest of the tour will have to wait," Jacob explained.

"Cool. See you guys next time," The guard said.

Vince and I nodded and hastily walked the way we came. As soon as we turned the corner, the walking turned into a track meet. We ran all the way back to the bus stop just in time to catch it back home. We scurried to the back of the empty bus. I put my face in my hands and started to laugh as I remembered the text from Jean, but Vince still didn't know.

"What's funny man? he asked. "My whole plan fell apart. We didn't get the money. Now, what are we going to do? I'm sorry for ever putting you through this brother,"

"Remember that ringing phone?" I asked after taking a breather from the laughter.

"Yeah. What the hell was that about? Your girlfriend?"

"Yep, OUR girlfriend. Jean. It's on man! That was her. She said to meet her at the Florida Central Bank tomorrow at noon to collect our online earnings. That's why I was like let's get out of here ASAP!" I explained.

Vince was quiet for a second, and he let out a huge laugh and came in for a hug.

"We did it man," I said.

The few people on the bus were looking at us due to our commotion.

"We did it!" Vince screamed at them.

We got off the bus at our stop, and before we split ways, we discussed meeting up the next day. Then I decided to stay at Vince's place to make it easier for us. Jean wanted us to be there at noon. To me that's 11:30. We could barely sleep because of the nervousness and excitement. The next day my annoying alarm woke Vince at 9:30am. I reached under the pillow to grab the burner phone to check any messages for additional directions.

"Jean says for us not to forget that folder," I told Vince.

"You still got it right?" he asked me.

"Of course," I reached in my bag to show him the black folder. If I had lost that folder Vince probably would have killed me if I didn't kill myself.

We did our best to try and treat the day like any other day. Eating cereal, doing push-ups and playing Call of Duty, but our excitement was ruining it. We were looking at our watches every minute counting the time before we needed to head out. It was like being in class and waiting for that final bell to ring so you could rush out of there. We decided not to fight it anymore and just concentrate on playing COD.

"I set the alarm for forty-five minutes, bro," I said. "That's when we need to leave out so we can beat any potential traffic and or car trouble,"

"Yeah because with your car you never know!" Vince laughed. "But No worries, we can both get new cars soon!"

A new car was way overdue for me and getting any car was overdue for Vince. I would dream of having a new car to drive and be free of the misery of hindrance by my old Camaro. The transmission was slipping. It needed multiple cranks before starting. I had cables basically holding the front end together. Not to mention wherever I go people would point and laugh or either talk about me and my Camaro. To the naked eye, I was an example of what not to be in life.

My alarm was finally going off, and it couldn't have been at a worse time. My girlfriend was calling me too. I signaled to Vince it was time to go, as I answered the phone. The conversation started off normal. But, soon it turned into annoyance. She started to nag me about my lack of communication with her. Sure, I could have probably done a better job of making an effort to call her, but I had a lot on my plate, and she would never understand. I wanted to tell her what was going on, she's too much of a good girl though. She would freak out and probably call the cops on me.

If I was to be with anyone, I would want them to be down for and with me. More than anything, I always felt like I was holding her back in life. Toya was on her way to being a well-known artist. She has always been an overachiever, and I couldn't understand why she's wasting her time with a misfit like myself. Was it love? Or stupidity? She even wanted me to go California with her to find a new life. The more my girl nagged, the more I was ready to call it quits. We're not married with kids or anything, so there wouldn't be any hassles or attachments, just a minor heartache that would heal in due time. I just wanted to be free, so I could focus.

"Baby, I am sorry, but I have been extremely busy. I'm working hard for us," I assured her.

She started to preach to me about how I've changed and how I needed to balance out work and family, and she was absolutely right, but I just didn't have the time. I started to feel bad because I was assuring her of something that was false. I wasn't sure if I was doing this for me and her anymore. I just wanted to take care of my mom and my debts. Toya was not on my radar anymore, and quite frankly I was just a kid starting to outgrow his old toys or simply put, just starting to not care anymore.

"I probably should have told her how I'm starting to feel huh?" I said aloud in the car with Vince.

"I mean, no sense in prolonging it right? Set her free if you don't want it anymore."

"You right. Just don't have the heart to break hers. You know?" I continued.

"I hear you brother, but you are kind of already breaking it."

He was right, I should set her free, but that is easier said than done. I didn't care enough to do it at the moment.

"Anyway. We are here. Now we wait."

It was 11:25am, thirty-five minutes shy of our well-deserved and overdue payday. I had the black folder with all the directions and paperwork she gave me during the job. Time was dragging by like it didn't have any business elsewhere in life. Then finally, noon came around and as soon as it did, the burner phone started to ring. It was Jean, right on time, like clockwork.

"Hey, you two, come to the front and bring that folder with you."

"We're coming!"

The Camaro doors made a loud squeaky noise that alerted close bystanders as we got out the car.

"There she is." I squinted my vision towards the bank. Jean stood out like the center of attention. She was wearing all white. White blouse, white skinny jeans and what really had me scratching my head was her shoes. She wore a pair of all white Jordan 11s to compliment her fashion. These weren't any old pair of Jordans. The 11s are always rare to find which makes them really expensive. Well done, I thought to myself. Being from Chicago, I was impressed. My mom always told me you can learn a lot just from the shoes people wear. We hurried to the front door of the bank as commanded. Jean was really straightforward, and that's what I liked about her handling the transaction the most.

"Sorry, we were so late with this. Hope it didn't put you guys in a bind," Jean said.

"You have no idea," Vince responded. "Six weeks late but no worries, right?"

I looked at Vince with a face that said chill out.

"You are here now, and that is all that matters. Nice elevens by the way," I complimented her on her shoes. She looked down at her feet like she didn't know she had 14K gold bars on her feet.

"These old things? Thanks. I actually just bought them today before coming here,"

I looked around to make sure everything looked legit before walking in. I wasn't trying to walk into an ambush or something which I guess wouldn't matter because I was already here anyway.

"Where's D and Viktor?" I asked.

She gave me a disgusted look, shocked, I had the audacity to be asking her any questions. "Viktor is in Germany and D is in New York on business. Any other questions?"

"Nah. I was just making conversation."

"Good. Get that folder ready. I'm about to call our guy. Come on," Jean instructed, while she held the front door for us.

We were amazed by the size of the bank. We were used to your regular walk in, walk out bank, no bigger than your average fast food restaurant at most. However, this bank was massive. Every teller was busy with a customer. There was an upstairs for those with personal bankers, and a special department for customers with special needs. It was an intimidating setting, to say the least.

"Can I help you guys?" one of the employees asked.

"No, we're good. Floyd is coming down to meet with us," Jean stepped in as she whipped her phone out. "Floyd, it's Jean. We're here in the lobby. Come down, you know my time is money."

Jean or D or any associate of Viktor's must light a fire under people, because right when that phone call ended, Floyd was coming down those stairs like he had a record to beat.

"Hey, Jean. I should have been in the lobby waiting for you, but I had to finish some paperwork. How are you? How is everyone?" Floyd greeted, reaching for a hug.

"Everyone is good. Here, meet our two new associates," Jean pointed him in our direction.

I approached him reaching for a handshake. "Temar is my name, and this is…" I ran into a roadblock as I didn't want to give Vince's real name away.

"Uh, Owen! Name's Owen," Vince stepped in, saving us from an awkward moment. "Nice to meet you, Floyd," Vince said.

"Good. Now that everyone is acquainted, business shall we?" Jean prescribed.

"Of course, right this way," Floyd said, leading us up the stairs to his office.

As we got into the office and sat down we let Jean do most of the talking. They had history together which saved us the trouble of awkwardness because we had never done anything like this before. I was taking mental notes during the whole transaction just in case I ever needed to do a transaction like this by myself. I picked up on how to talk, especially making them comfortable with small talk and compliments. Next, just beating around the bush with talks of the weather and so forth then, the negotiations begin. They spent most of the transaction talking about online winnings, what games pays the most, which game has the most risk and how Vince and I were wizards at math and betting. I wasn't sure if that was a front for people nearby that could be listening or does Floyd really think this money is from online winnings. I was praying it was front anyway because I sucked at real math. If he asked me a basic algebra question, the cover would be blown. I didn't pay my thoughts too much mind though because Jean was doing the deal anyway.

My daydreaming and note taking ceased when Floyd grabbed a small book-bag out of his drawer and put it on his desk. He did a 180 turn in his roller chair turning to his drawer behind him. He opened it and to our surprise laid a pretty hefty safe about the size of a dorm room fridge.

Vince tapped me out of excitement as he started to turn the combination lock wheel and enter his pin code. Two little beeps and the safe door popped open like a jack in the box. What stood behind those doors were blocks of cash stacked from the bottom up. Floyd started grabbing the cash block by block and began loading the book-bag nice and slow. I looked over at Jean who was filing her nails in the middle of what I considered to be a big deal but perhaps not to her. She glanced at me and smiled and as she continued to file those nails. I guess to her, this was chump change or something but not to us. This was a billion dollars to us.

"Alright. Three hundred and fifty thousand dollars cash for our sport betters," Floyd said, as he zipped up the book-bag.

He slid the book bag across the table into my hands. I felt like I caught a Hail Mary pass in the end-zone to win the super bowl. I cradled the bag in my hands like a precious child.

"Thank you," I uttered. I felt so thankful in the moment. It felt unreal to have that bag of cash in my hands.

"So, will I see you guys again?" Floyd asked.

"Uhh-"

"Sure. As long as these guys keep winning, we will be back," Jean butted in, rescuing me from my stalling.

"Winning is what we do best, and I can't wait to come back," Vince chimed in.

I started to think to myself. See us again? Can't wait to come back? This is a one-time deal for me. For us. This is to only to take care of my mom, pay off my school loans and go back to school. I don't think I can pull this off again I thought to myself.

"Alright. We'll be in touch," Jean said. Yeah, she will be in touch. Not me. Not Vince. I continued my thoughts to myself. We stood up, shook hands and proceeded to leave the bank. Now, I'm waiting on the authorities to ransack the place and hem all of us up and place us under the jail, but it didn't happen. Here we were standing outside with not a cop in sight.

"Soooo that's it?" Vince asked.

"Were you expecting something else?" Jean responded. "Go have some fun but be smart with your money. But have fun. And pay it forward. We like to think of you guys as family and partners now. Viktor or I will be in touch. Give me that old burner phone and take these." She gave us these small candy bar style phones that looked like a child's toy and proceeded to her Audi A6, leaving us behind. Vince and I looked like we just got dropped off at college for the first time without saying goodbye to our mom. We were standing outside the bank lost.

"What just happened?" I uttered.

"I don't know. We should probably go, though." We scurried to my tin-can of a car and just sat there for a second. My hands were sweating, and I started to lose feeling in them as I realized I was clenching the book-bag so tightly. I screamed loudly as my vocal cords would allow. Vince followed in my footsteps, letting out a scream. I pumped my gas pedal and anxiously dug in my pockets for my keys to start my car. A couple cranks and she started for me.

"Ok. Ok. Where do we go? My house. Yeah, let's go to my house. My mom should be doing her exercise walk around the block right now," I said.

"Make a quick stop for me?" Vince asked.

"Seriously? Now? Where to?" I said with a confused look on my face. We just netted a load of cash and Vince wanted to run errands.

"We need to go to OfficeMax," Vince said.

"OfficeMax!?"

"Trust me. We need to go to OfficeMax," He assured. I made the quick detour to OfficeMax for whatever odd reason Vince needed to go.

"Ok. Hurry up," I expected to see Vince come back out holding bags but he came out cradling a box like a football.

"What's that?" I asked.

He pulled back part of the bag the box was in to expose the name. `Cash Counter Machine.`

"Let's count this money and break bread the right way," Vince said smiling.

"I like your style brother! Can we go home now?"

After about twenty minutes, we finally reached our neighborhood. I made a quick circle around the blocks to see where my mom was in her walking routine. I was coming down our block doing about 5 mph when I saw her going away from our house which meant she probably had just started. I let the car sit until she turned the corner. If she saw us, she would have flagged us down, and forced Vince and I to do the walking rounds with her and would not have taken no for an answer. The last thing I need at this moment is for moms to find out what we're doing. She would be so disappointed in me. As soon as she turned the corner, I sped up and parked in front of our place, then headed in.

"We have money bro!" I exclaimed. "We have fricking money!" I hugged Vince as tightly as I could. I was just so happy. I could kiss him I was so happy. He had tears in his eyes as I dumped the cash on the bed. "What are you crying for man?"

"I just wish my father was here. With this money. Man, I could have saved him. Life could be just that pinch better," He explained. "Don't get me wrong, though, I'm happy as a duck!"

"I hear you brother. Just do right by this blessing. Take care of your mom and continue to be a man. That's what he would want from you, you know," I said grabbing him by the shoulder. "Now how in the hell do you figure ducks are happy?"

"Their faces just look happy all the time," He laughed. "I love you man, you always been there for me. Anyway, I don't mean to be a killjoy, let's bust this money down. That money counter coming out of your cut!"

"Yeah? You better get your soft ass out of here! That's your counter!" I laughed. "I'll always be there for you kid,"

After fumbling with the money counter and figuring out how to program it, we finally got busy on counting the cash. Although we knew how much it was and how much we were getting each, it was something about counting it and dividing it. Maybe we wanted to play mob kingpin or something. In the movies, they always had a ton of money just lying around and a team of naked women counting it. We didn't have any naked women, but it still felt damn good! The way that money counter was counting cash, you would think it was going to overheat. We were counting Vince's cut first. Feeding the machine stack after stack, about 300 bills per minute. Every time the counter beeped it read $30,000. Six minutes in and Vince had his share in one hundred and seventy-five thousand dollars. I put his cash back in the book-bag and right in his hands. Since it was evenly divided, I didn't have to count my half, but I did anyway just to keep the Broadway play going. Three minutes in, and ninety thousand dollars deep, things got a little hairy.

"Yo. You hear that?" My voice trembled.

"Shhh! Wait, be quiet," Vince whispered.

We both ceased talking to focus on the noises we were hearing.

"Son?" We heard a close but distant voice say, footsteps behind it.

"Shit! That's your mom!"

"Ok. Ok, think. Think. Quickly turn that PlayStation on," I said.

Mom was on her way to my room, and there was cash everywhere. How would I explain this scene to her? The best way was not to explain it at all. She was walking at her normal pace, but it felt like she was coming faster than a bat out of hell which left me with mere seconds to spare. I scooped all the cash blocks and loose cash up and stuffed it in my rucksack. There were still a few bills left in the counter, but I didn't have time to get those. The infamous *Knock knock* from mom. She was at the door. Those are the two knocks that let me know that she is about to enter the room. I left those bills in the machine and placed the counter behind my TV just as the door was opening

"Hey! Oh Hey, Vince. Didn't know my other son was here. What are you guys doing?" Mom asked.

"Hey, mom! Just trying to fix this stupid router so we can play a little Call of Duty. You?"

"I swear that is all you two do. Anyway, just finished my walk. I was going to make a salad. You guys want some?" She asked.

"I'm fine,"

"Vince?"

"Umm," It sounded like Vince was leaning towards yes in which I couldn't blame him because mom made a pretty bomb salad. I cleared my throat and prayed he got the clue.

"Actually, I just ate not too long ago, so I'm fine for now. Thanks, mom."

"Suit yourselves," Mom told us. I sighed and shook my head as mom headed back to the kitchen.

"That was close, man," I whispered. I took my rucksack and put it at the top of my closet and prayed nobody will find it. "Want me to put up your cash too?" I asked Vince.

"Nah. I got it. I'm going to put mines in my closet as well," I wanted to hold his cash just to make sure he didn't make any silly decisions, but I had to let him live. That was his money, and he is his own person.

"All this money. So, what now?" Vince asked.

"I don't know, but I got this crazy idea. We always play those casino games online and dreamed what it would be like to play in real life right? Ever been to the city of lights?" I smiled. Then we both burst into hysterical laughter, until I remembered mom was home, and I put my finger up to my lips, hushing us both.

"Let's go to Vegas bro," I whispered.

Sin City

Vince and I hopped out the cab and ran into the airport, running late as usual. Lucky for us, we didn't have any luggage beside our backpacks of toiletries underwear, socks and fifteen thousand dollars cash. So, running to board the plane was a breeze. We made it to our gate with about fifteen minutes to spare. I went into the convenience store to grab some snacks and a couple magazines to ease the pain of flying. As soon as I walked in the store, our boarding number was being called. I grabbed a Robb Report magazine and hurried to the line.

"Now boarding C-Pass. All with C-Pass, please board the plane," We heard over the intercom. My nerves were starting to flare up with the thoughts of getting on the plane.

"Here we go, baby! Don't get scared now!" Vince teased when he saw the uneasy look on my face. I gave him the dirtiest look I could as he laughed. As the plane start moving and gearing for takeoff, I said a quick prayer to God and my grandmother to watch over us during our air travels. I felt a little better after sending that prayer up, but nothing could truly make the terrorizing feeling of flying go away.

"Man, if you can fly to Germany, you can do this trip. This is only a fraction of that trip!" Vince reminded me.

"Yeah, you're right. I had sleeping pills remember? I feel like I will never get used to this. We could fly across the street, and I would still freak out."

"Tough. Crack that magazine open and relax, man."

I opened my Robb Report Magazine to let the love of expensive cars and toys ease more pain. For the most part, it worked. I came across a page that had Las Vegas attractions on it and boy was I attracted. The attraction that caught my eye was the exotic car rental establishment. They have every exotic car a man could dream of. The rental wasn't cheap, but I wasn't broke either. I turned to Vince to show him, but I guess someone punched him out while I was reading, he was totally knocked out. I planned to just show him when we landed. I kept reading and reading and playing games on my phone looking for things to kill boredom with while we surfed the air, because it was impossible to sleep. A couple more hours of twiddling my thumbs and we were landing. I looked over at Vince who was still dead to the world with his mouth wide open, and head tilted back, awaiting a baptism.

"Wake up, chump," I said, flicking him in his Adam's apple. He let out a loud snore noise right before he opened his eyes. "We here baby. Let's go have some fun!" I said with excitement. "Check-in at the Mirage hotel is at 1:30pm so, we got about an hour and thirty minutes to burn. Wanna go to Fatburger?" I asked.

"You know I want to go to Fatburger baby!"

I guess after hearing about Fatburger all the time from other people, our expectations were too high. They had really good french fries and margaritas. The burgers were good but overrated. We would take a burger from home any day. Aside from Fatburger, Vince and I were marveled at what we were witnessing in Vegas. It was truly the entertainment capital of the world. It was like a 24-hour party. People everywhere, on every corner, trying to get you to go to every attraction available. The unique architecture was unlike anything we had ever seen before. Some buildings gave Jack's beanstalk a run for its money. Even buildings with roller coasters wrapped around it like a boa constrictor. We had to flag down a taxi to get around.

"If we going to go out tonight, we have to go out in style, and I'm talking formal. Driver, can you take us to the nearest mall?"

"Sure. It's one just right up the street," His Arabic voice responded.

At the mall, we were looking for the freshest fashion we could find. Neither of us had worn suits outside of our high school graduation, so this was going to be a task because we did not know what to look for.

"Excuse me," Vince said to one of the ladies working in the Macy's men department. "Emilia? Yes, Emilia," My brother and I totally suck at picking formal wear. We want to look good tonight. Can you help us?" I sat back and let Vince do his thing because if it were up to me to pick stuff out, we would be out there in a t-shirt, blue jeans, and Chuck Taylors.

"Sure! In fact, if you want to get the latest fashion, men's leggings are in heavy rotation now. Here, let me show you," She said with the straightest face. Vince and I looked at each other with the most confused faces before we were relieved with her laughter. "Jeeze, I wish I had that reaction on film!" Emilia said. "I'm joking. Ok, do you guys know your sizes?" We gave her another reaction she would probably want on film. "Oh nevermind. Come on let's get you fitted," she said while whipping around her measuring tape like a slave owner.

"I was looking at the two-piece suit right there," I said, pointing at the mannequin. "The black one."

It was a dark black, two-piece suit, with a black under-shirt and a skinny black tie to go with it. The suit fabric felt so good, so smooth and shiny. The shoes were black too but suede. Vince chose to go with a gray two-piece suit. He emerged from the dressing room looking like a slab of armor. His suit looked like sheer gunmetal. It looked great on him. If the two worlds collided, he would be Bruce Wayne, and I would be Tony Stark with the suits we had on.

"Ooh, la la look at you fine gentlemen," Emilia complimented.

"Thank you, thank you," Vince said. "You know Emilia, you should come out with us tonight. I need a pretty lady by my side," She started to blush instantly at Vince's offer as if she's never been extended a compliment accompanied by invite before.

"Oh, I don't know. You guys seem pretty cool, and I'm kind of square you know?"

Vince tapped me as he pointed to her. "Bro, is she kidding? Tell her we are the biggest geeks she could meet." I co-signed as Vince needed.

"I got to tell you Em, he's right. All we do is play video games."

"I'm not buying it, but I could kill you guys in Street Fighter!" She challenged.

Both Vince and myself laughed hysterically at the thought. We basically grew up on street fighter, one of Earth's most prestigious fighting video games.

"I highly doubt that dear," I butted in.

"Only way to find out," Vince said. "Here's my number. You're invited to hang out with us tonight. We going to be at the MGM Grand pressing our luck. Also, if you want to press your luck in street fighter, give me a ring. Ken Summers and I will take on whoever you want," Emilia looked seduced as Vince laid down his offer. Either Emilia was an actress in training or Vince had some business to attend to tonight I thought to myself.

"I'll keep this. I might get bored tonight and might need a victim," Emilia said smiling. "You guys paying for this together or separately?"

"Only one way to settle this," I said. I opened the palm of my left hand as I turned to Vince and pounded my right hand into my left palm like the hammer of Thor. "You ready?"

"Rock! Paper! Scissors! Shoot!" We shouted.

"Dammit!"

Vince usually picks rock to start off with, but this time he changed it up on me. My paper was shredded into confetti by his scissors.

"Snip snip baby!" Vince said to rub salt into my wound. "Take that cash out!"

"Shut up foo, before I deck you!" I snapped back. "Emilia, how much do I owe you?" Emilia was laughing the whole time. She found our theatrics hysterical.

"One, you guys are total dorks after all. And two, someone owes me $631.55.

I paused for a second as I dug into my pocket for my knot of cash. It hit me that we had money for once. Just last week we would have killed for a hundred dollars, and now we were spending almost a thousand dollars for some clothes we were probably going to wear once. It was a surreal and a damn good feeling.

"Cash or card?"

"Oh yeah. Cash. Sorry about that, I totally just spaced out," I explained. "Losing is a tough thing, man,"

"We understand," Vince said laughing. "Emilia, as you can see, I'm a winner. Don't let this happen to you," I shook my head with a smile to his remark as I handed over $640.00 cash for tonight's attire.

"Eight dollars and forty-five cents is your change. You guys have fun tonight. Vince, right? I will consider your offer," Emilia said as she looked at the paper he gave her.

We burned another hour surfing stores in the mall, buying stuff just because we could. Vince spent eight hundred dollars on a Versace shirt. I tried to stop him because it just seemed so outrageous, but he had been waiting to acquire one of those shirts since he was a kid watching The Rock do his thing in his wrestling days. I shut my mouth and let him do it. The next store we visited was the Burberry store. I had never been so intrigued by articles of clothing before. Burberry's main attraction was their pattern design on the clothing. It was a plaid sort of design but arranged in different ways. I wondered how they could charge so much for clothing. Then I felt the fabric, and it started to make sense. There was a huge difference between something designer and something anyone could buy. Vince scolded me while I tried on multiple pieces. I chose a slate black shirt with a red plaid design.

"I'm going to get this, bro!" I said to Vince. He just shook his head and smiled.

"Do it. It's not like you don't have the money," he encouraged me.

I just tried to stop him from buying an expensive shirt and here he is encouraging me. He had a good point, though. It wasn't like I didn't have the money. I rang those two shirts out and spent five hundred dollars on them. Although it felt weird, it felt good to buy whatever I wanted.

As soon as we walked out of the mall my phone was buzzing from a weird number with a 702-area code. I gave an unsure "Hello…" as I picked up the phone. When the lady on the other end of the phone spoke, I instantly struck my forehead with my palm. It was the Mirage Hotel. We were supposed to check in to our room an hour ago, and now it's up for grabs on a first come first serve basis. I assured the lady we would be there before she knew it and not give our room up. I had put one thousand dollars on my debit card prior to coming here so we could hold this room. If we didn't get it, then we would run the risk of not renting a room because I wouldn't have enough money on my card to book anything.

"We got to hurry bro, or we are going to be stuck like chuck, looking for a room," I told Vince.

"We could get a room off the strip if all else fails," Vince suggested.

"Nobody comes here to get a room off the strip, man. That's weak sauce! I need to get to the Mirage as soon as possible. Come on, help me flag down a taxi,"

We flagged a taxi down quicker than a New York minute. Luckily this taxi was a van because we had too many bags that we didn't take into consideration in conjunction with traveling. We both had suit bags and about three bags each. Technically, the Mirage wasn't far from the mall. I mean you could practically see the Mirage on the road but the Vegas traffic turned a ten-minute ride into a twenty-five minute ride and I was willing to bet we lost our room. Part of me wanted to grab our bags and run for it with the way traffic was moving. I hate traffic with a passion. Traffic never made sense to me.

"If everyone would just fricken drive, everyone could get to where they were going," I said angrily.

My mood was ruined but not for long. Once we got to the Mirage I was marveled. For starters, it was huge. I got lost just by looking at it.

"Welcome to the Las Vegas Mirage," One of the doormen said as he opened our doors. "Do you need help with any luggage?" The doorman asked.

"Yes. The bags are in the trunk," I thanked our driver and gave him forty dollars to cover our ride and a twenty-one dollar plus tip. The doorman had our bags, and we followed him inside the Mirage to check in. There was a small line that both Vince and myself was thankful for at the moment so we can soak in what we were seeing.

"This is nuts. I have never seen anything like this," Vince uttered. There was grass and trees everywhere! It felt like we were inside a tropical rainforest of some sort. There were these brass mermaid statues that reminded you that mermaids were indeed real. When you looked up, there was a huge glass dome above, that you could see the hotel rooms from. To our left was our destination and one of the coolest sights in the check-in area. It was an aquarium with a ton of actual sea creatures. Being two inner city kids, we were blown away. Before we knew it, we were next to check in. Hopefully, at least.

"Hello. How can I help you guys?" the receptionist asked.

"Yeah. Uh, we had a standard two bedroom on hold. It was for three o'clock. I know it is four seventeen now. Can we still have that room?"

"Well, it is quite late. Do you have any documentation?"

"Sure, here is my ID and here is the email you guys sent me," I said while giving her my phone. She was typing a thousand words it seemed. Considering how late we were and the size of the hotel, I guess it only made sense that she would be able to type like that. The longer she typed, the more I became worried we were not going to get a room.

"Okay," She said dryly.

"Okay?" I repeated matching her dry tone.

"So, the room you originally booked did get taken. I am sorry. We do have single rooms though and if you need two rooms you could upgrade to our penthouse."

"Dammit! Penthouse? What's that? How much is it?" I said with disappointment.

"Well, our penthouse is 1600 SQ. FT so in layman's terms, that is huge. Two full baths, king size beds, 50-inch TV, living room area and a small kitchen. That would cost you seventeen hundred which is a steal may I add, this weekend is a special, so regularly it would cost about twenty-five hundred," she explained with a grim face.

We went from spending six hundred dollars at three hundred each for our room to being on the verge of spending seventeen hundred at eight hundred and fifty each. I wanted to choke myself for being late, and I wanted to choke Vince too, just because.

"Jesus. That's eight fifty a man bro," I told Vince. "What do you want to do?"

"Like I told you earlier…it isn't like we don't have the money," Vince said. I shook my head. He was right but damn, that can't be the answer for everything. I couldn't help but feel the same way at the same time.

"Okay, mam. We will take the penthouse," I told her.

"Awesome. I will get this processed for you. One minute."

She basically maxed my debit card out. I had to put a thousand-dollar deposit down to get the room, and we could pay the difference in cash any time before we left. We followed the doorman to the private elevator that takes us to the penthouse. The elevator was so spacious. We were taken aback by how fast it traveled to the 25th floor. If it went a little bit faster, we would have had to squat down to account for the pressure it put on our legs.

"Got your key cards? That's your room right there. Enjoy," the doorman said. He stood there before getting back on the elevator creating an awkward silence, then it hit me.

"Oh! Right. Your tip. Sorry. Here you go," I said as I gave him a ten-dollar bill.

"We got to get used to tipping people I guess," I laughed.

"Open the door baby. Let's see what we are paying all this money for."

"This damn card doesn't work," Vince said as he slid the key card in and out.

"Mannn give it here! Watch out," I put the keycard in slowly and *beep beep* a green light flickered.

"See! You have to be gentle. You can't just rush into it, you know. You'll hurt it if you just ram your keycard into her keyhole," I said with a smirk.

"You have a dirty mind," Vince said smiling.

We walked into the room only to once again be amazed. When the receptionist said 1600 sq. ft., I didn't really think too much of it, but when we saw 1600 sq. ft. it blew us away. This room was huge. It was like having a house without the upstairs and the basement. Both our rooms were a comfortable size big enough to accommodate any college student. The kitchen came pre-stocked just in case one of us wanted to cook or eat something, and decked with the finest looking silverware and appliances. Our bathrooms were immaculate, done in white marble, with a shower/hot-tub combination, made a little more spacious than it already was. The best part of the room to me was floor to ceiling windows that showcased our beautiful view of the strip. I could see the Imperial Palace, the Flamingo, and most of the Caesar's Palace Complex. I also had a lovely view of the Mirage's large pool. I could even see the dolphin habitat off in the distance.

"Well it's 4:45pm. We should start getting ready around 7pm or so. I'm going to take a quick nap for the time being," I said.

"Word. Set your alarm, I'm going to explore this huge palace of a hotel," Vince told me.

I headed to my designated room for some shut-eye.

"Whoa," I said to myself as I sat on the edge of the bed. It was extremely comfortable, more so than it looked. I kicked each shoe off one at a time as I laid back. As soon as my head hit the pillow it was murder she wrote, I was out for the count.

I can't move. Where am I? Who are all these people and why is everyone dressed in black? Wait. There is my mom and Vince's mom...they look so sad. "MOM!!" Can she hear me? "MOM! Mrs. Owens!" What the hell? Why can't they hear me? I can hear my name being called, but it's faint. Sounds like Vince's voice. There's Vince. "YO, Vince! I can't hear you that good. Say it louder! What are you pointing at? The box is closing? What box?"

"Yoooo! Wake the hell up. Christ! Nothing can wake you up bro," Vince said after shaking my lifeless body.

"It's 7:45, and it's time to party. Get up!"

"Alright, alright. I had this weird ass dream man. It was like a fleet of black Cadillacs, everyone dressed in black like a funeral. Our mom was there, you were there, and I was there but trapped in a cube or box or something. Nobody could hear me, but I could hear them slightly. You were yelling my name and yelling the box is closing. I don't know what to make of it," I explained.

"Just a stupid dream man."

"Yeah, but it felt so real. Like more than usual. Like a foreshadow or something," I explained.

"I hear you, maybe in time, it will make sense. In the meantime, get ready!"

I hope it was a stupid dream. I remembered years ago my mom telling me about something I had called ESP. Mom said when I was born, her friend told her that I had ESP. I paid it no mind, but later I found out ESP stood for extrasensory perception which is considered a sixth sense, and by many, thought to be psychic. I never saw myself to be psychic, but when I was younger, I would see things, usually unfortunate things and no matter what, they always came true. It would freak me out, and I never could tell anyone because they would never believe me so why bother? It's always been hard for me to tell my dreams apart from the visions. I just hoped this particular one was just a dream. I snapped out of my thoughts and back to the focus at hand which was getting ready to hit the MGM Grand and party! Vince and I did our best to dress as good as Emilia did us at the mall earlier. Judging by the way people kept eyeing us in the lobby, I'd say we did a pretty good job.

"Want to flag a taxi?" Vince asked as we exited the main entrance.

"Uhh, let's walk. My GPS says it's about a twenty-minute walk. Let's enjoy the scenery," I insisted. "Besides, we didn't bring any small bills with us," I whispered to Vince as I flashed some of the cash that was in my pocket.

"The MGM is that way, right?" I asked one of the bellhops as I pointed left.

"Yes, sir. Keep that way, you'll see the green color illuminate the sky. Can't miss it!" the bellhop replied.

"Thanks," We both said as we proceeded to our twenty minute journey.

The weather was orgasmic. Perfect for a night out in the city, a dry 82 degrees to be exact. Back home, 82 degrees would have been humid as can be and would have had us begging for mercy. This Vegas 82 degrees though, had me praising Allah. The night really made the scene pop out. Vegas wasn't called the City of Lights for no reason, everything was lit up. When God supposedly said, "Let there be light," he was speaking about Las Vegas for sure.

We got to walk past a lot of amazing attractions and hotels. Each one looked like they came out of separate worlds. Every which way you looked, there were water eruptions designed like geysers that would shoot out the ground like a rocket when you least expected it. We got to see the Flamingo which was one of the hotels always shown in old Vegas movies. It was the pinkest of pink, hence the name. Across from the Flamingo was Caesar's Palace and it was just that, a palace. The hotel was huge, which made sense since it was modeled after the royalties of the great General Julius Caesar. On the outside, it looked like it could fit a million rooms inside it. Like most of the buildings, the water geysers that shoot water to the heavens were displayed in front of the palace.

"Every time that water shoots up, Caesar takes a sip," I joked with Vince. "Whoa! Look at that one bro," I said to Vince as I pointed to another massive hotel.

"How do you say that? Bell-ah-gio?" Vince uttered slowly as he was unsure of how to pronounce the foreign word.

"Bell-lage-gio" I corrected Vince. "I think that's how it's pronounced."

The Bellagio was even more massive than the previous palace we marveled at. This place was a mammoth. Before you can look at the front of the building, you had to look across what seemed to be a lake in front of the establishment.

"Got a boat?" Vince joked.

"Or Noah's Arc?" I stated as I laughed with Vince.

If a boat was actually the way to get to the front entrance, it wouldn't do anyone much good due to dancing water fountains in the lake that looked they were constructed by Captain Planet himself.

"You see that green in the sky baby?" Vince asked with excitement.

"We almost there!" I replied, matching his energy of excitement. You could see the green tint of light as we edged further down the infamous strip. After about ten more minutes of walking, we had finally reached the huge, impossible to miss, emerald green building, The MGM Grand.

"Man! I can't wait to get inside there!" Vince said bursting with excitement and rubbing his palms together.

"Let's do this!" I uttered aloud getting myself pumped for this moment we had been waiting for.

"Who is David Copperfield?" I asked Vince confused, looking at the banner above.

"Who's David Copperfield?! Seriously?" Vince questioned in disbelief. "The world-famous magician. Don't ask that question aloud again. Let's just go inside before you embarrass us any further," Vince suggested with a smirk on his face.

The experience began the moment we stepped through the doors into the main lobby. The first thing that we noticed was a distinct fresh scent that showered over us and almost immediately relaxed us. It is a combination of jasmine and rose aromatherapy oils dispersed into the air, and was very welcoming.

The lobby itself was an elegant semi-circular room with gold and white accents everywhere, including the infamous golden statue of a lion in the center. At the far end was the large check-in desk, with a huge LED screen behind it, that displayed the many events and activities the hotel had to offer. The MGM is broken up into four different wings, south, north, east and west. Directories were everywhere, constantly informing guests where everything is and what is offered during your time at the MGM. There were several theaters. The Ka Theater, which houses "Ka," one of Cirque du Soleil's most elaborate shows, and The Hollywood Theater, where performers like "David Copperfield" performed.

There was the MGM Grand Arena, the venue for musicians on tour. Also, several clubs to choose from. Most of the patrons were there for Tabu Ultra Lounge where all the major DJs perform. And, the Centrifuge bar, that had bartenders who pole dance for patrons.

"South Wing, that's where the casino is," I said to Vince over all the commotion that was swallowing the airwaves.

"Lead the way," Vince directed as he laid his hand out.

The casino was just what we expected it to be. The gaming area alone was massive, an endless amount of square feet, full of slots and table games to choose from. Of the twenty grand, each we came to Vegas with, we brought fifteen total of that just to press our luck at the casino with.

"I don't know where to start, I'm overwhelmed," I told Vince in a joking manner. "Do me a favor, change our bills for us over there where it says kiosk," I asked of Vince while handing him my fifteen-thousand-dollar wad of cash. "I'll get us loose with some shots."

"Word. Be right back" Vince confirmed of his small task.

There were so many women walking around with trays, serving drinks that I just wanted to yell "I need a shot!" aloud. Luckily, the servers were so skilled at what they do, they could sniff out someone looking for a drink.

"Can I get you anything to drink, hun?" a server asked me in the most enticing voice she could project.

"Yes. Can I order shots?" I inquired.

"I can tell you're a virgin here. You can order anything you want, dear. Drinks are free as long as you're gambling," she explained to me as if I had just been born. "Do I have to explain how to tip as well?" she asked sarcastically.

"No" I replied with a stone-face. I channeled my inner Viktor for my order. "Can I have two double shots of vodka?"

"Be right back," she said right before turning away to retrieve the order.

Vince had finally returned with the chips, in assorted colors and denominations. He had two small bags, one for him with his chips and the other for myself.

"Where are the drinks?" Vince asked as he handed me my new casino currency.

"The waiter should be here in a second with them. I wouldn't call them drinks though" I smirked. "See for yourself, here she is."

"Two double shots," The server said aloud confirming the order.

"Jesus," Vince whimpered, as he was about to face his doom.

Vodka for me, was almost like water, so it wasn't a big deal for me to down shots. Vince hated shots. After his double shot, he grew so much hair on his chest you would think he was about to become a werewolf. A double shot is tough for most people, but despite his reaction and my will to not drink a lot, we were vets at drinking. I decided to order one more round just for good measure just to make sure we going to be just the right level of drunk.

"Before you go, Grace?" I said confirming the server's name on her nametag. "Can I have two double shots of Fireball?" I asked, placing a twenty-five-dollar chip on her tray.

"Be right back," She scurried off.

"You good?" I asked Vince to make sure he was decent.

"I should be asking you that, mister double shot man," he laughed. "As long as my brother is with me, I'm always good," He said wrapping his arm around my shoulder.

"Okay listen, bring me my fireball shot. I have been eyeing this blackjack table in the corner over there, and two people just raised their asses up, so I'm going to lower my ass over there. Cool?" Vince said looking in the direction of the blackjack table.

"Cool. I got you. I'll be over there in a minute."

A familiar scent struck my nose and sparked befuddlement as my mind raced to put images with the aroma. My mind stopped racing as soon as the scent spoke.

"And don't you certainly look familiar?" I heard a voice say from behind. It was if an angel had graced me.

"Ah. That sounds like the voice of this sweet young lady I know named Renee," I said as I turned around pretending to be cooler than cool.

"And lucky guess. What a surprise. It is Renee. How are you dear?" I said, as I went in for a hug. "What brings you to the city of sin?"

She kissed me on the cheek as she came in for her half of the hug. She was wearing an all crimson dress that stopped about eight inches above her knees, giving just the right amount of exposure. Her fragrance was like nothing I've ever encountered before. It was like a pheromone being released in the air but only to me. I was a slave to this woman. She was a genie in a bottle.

"Well, you know us models get paid to travel the world. I have a couple of shows here in Vegas. When duty calls, you must arise right?"

"Ah yeah, I hear you loud and clear there."

"So why are you here, mister?" She asked.

My thoughts were so jumbled from lack of concentration due to her beauty. Not to mention, I was here because I could afford to be here, in account of to my illegal activities. I didn't have a clear answer to give her.

"We're just out here," I responded.

"Oh. Ok. Just out here. I guess that makes sense."

She looked dumbfounded, and I felt just plain dumb. You could not have thought of something better to say, idiot? I thought to myself.

"Who's we?"

"You remember my buddy Vince?" I said, pointing in a far enough direction for her to look. "He's over there on the craps tables trying to get lucky. I'm going to join him shortly and probably do a little gambling on the roulette table. Care to join me? I mean us, join us," I asked, shooting her my best charming smile.

"Eh. I don't really gamble. I don't know how actually."

My eyes lit up with enjoyment, like she had just said yes to my date invitation.

"Come on! It will be fun, I will teach you. Besides, since you are new, you have beginners luck so I need you by my side so you can win me some money and some for yourself too."

She grinned, gazing down at the ground, showing that she was thinking deeply about it. "Oh, what the hell. Let's do it."

I clapped in excitement and reached for hand, to show her off, as if she was the only woman that existed on the planet. We made our way over to where Vince was. He looked so lost and nervous at the same time. He had the dice in his hand with a crowd of people around him. I could only think of the situation he was in. Either he was on a hot streak and lost it, or he was building a streak. From the look on his face though, it was more of someone who has just lost all their money and doesn't know how they are going to get back home.

"Look who I found bro!" I said in excitement.

"I know her from somewhere, and I would love to talk, but I am kind of in a nerve-wracking situation. I have to place my chips on this. Where that shot at I'm going to need it."

"Damn, I forgot I ordered those. Never mind that, what have you done man?"

"I kind of just lost twelve grand," He sadly uttered like he delivered news of running over a neighbor's dog.

"Twelve Gs?! We only came here with fifteen!" I reminded him. "I knew I should have held the money man."

"I know I know! I was on a streak just betting five hundred here and there, but I dug a hole and, yeah. Now I'm here. I'm going to go all in."

Renee and I looked at each other confused, because his mind was made up.

"So, he is betting on a number?" Renee asked.

"Yeah. One of the many ways to win is to bet that your number is rolled. That's what he is betting on. I'm sure he is betting on eight because that is his favorite number."

"Hmmm. Hey, bet on 4!" She ordered Vince.

Vince looked at her, then me, and shrugged. He knew he had nothing to lose. He slowly placed the rest of his colored chips on the green number four and held the craps table for dear life like he was riding the world's most terrifying roller coaster.

"Close your eyes!" Renee said. The guy throwing the dice made a dramatic roll every time he would roll the dice, screaming "We rolling!" before every throw.

"Here we go, bro! I'm going to kill you both if this number isn't four. And since I can't eat because this is the last of our money, I will have no choice but to go full zombie mode on you both, but hold that thought!" Vince said.

"We rolling!"

"Four!!!!" The dealer shouted.

Everyone around started clapping. They could feel Vince's desperation to win like a +1000 underdog.

"That's crazy. Renee, you are a genius!" Vince said.

"Eh. Lucky guess. Glad you won, though. I wouldn't want us to be zombie food, you know?"

"Good point."

"Yeah, yeah. Listen, hand me my cut mister, before you spend it all," I said, reaching my hand out.

"Here. Don't go spending that all in one spot,"

Vince gave me eight thousand dollars' worth of chips.

"Shut up punk and win our money back. We're going to the roulette tables. Meet at the bar in an hour or so?" We all looked at our watches to confirm our meet time and separated.

I was two grand short now, thanks to my best friend, but I was determined to win more than that back. Roulette was my game for some reason when my grandmother took me to the boat. It was time to see what I had, and losing in front of the world's most gorgeous woman was not about to happen.

"So. How do you play roulette?" Renee asked.

"Well like craps, there are different ways to win. I'll go throw the few that I play and if you like, you can play too. Cool?"

"Yep. Go on,"

"So, in roulette, you have odds for the different ways to win. So basically, you see that little white ball right there spinning around? You can bet on that ball to land on a specific number. Out of thirty-six numbers, that is not easy, and it's thirty-seven numbers if you count the zero," I explained.

"So why would anyone want to play a game like this? It looks like all the odds are against the players. Especially by betting on one number,"

"Well yeah. That's gambling in general, though. So the odds suck, but if you can win with your number, the payout is thirty-five to one!"

I looked up to make sure she was understanding, but the soulless stare at the spinwheel told me enough. I had to reset my teaching process.

"Ok, thirty-five to one means if you bet one dollar on say, your lucky number four like the previous game, you would win thirty-five dollars,"

"Ohhh okay. I got it now,"

"Good. So, you can bet on colors and a range of numbers, all even or odd numbers, which is usually what I do,"

She began to reach into her white clutch purse. She began fiddling around looking for something.

"I'll take that bet," She said to the dealer.

"Wait. What bet? We haven't talked about a bet yet."

"I want to bet on the number four again."

"Well. I mean, maybe you should warm up with a lighter bet first. I wouldn't jump right into the highest of bets just yet you know. Maybe-"

"How much would you like to bet?" The dealer asked.

"A thousand," She said with uncertainty.

The bystanders awed in amazement as they were about to witness someone either blow their wad or come up nicely on a new stack of cash.

"What? Renee, just wait a minute,"

Trying to reason with her got me nowhere. She didn't say anything, she stared at the roulette table fiercely with laser focus.

"Last call for bets!" The dealer shouted.

Everyone around was looking at me to see what was I going to do, chicken out or press my luck. Just in case we lost, I bet more than her so I would look worse than she would.

"Bet even," she whispered. The stone gargoyle look on her face made me listen without hesitation. I put two black chips on even, and five black chips on 1-12 totaling in seven thousand. This left me with one thousand to my name while in Vegas. My odds were slimmer than an anorexic, but I was prepared to face the consequences.

The wheel started to spin, and the ball dropped. Renee and I clenched hands tightly. All we could hear was the white ball tacking against bridges between each number, each tack growing in sound as the frequency slowed down like a slowed tempo record. The tacking noise suddenly ceased. The crowd ooh'ed and ahh'ed. Renee and I scanning the spinwheel, looking for the little white ball like an Easter egg hunt. We were too late, as the dealer beat us to it.

"Four!" The dealer shouted. We both screamed and yelled in excitement and disbelief since the odds were so heavily stacked against us. Thoughts of winning seemed like a mere dream.

"You realize you just won thirty-five stacks right!? You had me so worried!" I said to her in excitement as we gazed into each other's eyes. After three seconds of gazing she spoke.

"I wasn't too worried. If I lost, I had this handsome guy dressed in all black to cover," She said, biting her bottom lip.

"He must be a real guy then," I replied as I smiled, continuing to look into her eyes. The dealer handed her three gunmetal colored chips which were $10,000 each and six black thousand dollar chips. He handed me one gunmetal colored chip and nine black chips.

"Congrats on your winnings guys. You can change out for lower denomination chips at any table or cash out at the booth. Up to you," the dealer explained. We looked at each other and then back at the table and shrugged.

We were feeling lucky tonight. I tipped the dealer, and we continued to press our luck while we could. Most people would just quit and go home with their earnings or whatever because they are afraid to lose their money but not us. I understood now that scared money didn't make any money. We were young, and fear didn't really exist for us yet, and we were in it to win it. I grabbed Renee by the waist and pulled her close.

"Why would we come to Vegas and not push the envelope!" I said aloud, giving the people around us a show.

"Since this whole thing is peculiar, give me five grand on odd!"

"I'll take the same bet!" Renee told the dealer.

"I want that bet too! But ten grand!" We heard a raspy voice order. "I see my buddies getting cash, and I want in!" Vince said.

We all made our bets and joined together at the waist like Siamese triplets as the dealer dropped the ball on the spinning wheel.

"Seven. Winner!"

"Incredible," I whispered to myself. I didn't know if the stars were aligned in a certain pattern or if Renee's beginner's luck was rubbing off on us, but I had never had such luck before. We didn't win every bet as we continued to play, but we won the bulk of them. If a person didn't know any better, they would have thought we robbed a bank. We were shooting for half a million but we fell a bit short. We were still satisfied.

Altogether, we walked away with a quarter million dollars of the MGM Grand Casino's money. It took us all night. We started around 9:00pm, and we didn't stop till about 1:00am. We finally called it quits. We were dog tired. It felt like we just ran suicide drills for basketball tryouts. The cash teller gave us our own small bag of our earned cash. Renee took $50,000 in five blocks of hundred dollar bills sealed with a yellow seal displaying the number $10,000 on each seal. Vince and I were splitting $175,000 50/50. I called for a limo driver while we headed for the exit.

"I can't believe I have to work tomorrow. I have to be up in four hours," Renee said. I knew I shouldn't hang out with you guys," She smiled, so I knew she wasn't too serious.

"That sucks man," Vince responded.

"Yeah but you know what doesn't suck? Turning a thousand dollars to fifty thousand in a matter of hours! So, you are welcome. Now you can afford to be late," I butted in. She gave me a side eye.

"What makes you think I can afford to be late?"

"You just made an important person's salary in a few hours! Hell, that's enough to at least call in sick," I said chuckling.

"Where are you guys staying at tonight?" she asked.

"With you," I uttered smoothly. The smile we gave each other showed that we may have been thinking the same thing, not wanting the night to end just yet.

"We got a room at The Mirage actually," I corrected myself. "Speaking of, we have just arrived," I said looking out the window.

"Awesome. I'm going to head to the Travelodge then," She said to me with instant silence behind her sentence. She was anxiously awaiting my response.

"I thought you were going to stay with me a while? I would have had the driver drop you off first. You are more than welcome to stay with me for the night."

"Well, thank you. I don't want to impose on you two and besides, I don't have any pajamas."

I laughed and offered out my hand to assist her from the limo seat.

"Well, you wouldn't be imposing. We have separate rooms. Vince's feet stink, there is no way I could stay in the same room as him," I laughed. "Besides, I have some clothes you could wear. They might be a little big but just pretend you are modeling them for someone."

"Fine," She said with a smirk. "You better not be up to any funny business."

I felt like she couldn't resist. I also felt like who could. I mean, I was dapper from head to toe, professionally styled. I had money, well-mannered, I'm handsome, and I'm a nice guy. Why would she or any other woman resist? And with this confidence, I couldn't live with myself if I didn't shoot every shot. I had to get her to my room. The kicker was, I wasn't trying to get in her pants or anything like that. I just wanted her company and her trust. I wanted her to feel welcome around me, I wanted to be friends with her.

"Hey, I'm not having fun guys, so I'm going to have the driver take me out," Vince said. "Here. Take care of this for me," He gave me his portion of the casino winnings.

"You want me to go, bro?" I asked.

"No no, it's all good. I'm going to hit a few bars. Just scoping out."

"Alright, be safe."

"Bye bye," Renee said.

As Vince left, I proceeded to head to the 31st floor of the hotel with this beautiful woman. We finally got to the room, and her breath was taken away. She was wowed by the room.

"What on earth? What kind of room is this? Look at these windows! The view you have! This is amazing. I can't stay here, take me home. This is out of my realm."

I laughed before explaining.

"I had a chance to do something nice for myself for once, so I said why the hell not you know?"

"How much does something like this cost?"

"Just depends. It can vary with the style of the room, the number of rooms. They have some that are nicer than this for about eight grand for a weekend."

I changed into something a little bit more comfortable. A pair of Adidas sweatpants and a tank top. I gave her some clothes to change into as well.

"Here you go. A shirt for you to change into."

"Where's the rest!?" She yelled at me.

"Rest of what?" I busted out laughing while looking at her facial expression. "I'm just joking! Smile! Here are some shorts for you. The ass part is see-through, though," I laughed again. "Just joshing. The bathroom is over there," I directed her.

She came out the bathroom looking like a younger sibling with hand-me-down clothes from an overweight relative.

"They are too big!"

"Heyyy no worries, they give you a cute look. That might be the new style one day, and I'm your witness that you started it," I joked with her.

"Movie time?"

"What do we have to watch?" she asked.

"Let's see," I started to flip through the TV channels. "Oh! Terminator 2 is on! This is like one of my favorite movies!"

"No way. I love Terminator! Sarah Connor is my hero!" She explained.

"Say no more!"

We were in deep silence while we watched one of our favorite movies of all time. I couldn't believe she loved the Terminator movies. I was falling for her now. I could tell she was beginning to get more comfortable around me as she closed in to lay her head on my shoulder as she started to get a bit more relaxed.

"So, what's your story? Who are you? What do you want from life?" She asked me. "You particularly come off very mysterious to me." "What you see is what you get with me. I'm just a guy that's trying to get a fair shake in this world and help my mom," I responded.

"What's wrong with your mom?"

I sighed.

"I wouldn't know where to begin. But the short of it is that she has this rare form of arthritis that will cripple her if she doesn't get the right medication and treatment."

"What kind of treatment?"

"Well. The illness attacks her joints very violently which causes her knees and hands to swell and even her legs and feet. Sometimes she can't even walk. So, the doctors use a needle to drain the fluid build-up from her joints. I can never watch or be around, you know? Can you imagine watching the life sucked right out of your mother? Breaks my heart."

I looked away from her eyes and then down in sadness for a second as I thought about my mom. Then I felt extremely sick like I was about to do a presentation to a million people. I had butterflies. Renee had grabbed my hand.

"Jeeze."

"Yeah. Guess what I'll be doing with tonight's earnings," I smirked as I looked back into her eyes.

"Man. I have so many issues right now, but my mother is my main focus. I just have to get enough money to pay for everything and then keep the maintenance going."

"What about your partner?"

"Vince? That's my day one right there. Working for Viktor was kind of a new chapter for me and life changing. I decided I want my best friend by my side to experience a new chapter too.

"I see. I see. Cute."

"Cute huh?" I laughed. "I hope he comes in soon so I can stop worrying about him. I worry too much anyway." I turned Terminator down a bit because we would be talking for some time.

"Why do you worry about Vince?" She asked.

"Like myself, he has his issues too. We deal with them differently. Vince likes to drink. Especially when he gets in his thoughts. He lost his father when he was little, and things go downhill from there when he starts thinking about his dad. He wants to do right by his mother just as I do. She's all he has."

"Man, you guys are warriors," Renee said. "Humble beginnings you know? So, when you and I first met it was a little wild…"

She took her hand back and covered her face.

"About that. I'm not that type of a girl. That night my friend Sasha talked me into letting loose. That was my first and last one night stand. So, don't you even think that's what about to happen right now!" She pointed at me.

I threw my hands up in defense. "Hey man, I'm not judging or anything like that. We don't even have to talk about it," I explained.

"Do you know Viktor?" I asked.

"Who's that?"

"The owner of the club we met in?"

"Oh no. We had a show that night, and Sasha just talked us into the club. He just happened to be the owner, and he liked us, I guess. That's why we were upstairs hanging out and what not."

"Ah, I see." A big part of me was relieved that her and Viktor didn't know each other because if they did, I would have to cut off my feelings right then and there. I am a firm believer in not mixing business and pleasure.

"So, your turn. What's your story?" I asked.

"Well. Nothing like you two guys but I grew up over in Brazil for most of my childhood. I grew up in poverty, some nights not even knowing if we would eat dinner or not but my mother and father always made a way. One day an American guy comes through the slums, and he is taking pictures of everything and everybody, you know capturing the experiences and he captures a picture of me too."

My mind, body, and soul was totally immersed in her words as she continued to tell her story.

"After he shoots the photos, he tells my mother that I was beautiful and that I could make it big over in the U.S. with modeling if I chose to pursue it. He gave us his card and told us to call him one day. I had to be 10 or 11 at the time. When I turned 17, my mother and father showed me a pot of cash they had been saving up since that day. That cash paid for my ticket to America and my way into modeling. I got seven years of experience now, and I'm global. Not famous yet though, and I'm not sure I want to be. I'm just looking to continue to grow in the industry."

"Wow. That's amazing. Just hearing your story makes me want to say, I'm proud of you. I know your parents must be so proud," I told her but she looked kind of down.

"What's wrong?" I asked.

"Well, yeah they are proud, but I want to move them to a better place. Everyone thinks I have forgotten them, but they are misled. When people see your face in magazines and stuff they think 'oh you rich now,' but I am not rich. I am not poor anymore, either. So, I always send them money and stuff. I just want to do more,"

This time I grabbed her hand as she looked up.

"I'm sure you will be moving them around soon. You're doing the best you can, no?" I asked.

"Yeah. I am."

"Then that's all that matters. You can't beat yourself up about it if you're trying your hardest," I explained. "That big break is coming for you and your family. Believe it,"

"I guess you're right."

Renee and I were on the brink of falling asleep on the couch when all of a sudden, a loud thud hit the door.

"What the hell is that?" she asked.

"Sounded like the door."

I started creeping to the front door, quiet as a ninja on his initiation mission. Whatever it was behind that door, I needed to have the upper hand. I looked through the peephole only to see some legs attached to some nice shoes.

"Shoot! It's Vince!" I opened the door as fast as possible. "Help me get him in?" I asked Renee as she watched. "I can smell the liquor. You just couldn't resist, huh?" I said while trying to get him in his room.

"Should I leave?" Renee asked.

I dropped Vince right where we stood like a heavy sack of bricks.

"No, no. You don't have to leave. I need you to help me take care of this guy," I said.

If she left because of Vince, I was going to suffocate him with a pillow while he was out. Not seriously of course, but I would have been upset.

"Ok, let's get his shoes off and get him lying on his stomach," Renee said as she went for his shoes. We sloppily dragged him to his bedroom by his arms, body sliding on the marble floors. We looked like two first time killers trying to cover up a murder.

"Give us a little help brother, we got to get you on this bed," I said to him giving him the best encouragement I could.

"Just leave me right...here. The floor is fine," Vince told us. His voice slurred and weakening with every word, giving up on making it 2ft to the bed. Renee and I both looked at each other for a split second, and both non-verbally agreed to Vince's wish and left him on his bedroom floor a couple feet from his bed.

"He will have some explaining to do tomorrow," Renee said as she dusted off her hands.

"Yes, indeed, he will," I confirmed. "Out of sight out of mind, for now, I'm going to bed. You can have the bed, of course, and I will take the couch," I explained.

We went to our designated locations, and I couldn't help but think about how we almost fell asleep together, and Vince came in and destroyed everything I had worked for. Renee made me feel like a schoolboy again with her beauty. The schoolboy that sees the most beautiful girl walking the hallways and he is just wishing, praying and hoping that she notices him and praying that he would get the opportunity to talk to her. When she does talk to him, he is wishing he can go that extra step every interaction whether it is walking her home, or just a wave every time their paths cross. That schoolboy feeling is what she gave me, only this time this schoolboy wishes he could climb up the side of her house and be welcomed into her room and into her bed.

"Hey! It's cold!" Renee said from the bedroom.

"Okay!" I responded to her call. I paused for a second collecting my thoughts.

"There is a God," I whispered to myself.

She had only been in the room for a few moments, but that's all the time it took for the room to be fermented in her scent and for me to be drugged.

"Mom, I had a bad dream, can I sleep with you?" I said joking with her as I climbed into the huge bed. I lied there, stiff as a board trying not to be weird or awkward. All I could think about was not getting a woody. She was so spicy and sexy. I don't think anyone could blame me if I did catch a woody but I didn't want to risk it. I started to think about boxing to calm my sexual nerves, and as soon as I got a lid on things, she turned the opposite way, said goodnight and placed her perfectly shaped ass in my pelvic region and that was it. Woody was in full effect. I quickly turned the other way so that my ass was up against hers. I was too old to be feeling like a little boy again, but with me thinking too much, I couldn't help it. The man in me wanted to turn her over right then and there, rip our clothes off and get busy, but the kid in me won the battle, and I went to sleep right there next to her.

"Wake up!" I heard a dry, raspy voice call out. My head was still foggy from the alcohol and lack of sleep. I opened my eyes and blinked like a shutter camera, clearing the blurriness to see whom this person was.

"Vince? Welcome back from the dead you animal!" I said as I sat up on the bed yawning. "What the hell happened to you? Who gave you that black eye? Whose ass do I need to beat? Wait. Where's Renee!?" I asked intensely after searching the bed, hoping she was lost in the covers.

"Here," Vince uttered, handing me a piece of paper. "Looks like you got hit and quitted buddy," Vince laughed.

I gave him a stone-face as I looked up. On his deathbed, he still had douchebag jokes. It was a note from Renee

I had a blast with you last night. I wish I could have stayed with you, but duty calls. I have to fly to LA tonight for another show. Hope we meet again, call me sometime. PS, thanks for respecting me.

I grabbed my phone and placed her number in my contacts for the day I choose to contact her. I looked back up at Vince and I put my phone back down.

"So anyway. Carry on," I egged him on to continue his story.

"Bro, last night was crazy. Damn my face hurts," he grabbed and wiggled his jaw. "Anyway, I don't remember how I got back here. Like I don't remember at all. But let me tell you what I do remember," Vince said. His voice was desert dry. He sat on the floor near the bed, his way of telling me this was going to be a story to remember.

"So, after we split ways at the hotel, I had the driver take me sightseeing you know. So out the blue, I get a text message. Guess who? Emilia! So, she's like, 'hey, I haven't played in a while because there aren't worthy challengers out there but it's not often I get to play a foreigner, so if you're up to it, Sagat and I will take you and Ken down.'

So, I'm there, blown away that she even texted me back although the ladies always hit my phone because I got the juice, but it was so late at night. Anyway, I accept the challenge, of course. As soon as she sent me the address I got the driver to drop me off there. I get there at her place and whatnot, and it's a nice little low-rise apartment building, so she comes out to get me. I took the taxi driver's number just in case I needed a ride back. Man, I thought she was sexy with her wild leggings she had on at the mall but she took it to another level last night. She had on a loose-fitting Street-Fighter t-shirt with these little blue and red muay-thai shorts just like Sagat wears in the game. I didn't know if she was trying to seduce me or what but she had those beautiful legs out, and I was ready to forfeit and pounce on her. I can't lie, though; she had me worried at first. It's not every day your opponent is dressed like their favorite character you know? I was thinking to myself like man, I just might get creamed, not to mention I was rusty.

Once inside, she tells me to get comfortable, and she will be right back. She had a very cozy home, so it wasn't hard to get comfy. I was hoping she was gonna come back with no clothes on and tell me to get in her room. She came back only to meet me with a jaw opening facial expression. She brought out an Xbox bro. I hate Xbox. I begged her to go back in her room to find a Playstation, and she looked at me like I had an upside-down face. We argued for a few minutes on which system was better and why just like any opposing gamer would. After a while, we got the game going, and I let her get her moves in. I was just playing like a beginner, throwing fireballs and whatnot but just really seeing how she plays and what she knows. After I got comfortable with the controls, it was pretty much a wrap. I thought I would make things a little bit more interesting with a wager. I was winning all night, why not right? So, I say ok if I win, you gotta come to a bar with me and have a drink. She sucked teeth and said, 'I'll bet anything because you suck, no way you can beat me'. She's laughing and whatnot, but I'm just smiling because she doesn't even know what's about to happen to her. So, I make it even more interesting. I say if that's the case, if I win, then you have to kiss me too. She just replied with a 'sureee' like I was out of my mind. The match begins, and I totally wipe her out bro, like, I nuked her. She's was so mad, it was so funny. But she was legit and kept her word.

I called my driver to come and get us, and we headed out for the strip. I have her pick a spot for us to go to since I wasn't from here and she takes us to this spot called Ghostbar which was a little off the strip at the Palms but close enough. This wasn't your average bar, though; it was on the 55th floor of the hotel. After the bouncers checked our IDs and hit our pockets for forty dollars…well my pockets since I paid for her entry, too. The bar was live, super crowded but dope. Dark but the neon lighting and many TV screens kept the club lit just right. The DJ was spinning all the latest music but remixed with sped up-tempo. I swear it felt like everyone in there was on ecstasy. The 360-degree view she was telling me about was the coolest part. The windows were floor to ceiling like we got in here in the hotel room, except you can see just about all of the strip in there.

We sat in a corner by one of the windows, a little secluded from the bulk of everyone. I flagged down a waitress to get us a bottle of Fireball to sip on while we talked and what not. After talking with her for some time, I found that we had a lot in common besides Street Fighter. Like I lost my dad, she lost her mom a couple years ago. We didn't mean for the conversation to take a sad turn, but it did for a second, so we took a shot of fireball for the pain and another shot right behind it in their name. We played rock, paper, scissors for a wager on who was going to take a double shot. She was so competitive, and that was a turn on for me. She lost the round, but I told her I wouldn't let her take it alone, so I took a double shot with her. The DJ put on that "You" record by Lloyd and she grabbed my hand and whispered, 'Dance with me' in my ear. Drunk and already in love with her, that put me in a trance. Maybe Lloyd was performing, and I didn't know because the DJ mixed another Lloyd track right after that one. It was a lot slower and she matched the tempo, giving me the captivating version of her, grinding her body on mine. Placing my hands on her hips while she danced her body on mine. I backed up a few inches turned her around facing me and put my index finger in her pants right where the seam met the navel, pulled her back in to me, and kissed her. Her lips were so soft, the best kissing I ever experienced, man. So, after we tried to eat each other's faces she says I should come back to her place and beat her in Street Fighter again, so you know what that means. But first she says she has to pee so she stumbled her way to the bathroom and at this point, I'm feeling really good you know, not too drunk but drunk enough, I got a beautiful girl loving me and I'm loving this moment you know? Now here is where the night takes a turn. I'm just people watching, sipping some fireball on ice. I notice her coming back. Emilia was about twelve feet away when some guy grabs her, says something to her then forces himself on her. I guess he was looking for a dance or something, but

Emilia was not having it. The guy had a hold of her. So, I run over there and pull her away from the idiot and push him away. His two buddies come out of nowhere looking like they're itching for trouble you know, calling me Chinaman, which was kind of funny because my mom is Filipino, but anyway. I was outnumbered so the only logical thing to do was to talk my way out of it. Emilia and I just came to enjoy ourselves, not bothering anyone and definitely not to fight anyone. I explain this to the idiots, take Emilia by the hand and tell her we out of here. These guys pushed me to my breaking point brother.

We head for the door and one of the guys was like 'I love that little tight ass you got.' And smacks it bro. He smacked her right on the ass and high-fived his buddies. I totally blacked out. I walked Emilia to the elevator and told her to wait there. I grabbed a drink from a nearby table where the three stooges were and threw it in the first guy's face and pushed him down giving me some time to make my way down the line. I decked the guy in the middle, who was mister hot hands himself. I winded that punch up like I was on the mound of the World Series, 9th inning bases loaded with two strikes! I tried to fly his head to the moon! He went to sleep instead which was good enough for me. The last dude and myself had a stare-down, and he didn't know what to so I just kicked him in his balls like a schoolgirl and watched him fold to the ground in pain. The guy with the drink in his face tackled me from behind, turned me over and planted a nice one on me right before the bouncers snatched him off of me. That's where I got this nice little shiner. After the scuffle, the bouncers threw us out of the hotel. Outside, I see Emilia, and she started apologizing for some reason. She had no reason to because she didn't do anything. I apologized for getting us kicked out the hotel, but those guys had a beat down coming. She thanked me for protecting her, so it was worth it. She offered to ice my bruised eye at her place, so I called my driver to take us there. At her place, she laid me down on her couch and put a bag of frozen peas on my eyes. I laid my head back from relief and before I knew it she was kissing my neck, so I threw the peas aside and got on top of her. Kissing her from head to toe, undressing her in the process. You pretty much know the rest, we did the nasty, and I put her to bed. She had a bottle of Jack Daniels whiskey on the top of her fridge, so I took a big hit of that on my way out and that kind of put me on drunken monkey mode, in fact, I don't remember anything after. How did I get here?"

I put my hand on my head trying to process everything that I just heard. "It went down like that?!" I said with excitement, pounding my fist into my palm. "I'm guessing your drunk ass had your driver drop you off here, and you stumbled your way to the elevator. I don't know," I explained. "All I know is I wish I was there to rumble with you! I hate that I wasn't there."

"It's all good. I handled business," Vince said, laughing at the flashback.

"So, let me get this straight. While I was being mister romantic, you were out having a blast, huh. Beating ass, playing video games and slaying women and all I get is a callback number that probably isn't real?" I laughed.

"It's just like that sometimes, bro. So, wait a minute. I left you alone with Renee, and you didn't do your job? You didn't sex her up and down? Have you not learned anything from me? You got to stop being so nice and overthinking baby!" Vince said shamefully.

Vince was right. I was a dork when it came to getting lucky with women.

Generally, Vince would always get lucky, and it baffled me because he isn't overly nice or anything, He's a bit brash, but charming at the same time, which seems to win the ladies over. It was like a gift. On the other hand, I'm overly nice and kind, yet I always get played to the left. Nice guys finish last is perhaps true.

"So, what did you guys end up doing? Looks like you guys at least slept in the same bed" Vince said jokingly.

I shot him my trademark stone-face as I begin to tell my half of the story.

"I mean, it's nothing to the caliber of your night. When you left, we watched Terminator, which she's a huge fan of, and we chatted about our lives and how far we've come from our past and whatnot. She explained the last encounter we had was not who she was. Her friend drugged her or something like that."

"Sureee. That's what they all say. Next thing you know, they got their face in your lap," Vince abruptly butted in.

"Well, not her," I said, refusing to believe such antics from her. "Maybe that would have happened, but I never got a chance to make my move because guess what? Vince happened to crash the party!" I shouted.

"Well from the looks of it, your night sucked, and I did you guys a favor by adding some excitement!" Vince remarked. He stood up and patted me on the back."

"You must want two black eyes," I jokingly replied. "So yeah. That's my night. Let's grab something to eat, my head is pounding, and I'm sure yours is, too. I overheard someone in the lobby say the BLT Burger joint downstairs has the best burgers in Vegas. Got to be way better than that Fatburger we had. We probably should stop at the gift shop first so we can cover up that ugly face of yours," I joked, followed by both of our laughter.

We slept most of our Saturday away, and we were still hung over for the most part, so the rest of our trip consisted of just walking around the strip and spending hours in the world M&M arcade. They had every game imaginable there. I showed Vince who the real boss of Street Fighter was He didn't win one round against me and Ryu. We played until our eyes burned. Our flight was at 8am, we didn't return to our room till 3am. It's like in Vegas, we didn't sleep unless we drank ourselves to sleep and for whatever reason, we didn't mind those stipulations. We stayed up till it was time to catch our flight. Surprisingly, we caught our flight on time. As soon as I sat in my seat, I felt the anxiety from the fear of flying, but this time it was different. It was settled, it didn't attack me. Maybe I was becoming used to it. Instead of attacking me, it just sat next to me, letting me know it was still alive. I took advantage of this and just started to reflect on Vegas and all the wonders and pleasures of the world that are hidden from inner city kids like Vince and myself. I was curious. What else does the world have to offer us visually, mentally, socially or spiritually? I thought to myself. I couldn't wait to find out. Opening this Pandora box has been a good choice and a blessing.

You Know the Quote

A few weeks home from a well-deserved and an unimaginable time in Vegas, it was time to get back to work. I was tired of sitting at home just watching TV. The only problem was, we didn't have jobs. Vince never really worked outside of selling nickel and dime bags, and I quit the dealership. I was bored, but it beats being bored and broke by a long shot.

I wanted to make sure I stayed true to my plan of going back to Massachusetts Institute of technology (MIT), so I decided to enroll in a community college and take a couple of business courses for extra credits. The worst part was, it felt like I was in high school again. I never got much attention in high school, but I got plenty attention here. Mostly girls just trying to get a ride home and secure a boyfriend but I had no interest. I never cared for much attention anyway. My mind was focused on taking my classes and going home. I was taking economics and accounting to see how money works. Why do the rich get richer and how could I take advantage of it? Supply and demand and mass selling was the answer. The professor made it sound so simple. Find a mass of people, create a large desired demand for that mass and supply them with a sample of whatever product you're selling and then flood them with that product. When that demand returns even higher, the money starts rolling in. I was fascinated by the formula. I just wanted to learn as much as I could as fast as I can. I bought a few extra finance books, just to learn more about it.

I tried to teach Vince, but he was too focused on fashion and women. He went from old beat up Reeboks and worn clothing, to Gucci shoes and Versace shirts. As long as he was happy, I was happy.

Out the blue, I got a text from the heaven! It was Renee. I was so happy, I just stared at the text thinking of the perfect response. All it said was

hey punk :)

I responded,

hey loser :)

That's all it took for us to connect and start a whole conversation. The more we talked, the more I got the urge to do what I had been prolonging and contemplating for so long. I scrolled down my contacts and hit "Toya."

"Hey, Toya…" I uttered dryly.

"Hey," she said matching my tone.

"I haven't been a very good boyfriend to you. I'm sorry. I could justify everything but I won't. I'm just going to cut to the chase," I explained. "I'll always love you, and if you ever need me, I'll be there for you."

I could hear sniffing on the other end, she was crying, and it pained me. It pained me to break her heart. It pained me to hurt my best friend. We had been friends for ten years before we got together for another five years. I still remember the moment when we first met. It was very unusual how we met. It wasn't a bar, or church or school, it was on a video conference. I was at a buddy's house that day, and he just happened to be talking to her as I walked past the camera. She shouted out 'Hello!' and the rest was history. From the next day forward we were peas and carrots, constantly going out every chance we get. It wasn't an average friendship. It was odd because we weren't attracted to each other in that lovey kind of way. We didn't hold hands, we didn't hug or kiss, we just enjoyed each other's company. I remember the time I knew I was in love with her. She crushed me. She graduated college accepted a job offer all the way across the world to teach English in Japan. I remember holding the phone just hearing the reasons why she was taking the job, but I wasn't listening. All I retained was 'I'm going to Japan.' I asked her to stay and find work here, but I quickly changed my request and told her to take it because I would never want to block someone's potential. I told her I was happy for her and I was proud of her for taking such a big next step in her life, but I was truthfully sour because she was leaving me and I couldn't stop her. I told her I would be here when she returned and then she really crushed me. She told me not to wait for her. That's when I knew she didn't love me as much as I loved her. I spent a year trying to forget about her, trying to keep busy with work, school, and dating as many women as possible.

A little over a year had gone by since Toya had left for her new job and randomly, one sunny day, my mom handed me a piece of mail from Japan. It was Toya. She was coming home in a month. My stomach instantly filled with butterflies, my heart sped up to match a pace runners', and I was unprepared. I had less than a month to cut my workload in half as well as cut ties with all the women I've accumulated. I didn't want to let my newly found woman go, but for Toya, I did it. My love for her blinded me more than an all-white winter on a sunny day. When I was a kid, my grandmother told me 'If it is meant to be, then it will be' and I thought the day she came back was our calling. I remember her running and jumping into my arms. You would have thought we had just gotten married. From that day forward, we hugged, we kissed, we made love, and we kept the things that made us best friends intact. We were each other's soulmate.

"So that's it?" She asked. "After all these years. I came back to the states for you, and this is the thanks I get?"

"I can't explain this baby. I'm sorry," I said.

As I continued to speak, my voice began to crack, and she began to cry even harder. I didn't know how to tell her that this was my way of protecting her because I have entered a new world she cannot be a part of. I don't want her to be. She's got so much going for herself. It would be unfair of me to ruin that for her.

"Toya, I just need some time alone. I hope you can understand that as confusing as it is. You can hate me. You should hate me. I need you to be the best you can be in life and without me for the time being. Who knows? You came back to me. I just might return back to you" I explained through my own fragments of crying.

By now she had become silent on her end, so I figured this was just as good a time as any to take a page out of my grandma's book and end the call.

"Toya listen, I got to go but just know if it's meant to be, then it will be. I will talk to you later," I told her after I muscled up the courage to hang up the phone.

I plopped down on the bed and let out a huge sigh of relief. I finally did what needed to be done. I couldn't live my life this way, as a criminal, and keep her by my side. I truly felt it was the right thing to do. Matter of fact, I knew it was the right thing to do.

A New Beginning

It was three days since the heartfelt breakup with Toya. I was just getting used to it and had started to push it to the back of my mind. I still didn't have a job or anything else to do, so I figured I'd lend my mom my car so she could run her errands. Since she was feeling good, I would just kick back and watch one of my favorite movies, Scarface. As a favorite movie, of course I've seen it a thousand times. It's always just as enjoyable as the first time, but this time it was different. This time the movie was speaking to me. I felt like I was Tony Montana, Vince was Manolo and Viktor was Frank Lopez, of course. Something about watching those mob films, they always get you thinking. I was doing a lot of thinking and just like Tony Montana, I wanted it all Chico. I wanted to capture that American dream.

"Damn!" I said to myself as my phone started to ring, interrupting my movie since I clearly had never seen it before. 'Mommy' read across the screen.

"Hey, mom, what's going on?" I asked.

"Hey, baby. So, I was doing some research on COPD and this rheumatoid arthritis, and as I was about to leave, I'm stranded" she said, sounding sad as ever.

"Stranded where!?" I responded with concern. Then it hit me. What could I do? We only had one car. I couldn't do anything, and it started to kill me. My mom needs me, and I'm useless. I'm worthless to her right now, and I'm sick of feeling this way.

"I'm at the library, so I'm not that far. I'm going to walk," she said with disappointment.

"You're not walking anywhere. We will not risk you having a flare up. Stay there. I'll be there" I ordered.

"I will be okay, baby."

"Absolutely not mom. Stay there and continue what you were doing," I reinforced after her reasoning.

After going back and forth with her, she finally agreed to stay. I thought of calling her a cab, but then I thought to myself, what would Tony Montana do? I wasn't going to buy a new car, I was going to buy two new cars. One for me and one for her!

I called Vince to see if his cousin still worked at this dealership on Western Street. This wasn't your type of dealership like the prestigious Ford or Dodge. This was your come with the money, and you drive off the lot kind of dealership. Vince had told me stories passed down from his cousin, of drug dealers and hustlers buying cars from them because they didn't have to worry about questions like where you work or what's your credit score. I was bummed out because Vince said his cousin didn't work there anymore but he's optimistic enough because of his cousin's connections. We were going to see a guy named Pauli. I told Vince to meet me over there as soon as he could. I needed a favor, drive one of the cars back home for me. I didn't know what I was buying, but I wasn't leaving without two cars. I went to my room, grabbed $30,000 from my stash, stuffed it in my bag and was out the door headed to the dealership.

Having 20, 50 or 100 dollars in your possession is one thing when you're walking around in public. For me, walking around with cash always made me feel a bit uneasy. At the same time though, also secure because cash is king. But, when you're walking around with 30,000 dollars, it's a totally different atmosphere. A 25-minute train ride feels like an hour and everyone around me felt like a potential threat. Like a flesh-eating zombie and I just want to get away or kill them all to avoid the potential chance of anything happening to that money. I don't even care about my own well-being, I just want that cash to make it to its destination.

After my 10-minute walk from the train station, I was finally at my destination, We Got Autos. It was an interesting setup they had. I was used to the traditional dealership from working there before. Where you have a huge facility, a garage for repairs, and all the cars surround the place. This dealership literally had a shack no bigger than a trailer home and about 50 cars surrounding it. Vince was nowhere to be found, so I just glanced at the cars. I loved cars, I could look into them all day if I wanted to.

They stayed true to their name, they had almost everything in their large inventory. They didn't have Lamborghini or Ferrari, but they did have BMWs and Mercedes to name a couple, and everything American including old school models. I was pretty content on the choices they had there and was eager to buy. Roaming around, I stumbled upon a few old schools that caught my eye. A 1979 wet, deep gray Chevy Malibu with modern, red bucket seats. Someone knew exactly what they were doing and how to handle a true Malibu. They modernized it by having the bench seats removed, and the middle gear shifter replaced. The body was sleek as a Victoria's Secret model, and I'm instantly in love. Also, there is the 1969 dipped in black chocolate Camaro, that looks perfect for mom.

I was just about to cup my hands over my eyes to look at the interior through the glass when I heard the old wooden door creak open.

"Can I help you, kid? Unless you want a job washing cars, I suggest you don't touch them too much. We're not hiring either" I heard an old man's voice say aloud with slight aggression.

I raised my face from the driver's side of the window to see who was doing the talking. It was some old fat white man no younger than 65, favoring Danny Devito. It must be hot in that little office shack because you could see sweat spots on his loose-fitting button up shirt.

"Well, fortunately, I'm not looking for a job or to wash cars, but a formal greeting and some respect would be nice," I countered back at him.

"Well, what do you want? I'm tired of you kids coming here wasting my time" the old man complained.

"Well, if I'm not looking to wash your cars, or fill out an application. Hmm let's brainstorm for a second," I said, facetiously rubbing my chin in thought. "I got it! Maybe I'm here to buy a car!" I said oozing with sarcasm hoping that he would feel as stupid as sounded.

"Kid, how much money ya got?" He asked, letting out the world's largest sigh. He evidentially runs into this scenario every day.

I was about to say a number aloud, but then I stopped as the number appeared in my head. I didn't know this dude, and I don't know if this is who I'm here to see or not.

"I got enough. But listen, I don't have a lot of time. Is Pauli here?" I asked.

"Ah you're one of those customers" he responded. "Pauli! Get out here, someone's here to see you," he yelled.

Jack Williams

The old man went back inside, and I went back to placing my hands on the driver's window, looking at the interior some more. I was going to buy this car anyway, so I was going to put my hands all over it if I wanted to.

"Yo!" I heard from a small distance away. It was Vince.

"Finally, chump. I have been here for like an hour," I joked with him.

"Damn boy, you loud" I uttered as I sniffed him. "That's why you got that silly grin on your face huh?"

Vince smelled like he had just got off a cannabis boat and ran right over here. He was high as a cloud.

"You called me right when I finished a joint but you needed me so I'm here," Vince explained. "You meet Pauli? I have no idea what he looks like," He asked.

"Not yet. He's supposed to come out here, and here he comes, I think."

The old wooden door creaked open again, this time a slim young Hispanic guy came out. Looked to be no older than 30 years of age. He was wearing a wife beater, exposing his three gold chains and snake tattoos on his arm. Hair slicked back into a ponytail. He had on six gold rings, three on each hand. Oddly placed in my opinion, one ring on the thumb, middle and pinky finger.

"Who needs to see Pauli?" He asked with both his arms raised in the air waiting on the response from us.

"Hey, our man Jin told us to see you if we needed to buy some cars, cash," I explained.

"How do you two know Jin?" Pauli asked.

"Family," I said giving him a simple one-word answer.

"Well dig this. I don't know what you plan to do kid, but the cheapest car we have here is ten grand," He told us as he sucked his teeth and exhaled on his rings, then cleaning them on his wife beater.

"That's it?" I responded with cockiness as I flashed some of the cash at him. I didn't know if it was the dingy clothes we were wearing or what. They just seemed like they didn't want to take us seriously. Or maybe they just truly get the runaround from younger crowds trying to buy cars. I tried not to take it personally as I put myself in their shoes.

"Dig, what car were you looking at?" Pauli asked still standing at the top of the stairs connected to the shack.

"This here Camaro and that '79 Malibu over there," I pointed to the Malibu. "Can you grab the keys to both? I don't need a test drive, but I do need to see what's under the hood and hear these puppies run," I explained.

"I can dig it. I'll be right back with the keys."

I worked for the dealership we heisted for 6 years. I knew what sounds to listen for, in order to let me know if everything was good or not. If it had a clogged, dirty, spitting noise from the engine, then I would know it's no good, if it has none of that then I know it's clean. I would be looking for clean oil on the dipstick, no engine knocking, no water leaking from the tailpipe and no oil leaks on the ground. There were other signs, but these were the majors.

Pauli came back with the keys. I had Vince hop in the Malibu first and pop the hood then start her up. When the hood popped open, I was surprised to see such a clean engine. Usually, off brand dealerships only clean the exterior and interior to attract buyers, and when they get home, they see that engine is busted up and dirty, but this wasn't the case here. I was disappointed a tad because I was expecting to see a big block 5.0 V8, but it was a small block 4.7L V8, so it wasn't too bad.

"This small block should be putting out like 150 horses, right?" I asked Pauli, awaiting his confirmation.

"Yeah. Well, dig, the last owner installed an exhaust system so it should be getting about 250 horses out of her," Pauli confirmed.

Everything with Pauli was dig this and jack that. He was a slick talking, wild wild west gun slanger if you let him tell it. You'd think he grew up in the 70s the way he talked and dressed. I wouldn't be surprised if he was a pimping at night. "Vince, start her up for me. Let's see what that exhaust system sounds like" I ordered Vince. The engine shook a little as Vince cranked her and she started right up. It was a beauty. "Give her some gas baby!" I continued to order.

She sounded perfect. I couldn't believe how good she sounded. I was ready to blow my whole cash load for her as if this was my first time at a gentlemen's club. I couldn't wait to have her. Just like the Malibu, she started right up. I knew the Camaro had to be far more beastly than the Malibu. I popped the hood to see the Camaro holding a 5.0L V8 which I know was putting out at least 350 horses. As I revved the engine from tugging the throttle cable, I started to rethink the two purchases for a second and considered taking the Camaro and letting mom have the Malibu. "This might be too much power for her" I whispered to myself. "Nah, she'll be ok," I got out the Camaro just to marvel at it before I made the purchases.

"Ok, I'll take them both. If you the man to see for doing deals in cash, then get the paperwork and bring it out here. We're going to do the deal right here on the hood," I commanded Pauli as I shut the hood of the Camaro.

"I'm the right guy, and I can dig that jack," Pauli said, hurrying to the shack to get the paperwork like he had a fire lit under him. I looked at my wrist for the time, as I thought about my Mom. I hoped she was ok and not worrying about anything. I couldn't wait to get to her. I hated to see her in any kind of distress whatsoever. I started to picture her reaction when she sees the car I got her. I wondered if she would cry, would she laugh, or would she just not believe it. Knowing her, she wouldn't believe it until I put the keys in her hand and she got behind the wheel. I just want to see her happy. Life kind of decked her pretty hard of late. To go from the high life to being on welfare can't be an easy situation to digest and I feel like as her son and as her adult son, I feel like it's my job to change that. "Dig, here is the paperwork," Pauli said, placing the paperwork on the hood of the Camaro.

He laid out the paperwork to sign for the purchase and the bogus paperwork to stash in the glove boxes of the cars just in case the boys in blue wanted to see anything. He also gave me plates for the cars that when ran would show the dealership's name instead of mine. Everything was intact. "So how much I owe you?" I asked, reaching into my bag. "Dig, the Malibu is 12 grand and Camaro is 15 grand. So, 27 G's papi" Pauli confirmed. "Cool. Twenty-five, six, seven and eight because I appreciate you. Take care of us, we take care of you. Cool?" I stated, after counting the money on the hood. "Dig, that's great business. You're a good businessman. Come here first, I got you jack," Pauli said, displaying his happy customer service voice. "I'm going to hold you to it," I said. I slid all of the money across the hood to his hands, leaving me with two grand to my name for the time being.

I passed Vince the keys to the Malibu who still has the hysterical grin on his face through all of this. "Yo, smiley face? Can I trust you to take this home for me? Leave the keys in the mailbox. And most importantly...don't crash my shit man...you know how much I paid for this?" I joked with Vince, doing my best high roller voice impression.

"Shut up fool, you're welcome you know. You owe me a joint for messing up my high time," Vince laughed after stating. "Hit my line later, I'm about to wrap this around a pole," Vince said as he sped out of the lot. I shook my head and smiled as I shook Pauli's hand before getting into the Camaro to rescue my mom. As soon as I got in the Camaro and put it in drive, it instantly gave me flashbacks of that dark night, just a few weeks prior when we heisted a whole dealership. Hell, I think one of the cars was a '69 Camaro. The difference between driving those then and driving this one now, was that I was a nervous wreck then. I couldn't take in all of the feeling of a beautiful, well put together vehicle and now...I can. Now I have time to be one with the car, now I can take it all in. That gargly noise coming from the engine that sounds like heaven to my ears, that sweet but deadly gasoline smell, that old genuine American leather smell.

I threw gear in drive, slammed my foot on the gas and sped out into the intersection, fishtailing like a wild cod that just washed up on shore. I burst into laughter as the thrill tickled me. I hit about 60mph before I hit the first stop sign all of 100 yards away from where I pulled out from. All the nearby bystanders were staring at me as I drove like a bat out of hell, but I didn't care one bit. Anyone that just purchased this car and was sitting behind the wheel for the first time would drive the exact same way. I was only about 15 minutes away from the library where my mom was so I decided to stop at the nearby gas station for a little petrol. Everyone was staring, shouting nice car and a lot of older people asking me questions about it, trying to get me to come to car shows but I had no interest. I might even have come off as a douche, but I was irritated. I just wanted to get some gas and get mom. I asked the clerk for 30 on pump 4, and as paid, I saw a loaf of bread amongst other groceries. "Let me get a loaf of bread too," I asked of the clerk.

It's funny how a smell or a certain item can spark flashbacks vividly. I finished pumping the gas and got back on the road. Finally, I got to the library where mom was and shook my head in disappointment as I looked at my old piece of crap '92 Camaro just sitting there looking like an old rusted artifact. I remember when I first got her, I was so happy. On my way to work, a couple summers ago I bought her from this old man and a garage sale for $600.00. Although people everywhere pointed and made fun of me, I was so happy. I felt like I was Michael Knight from Knight Rider and the Camaro was KITT. I knew KITT was a Pontiac Trans Am but they shared the same body style, so it was close enough for me. The only difference from my Camaro and KITT was, it wasn't all black, it didn't follow directions nor talk back, and it damn sure didn't drive like KITT, but you can't blame a guy for pretending. All I had was my imagination! I parked right next to the old Camaro just for mom to notice her favorite car standing out. I called her to come out but played stupid like I had no idea whose car it was.

"Mom, come out. I'm here. I guess we will call a cab or tow truck" I said, smiling, because I knew this was a great joke to pull.

She came out, only to be startled by the ultra-mean looking 1969 Camaro SS.

"Now this wasn't here when I got here. Some nerve parking, next to our car when there are so many other parking spaces. Just making us look all kinds of bad," mom said with a bit of anger and envy. "One day I will get my old Camaro back that looks just like this. I remember I had an old Challenger that your stupid dad wrecked. I had a Chevelle that momma gave to me and a '71 Mustang. My favorite was still that '69 Camaro though boy, I tell ya," mom rattled off, going down memory lane, counting each car she had, on her fingers.

I figured this would be the best time to further lay the joke on her and start hinting at the car actually being hers.

"Mom, catch!" I said, tossing the keys in the air high enough for her to easily catch.

"What are these for?" she asked, confused.

I looked at her, and then nodded my head towards the aggressive beast, hoping she would get the picture.

"Baby, I don't understand," she uttered as her eyes welled up with tears. Deep down, she knew what I was hinting at, and she knew I knew. I saw the tears rolling down her cheeks! I smiled, they were happy tears, and I understood it.

My cheeks started to sting a bit, my throat started to feel tight. I did my best to hold back my own tears of joy. It was always hard to watch my mom cry. Even if her tears are happy tears, when she cries I cry too. All teary eyed, I walked over to the Camaro, and opened the driver's door, waving her to come over, solidifying the fact that this was real and this was her car.

"Come start her up, mom," I said, reaching down to pop the hood so she could see what the Camaro was working with.

I wanted her to look under the hood because she knew her cars.

"I can tell by the SS in the grille it's got to have that big block V8," she said while walking up to the Camaro.

I just kept smiling. I was stunned by how she could know that just off the bat. I thought I knew my cars, but she was one up on me. She took a peek at the engine and whispered 'gorgeous' then headed to the driver's side of the car. She started the Camaro up and instantly just fell back in the seat all relaxed and satisfied. Like she had been parched for days, and just had her thirst quenched. The rumbling noise of the clean engine put this look on her face that said it all. It said 'Yes, it's about time. I'm blessed, I'm lucky, I'm thankful, I'm back' and most importantly to me, her face said I'm happy, and so was I!

"Give it some gas mom! Don't be scared, it's yours!" I reassured her.

As she adjusted her mirrors, she looked at me and said, "Son, I love you!" She revved it high and hard, to 5000 RPM.

"Damn!" I said to myself.

Everyone was standing around staring at us and then it hit me that we probably shouldn't be doing all this loud commotion stuff right outside the library.

"They will be alright," My mom said, not giving much room for any care to interrupt her joy at the moment.

"Come on, let's take her for a spin. What do you say, we go old school and hit the lakefront?" I asked, showing her the loaf of bread I brought.

She smiled from ear to ear and agreed. I shut the hood, hopped in the passenger seat and let her navigate us to the destination. I could tell she missed the thrill of driving that old school American muscle, punching that throttle full force at every straight-away she came across. I might as well have sat in the trunk the way she drove. Constant speed from the beastly Camaro, throwing my back up against the seat, keeping my back and seat meshed together. Every red light that caught us and turned green was a race for her, and she won them all. About twenty minutes of this roller coaster and we had finally reached the lakefront. As we parked the car, flocks of birds were circling us, as if they have heard stories about us passed down from bird generation to bird generation about the bread we used to feed them.

"Looks like they have been waiting on the legend to return mom," I said.

"Maybe so," my mom said and smiled. "Do the honors," she instructed, while handing me the bread. It felt like we had literally turned back the hands of time.

When the birds saw the bread, it was a feeding frenzy. Squawking, telling each other that their supper had arrived. I ripped the bread open and began to throw pieces on the ground. In one motion, all the birds began to land by us fighting over the couple pieces of bread I had thrown. Once those pieces were consumed, they turned and looked at us anxiously awaiting the next piece.

"You better feed them before they attack you," my mom said.

"Nah, these are my little soldiers. They won't attack the hand that feeds them. Isn't that right my little birdies?" I asked as if the birds could talk back.

I handed half off the loaf of bread to mom so she could help feed them. I would just throw the pieces into the pile of birds, watching them mosh pit each other for a piece. If a bird didn't get a bite, then tough titty. My mom had a different view thought, she was so kind. She would make sure every bird got to eat a piece. Sometimes the smaller birds would get pushed aside for the food. It was really survival of the fittest. Mom would throw a small piece further than usual to lure the bigger birds towards the smaller piece and let them fight for it since they were usually the greediest. Then she'd give the smaller birds left behind big pieces. She would always say 'This will give them the strength to compete with those bully birds'. felt like a kid again, and it was a great feeling.

Mom and I headed to the big rocks by the lake to sit and just enjoy the sound of nature. I made sure to hold her hand as we maneuvered through the rocks and sand to get to the bigger rocks to sit. She could have a flare up at any time, and at this moment it could cost us our life because I couldn't swim and wouldn't be able to either.

"Ah, we made it," I said, letting out a huge sigh of relief. "How are you feeling lady?" I asked mom to ensure she was okay and safe.

"I'm okay. I just need to catch my breath. I'm not 33 years old no more," She said while breathing slightly heavy and bracing herself for a seat on the rock. Nonetheless though, still smiling, reminding me of the years when we came here often. I looked at her as she sat there a few yards away, staring off into the setting sunlight at the end of the lake, wondering what could possibly be on her mind.

"What you thinking about mom?" I asked out of curiosity.

"These rocks are huge. The pyramids in Egypt have rocks way bigger than this. We couldn't have possibly built them," she explained.

As I laughed, I couldn't help but ponder a thought.

"So, what are you suggesting? Aliens or something?"

"I don't know. I'm just saying think about it. No machinery in that time period," mom further explained.

"You do have a point mom," I said.

That was one beauty of our relationship. We were best friends. She could ask me silly stuff with no judgment, and I could do the same. One previous time, we discussed aliens and zombies. We were both obsessed with the thought of either of them popping up on earth. Although I was enjoying our fantasy talk, I knew the realistic conversation was coming.

"So where did you get the money for a new old Camaro?" my mom abruptly asked me, looking right at my eyes.

"Why you asking me all of this mom?" I responded in defense. "I went to Vegas. I played roulette, and I won big," I said as I flashed back through my memory bank, from the heist to Vegas, choosing the best answer.

"So, who taught you how to play roulette? I know I don't know and your dad doesn't know how. How much did you win?" She bombed me with another question.

"I am grown you know. I haven't graduated yet, but I am educated you know, and I happen to browse the internet a lot. So, I'm well versed in casino games," I further explained as I looked her in the eyes. I was confused whether I just lied to my mom or not. I didn't lie. I really did win big in Vegas.

"And I won enough," I continued. "I'm going to take care of your hospital bills, and go back to school next semester and get that engineering gig!"

"That's six figures!" She yelled with excitement.

"Maybe it is," I smirked. I put my arm around her and rested my head on her shoulder. "I love you mom, and everything's going to be okay like I said it would when I first left for school," I assured her.

We continued our conversation on the lake until we both got plagued with hunger and decided to head home. It was truly nostalgic hanging with my mom at the lake like old times. I wish I could just drop out of school and just hang with my mom or better yet just build a time a machine and make me a kid again. Those were the best times. She's just so fun to be around.

"Whose car is that?" Mom asked me, pulling up to our apartment.

"That's my new boo! Malibu that it is," I exclaimed, staring at it while driving past the machine. "I had to get myself something nice too you know. I can't take that beat up piece of crap no more," I grimaced with disgust as we both got out of her new Camaro.

"You got good taste boy. Where you think you got that?" she asked grinning.

"I have no idea actually."

"Yo momma!" She yelled as she tickled me like I was her baby boy again.

I was screaming with laughter as she rapidly tickled my whole upper body. My laughter quickly ended when she moved too fast.

"Ah! My knee!" my Mom screamed in pain. She collapsed. I quickly dropped my weight down, becoming her safety net.

"Mom! I got you. C'mon," I assured her.

We made our way to the door looking like war victims.

"I think a flare up is coming. Hurry up and hand me those pills," she ordered. Mom started shaking her hands out; she could feel the pain kicking in. I hurried and grabbed the orange tinted bottles, a glass of water and rushed them over to her. In that small matter of time, her left hand had already swelled up pretty bad. If you didn't know any better, you would think her hand was broken in three places the way the swelling looked. She was wincing in pain now. She downed a handful of pills. I hated the fact she was on so many different meds. She was taking Prednisone, Ibuprofen, and Tramadol all at once, which can't be safe but the pain was so strong I couldn't blame her. She had no choice. She would show me how odd the condition is all the time, like I didn't know. She just couldn't believe it.

"Look," mom whimpered while pressing on the swelling. Her arm had also started swelling up before our eyes. It was unlike anything the two of us had seen. When you put pressure on the swelling, it just leaves a dent where the pressure was, then slowly fills out again. It was like that on her hands and knees. I put some ice on her knees to try to alleviate any pain I could for her. The real treatment mom needed at this point was injections. Specialists would inject an anti-inflammatory medicine inside the affected area that offered relief for months. The only problem is that it's five grand per shot. She would need four shots each visit, totaling 20 grand. On the flip side to that, she was deathly afraid of needles not to mention relief isn't guaranteed but that was the least of my worries. It was worth the chance. I'd drug her and drag her to the doctor if I had to.

I sat by her side while she lay on the couch until the pain meds put her to sleep. The long process put me to sleep also. I woke up at about 2am confused as ever like any other time I wake up from a nap. Mom was still knocked from the meds. I got up and grabbed a blanket and put it on her. I grabbed my phone to see five missed calls from Vince, two missed calls from Toya and three text messages from Vince, Toya, and Renee.

I smiled as I looked at Renee's text. I started to reply to Toya's text but I was ignoring her. Out of sight, out of mind, I figured. I shot Vince a text to let him know the situation with mom and what happened, and I finally got around to the text that made me smile. I replied back to Renee.

Hey hot stuff, sorry I was KO'd. You still up?

I anxiously waited for her text back, feeling like a young schoolboy. After about ten minutes I gave it a rest. She's probably asleep I thought to myself before finally falling asleep again.

I woke up at 8:08am to my phone's ringtone loud as an alarm. It was Vince again calling my phone.

"Yo. You know what time it is?" I tirelessly asked, having just awoken from a lifelong slumber.

"Mannn wakeup! Come outside, I got something to show you," Vince said enthusiastically.

I let out a huge sigh. I was nowhere near ready to neither wake up nor get out of bed.

"This better be good, brother. I'm talking five naked women, good. Give me one second," I told him, angrily ripping the covers off of me.

I was a zombie, dragging my feet down the hallway to splash some cold water on my face, and barely brushing before going outside. I put my ear to my mother's door. Hearing the TV playing let me know she was ok. She probably watching some soap opera I wondered to myself. Heading to the door, I peeked out the window to see what Vince was doing, and my eyes almost bucked out of my face. I hurried and threw on my house shoes and ran out the house still in my pajamas.

"Yo! What!?" I said in excitement.

"I thought you might like this. You know what this is?" Vince asked me.

"Yes, I do. Why do you have a Mercedes Benz CL 63!? And how did you get it? You trying to get us busted? Take it back!" I fired off responses and questions.

He placed his hand on my shoulder calming me down.

"Relax. Everything is cool. I'm not going to take her back. I love her. I got her the same way you got yours and your mom's cars. I went to Pauli's to get a car, and I didn't plan for this one but a trucker was unloading a batch of new cars, and this one happened to be in there, so I bought it. 40 thousand, cash," Vince explained sincerely.

I couldn't deny, the car was a beauty. A total masterpiece, way different from mine. Which, it should be, considering my car and his car were almost 30 years apart. This car looked like a spaceship compared to mine. I just hated the fact it was so flashy. It was completely black on the outside, black alloy, 22-inch, starfish rims, with low profile tires that begged for attention from all. The guts of the car were peanut butter brown.

"Well, you just gonna stare at it or you play with it? Here, take it for a spin," Vince suggested, tossing me the key. I caught the key only to be mesmerized by it too. I was used to your typical car key, no different than the look of a door key. This Benz key though, looked like something you would stick into a computer to launch a nuclear missile. It was a black and chrome triangle with a tip that protrudes at the top. I hopped in finally. It really did feel like a spaceship, and it looked like one too. I was ready to take off into space to battle Darth Vader and save the galaxy.

We were both inner city kids. We only got to see cars like this drive by us. Vince and I used to play this game called, 'Mine.' When we would see a slick car we liked coming, the one that hollered out mine first, got to claim that car. Then we would begin to daydream about them, saying what we would do with it or where we would be in life when we got to own one. Never, in a million years did I think we would actually be driving one, and forget about owning one. Even if and when I did finish school, I'd be so far in debt I would be 45 years old before I got my hands on something like this Benz and it's already two years old.

In the average car, you use the brake to unlock the gear shifter, and you can shift into the desired gear. Not this magnificent car. In this spaceship of a car you just have a little spin knob that you turn left or right to select what gear you want.

"Hit the brake like you would in a regular to turn the gear wheel," Vince instructed me.

I let the windows down first just to be cooler than we already were just sitting in the Benz. I turned the wheel to reverse and then back to park as I heard a loud voice.

"Whose car is that!?" a voice coming from my place echoed.

"Shit! That's my mom! See, now how we going to explain this? How you get this car, Vince? Oh, I don't know mom, it just fell into my lap from the heavens!" I said, mocking an unlikely conversation between mom and Vince.

"Damn. Uh. Just throw it in drive and speed off! Pretend you didn't hear her!" Vince said panicking.

"You trying to get me jacked up? I gotta live here! She's not stupid!"

"I know you both hear me!" Mom yelled. I looked Vince dead in the face.

"See!" Confirming his speeding off plan wouldn't work. My mind started computing a million equations per second to figure out a solution of an explanation as to where this car came from. Lotto, found a suitcase full of money, an old will from a family member, casino.

"Casino." I whispered to myself. "You won big like I did in the casino okay? That's what I told her to explain the cars I got. Just be cool and follow my lead," I explained to Vince.

I was just hoping this explanation would work because once mom gets suspicious, she's not stopping till she finds the answers to her questions and they better make sense to her, or she will continue her quest for the truth!

"Heyyy mom. Good morning!" I said trying to deflect the whose car is this question.

"Don't good morning me boy, whose car is this?" She got straight to the point.

"It's Vince's car. Remember when I told you I won big at the casino? Well, I should have told you we won big because Vince won more than I did! Vince treated himself to this nice Mercedes Benz," I told her as I placed my hand on Vince's shoulder.

She stone-faced both of us before speaking. "So, you two just won big, huh? Just Miraculously, huh?" She questioned, not believing one thing we had said. We knew she didn't buy it but, we had said it now.

"Yep! Pretty much. It was just our night," Vince chimed in.

"You two up to something and I know it, and you know it, and you better not be getting in no trouble!" Mom said, pointing her index finger in our faces before walking back towards the house. "Put some clothes on boy!" She commanded.

"Ok," I said, and I waved her off.

We were pretty much screwed at this point because she knew. She played the same games in her heyday, she had to know.

"You can't bullshit a bullshitter," I said to myself.

You can't run game on a player either. She knew it was too good to be true but she didn't know what was going on or how we got our funds and I planned to keep it that way.

"She knows we're up to no good man. Don't think she doesn't!" I laughed and said to Vince. "I'd rather she knows than anyone else," I continued.

"True that," Vince agreed.

"Anyway, let's just go for a quick spin," I suggested, after coming to terms that my mom knows that I'm up to no good.

I spun the gear wheel to drive and sped off down the street as the car offered sheer happiness! In my book, this was as close to Heaven one could get!

"Wow." I said, approaching a stop sign.

The Benz was more powerful than it looked. Faster acceleration than I could imagine, and the engine combined with the sound of the exhaust was unlike anything I've heard before. It glided on the streets, even over bumps in the road. Felt like I was driving a cloud over the streets. This Benz made my new Malibu look and feel like my old beat-up Camaro. After roughly 30 minutes of cruising around, we stopped for a quick bite to eat at Ihop. Everyone was staring, assuming we were celebrities. My basketball shorts and wife beater outfit contrasted with the upscale driving machine we pulled up in, too much for the average citizen.

Altogether we were gone for about an hour. I decided it was time to get back home to work on some homework for my business course. I resist the desire to go buy myself a Mercedes Benz or something equivalent. I even contemplated going over to Pauli's to buy one, but I decided to just go in the house. Mom was already suspicious anyway, but I had no idea what was to come when I came in.

"Boy, why did some cops just leave here looking for you?" Mom asked as soon as I stepped foot in the house. My heart fell in my stomach as soon as she finished her sentence but I made my best poker face and tried to maintain my innocence.

"Mom what are you talking about?"

"Yeah, they said they had some questions for you and speculation that you are involved in some sort of theft situation at the dealership you worked at. What the hell is going on?" She demanded an answer from me.

"Oh my god, I already talked to those pigs! I didn't have anything to do with that!" I said with conviction.

I was lying through my teeth, but I didn't know what else to do. I didn't want to risk being disowned by my own mother or being kicked out of the house. I honestly wanted to tell her the truth because she never lied to me when I was old enough to ask questions about what she was doing for work.

"Ok. Follow me. How do you explain this?" Mom said as she pushed my door open.

All my cash was on my bed with the money counter and the burner phone. I was busted now for sure. I was defeated, but I wasn't going down without a fight.

"Why were you snooping around in my room?!" I asked furiously, pacing back and forth like a mad man.

"One, this is my house! I can snoop wherever I want when I want!" She yelled in my face. "Two. I wasn't snooping. That phone started ringing, and I traced it to your room. Now, what the hell is going on because that doesn't look like any damn casino winnings! I was not born yesterday, and you of all people should know that! I'm not going to ask you again!" she was irate at this point, standing right beside me yelling in my ear as I stood staring at my bed of goods. My eyes welled up with tears like a little kid getting yelled at for the first time. I didn't know where to start. I decided not to start at all.

"Don't worry about it, mom. I'm getting all this out of here right now," I assured her, as I grabbed my bag and started packing it with the cash first. "It's probably best that I leave huh?" I said.

She didn't say anything, and she didn't have to. I couldn't have the cops coming here bothering her. I did my dirt and didn't plan on bringing dirt to our home. She just stood there with tears in her eyes. I wrapped my book-bag around my back and kissed her on her forehead as I headed to the door.

"I'll be back for the rest of my things" I quietly told mom.

"How are you any different? What do you know that I or your father didn't?" she stopped me and asked.

"I don't know. It's just a different day and age," I responded, then continued my path out the door.

I felt like I wanted to throw up. Fighting with my mother hurt my soul. It happened so fast. I wanted to drive into an ocean; it hurt so, so bad. Those welled up tears soon began to fall down my cheeks. I thought about staying with Vince or even Toya for some time until I figured out what I was going to do. But, I didn't feel like explaining everything nor being a burden on anyone. I checked into a Motel a few miles away and stayed in my room all day. I turned my phone off. I didn't want to talk to anyone.

"Shit," I said, remembering what my mom said earlier, for what brought her into my room. I reached into my bag to grab the burner phone to check the messages. Jean reached out to us to book a video session with the whole team including Viktor tomorrow at 9:00 in the morning. I looked at everyone who replied 'accept,' not expecting to see Vince's name, but there it was. I wondered why he hadn't hit my phone to talked to me about it or even remind me. I hit 'accept' to confirm I'll be there as well and threw the phone on back in the bag and proceeded to lay back down and stare at the ceiling till I fell asleep.

My eyes opened at 8:55 am. I sighed, rolling over nonchalantly, and reached below the bed to grab my bag and get the burner phone out. I finally opened the link Jean sent hours ago, at 9:07 am.

"Whoa, someone is late!" I heard someone say.

I couldn't make out the voice as I was still trying to shake the confusion from abruptly waking up.

"Yeah. Sorry. Morning everyone," I greeted, and unapologetic for my tardiness.

"No worries," Viktor said. "Glad you could join us. I was just saying how I was fortunate to have such a great team and I wanted to say thank you," Viktor explained. "Everyone played a very important role, and we can't do this without each and every one of you."

I could feel it in my bones that this was much more than just a thank you conference. I just knew it had to be a build up for something else.

"I just wanted to talk to you guys about supply and demand. In short, demand is how much a product or service is desired by buyers and supply is how much the market of that product or service can offer," Viktor explained before pulling out a graph. "As you can see here, this is our product or our supply, which is not much but look over here, and you can see the demand for our product. See how high it is?" Viktor said, pointing to the graph.

It felt like we were in economics class all over again, listening to professors' drill us over and over with terms and graphing equations. I knew from all my courses in economics that anytime demand is high, it's time to get to work.

"Eh ahem," I cleared my throat to butt in as I had to voice my thoughts. "Correct me if I'm wrong, but if my memory serves me right, anytime demand is high, it's time for the factory to produce a lot of supply, right? Which means, in short, you want to pull off another job right?" I asked, already knowing the answer.

"Well in short, yes. I had no intentions initially, but the demand for our product is unbelievable. I'm talking at least double or even triple of what we made on our first job!"

I was thoroughly uninterested. Making double or triple did make me think about it really hard, but the work that would have to be put into it would be insane. We didn't have an inside man like the first job anymore, so a lot of scouting would have to be done on the streets to find certain cars. Not to mention I was already hot on the streets with the cops asking questions about me and my mom was heartbroken. I just couldn't.

"So, what do you guys think?" Viktor asked.

"I think we are all in. We could all use double or triple the money!" D said after breaking the silence of thoughts going through everyone's mind. Everyone agreed including Vince. I maintained my silence for a second before speaking. Everyone was happy to do another job except me.

"Sorry guys but no thank you. I'm out and Vince you need to be out too," I said, ruining everybody's joy. "The plan for us as discussed was to do this one job, and everyone goes separate routes. That was the plan, and we're going to stick to it. Besides, the cops came to my house. My mother's home and asked questions about that first job. I'm not in a position to do another job," I explained.

"They were only asking questions because you worked there man. Everything is cool. We need you bro," Vince explained. I went from being cautious to slightly angry when Vince questioned my reasoning.

"Where are you, Vince? From this video, I can see that you are in your room so yes everything is cool for you. See where I'm at? I fricken Motel! Because cops came to my home! And I have to protect my mother now! So, when I say I'm not in a position to do this, know I am not in a position to do this!" I yelled. "So, Vince, are you sticking to the plan or do you want people showing up at your place too?" I asked Vince.

Another period of silence went past before Vince spoke.

"I going to give this another go around bro. Sorry," Vince uttered to me. I let out a huge sigh.

"Suit yourself, dude."

"We really do need you," Viktor said. "What if I can personally guarantee you half a million dollars? Half now, half later? You're the brains kid, and we really need you to help us."

As much as I wanted the money, I just couldn't.

"I'm going back to school Viktor. I told you guys during the first heist. I told you that was my one and only time and we agreed. You even said you understood and it was the right thing for me to do, to pursue my dreams. Guys, I just can't. Sorry. I have to go," I told everyone as I turned the phone back off and laid back down. I couldn't stop thinking about my mom. I couldn't just leave her. I wouldn't just leave her. She wasn't in a position to be left alone, and I had to make things right with her.

Grim Clouds

First thing I did when I opened my eyes was to call my mom. I assumed she was mad at me because there was no answer. Then I assumed she couldn't answer the phone because she had a flare up. I hurried to the shower and then straight back home. I sped down the block our apartment was on, to see her still parked outside. I ran to the door as in a race for possibly, her life.

"Mom!" I yelled as I banged on the door at a constant pace Boom. Boom. Boom. I heard unlatching of the locks on the door which relieved my mind.

"Boy, what the hell is wrong with you!? Knocking on the door like you the damn police!" She yelled.

"I'm sorry. You didn't answer the phone, so I got worried," I said apologetically.

"You weren't worried when you left yesterday."

I stepped in and sat my bag down.

"That's why I was calling you but since I'm here, can we talk?" I asked her.

She waved me to the kitchen where she was brewing her organic green tea. The kettle started whistling as loud as a storm siren.

"Would you like some tea?" Mom asked me.

"Sure. No sugar, I'll have honey in mine," I responded. She sliced us both a piece of zucchini bread with our cups of tea. I moved some stuff off the small kitchen table, so we both had room to enjoy our small meal and chat.

"So, my son, what's up?"

"Let me just start by saying I'm sorry. I'm sorry I wasn't honest."

"Don't worry about it. Just be smart about what you are doing and do these dishes then we will call it even," she said, like I wasn't going to take that offer.

Since I made things right with my mom, I figured I'd make things right with my dad as well. I wanted to return the money he lent me with interest. I should have returned it a while ago, but I procrastinate too much.

"He's gonna think I'm not a man of my word," I said to myself. Hopefully, the interest on the loan makes up for that. My dad is a cash man, so the interest has to make up for it. I felt like I was late paying a mob boss back and now I had to make it double or else. I finished those god awful dishes my mom wanted done and headed to the Malibu.

"Be right back mom!" I yelled out, letting her know I was leaving.

"Bring me back a salad and some aloe vera juice!" She yelled back, giving me extra work to do.

Half the reason I haven't paid my dad back his money is because he lives so damn far. It was at least an hour drive without traffic, and there is never not any traffic. With nothing on my agenda for the day, I figured it would be best to go, otherwise I would procrastinate until I perished.

It was about noon when I left home, and I didn't pull up to my dad's place until two. It felt like a road trip. It took an additional fifteen minutes to find parking in his residential area. The area was weird, to say the least. "Okay, Darly Hotel," I said to myself as I walked up to the building.

My dad didn't live in a regular house or apartment. He stayed in an old hotel that was right in the middle of a historic neighborhood on the north side of the city. Imagine your old neighborhood, renovated and revived and then picture an old hotel that had seen its day, right smack dab right in the middle of a block. A hotel that had a history of gangsters and politicians using it and even movie stars in the prime of their careers. This place seemed to be constructed in the late 1800s and constantly renovated throughout the years. But no matter the renovation, nothing could hide the creepiness, staleness, and jailhouse-like appearance. The rooms might have been jail cells the way they looked when you entered each floor. When you walk in, your ID card is immediately requested by a receptionist, shielded behind a slab of bulletproof glass. It reminded me of when you go to the gas station at night, and you have to speak to attendant through the speaker and do transactions with the push out drawer.

Jack Williams

"Hey. Uh, Miss Harris?" I squinted at her name tag. She looked mean as hell, so I wanted to be exceptionally polite. "I'm here to see a Wayne Long," I said as I flashed my ID card.

"Hey," Miss Harris said, with no intentions of being at work any longer. "Room 508"

She handed me a visitor's sticker which was really a 'Hi my name is' sticker. I started to head towards the stairwell when I heard someone yell "Wait a minute!" insinuating something is wrong.

"Mr. Long isn't here anymore. I'm surprised nobody called you, I'm assuming you're his son since you look just like him."

"Yes, I'm his son. What's going on?" I asked quickly. My stomach was starting to feel weak, and my heart was preparing to drop.

"Mr. Long was taken to the hospital a few days ago. The cleaning lady went in to clean his room, and he was unresponsive. I'm sorry," she explained, still monotone.

It was like my mind was panicking but my body was a block of cement. I couldn't move, I was in shock.

"Is he-"

"I don't know," Miss Harris answered before l let the rest my fear leave my mouth. "They took him to Liretta hospital."

I darted out that hotel like there was a pack of wolves on me. I got to my car and called my mom, in route to the hospital, explaining the situation to her while I was shooting in and out of traffic. She was screaming a million questions at me, and I didn't have any answers to counter them. Her main question was like why they would take him to Liretta hospital, like I would randomly know why. I just told her to get to the hospital as soon as possible.

I could understand that question though. Liretta was probably one of the worst hospitals in the state, if not the country. Dad would not have a good chance of surviving whatever happened to him with the type of care, or lack of, that patients receive from this hospital. Their reputation was one of the worst ever.

"It is what it is at this point," I said to myself as I sped down a street not too far from the hospital.

It only took me 15 minutes to get there. I parked by a hydrant, not caring if my car got towed or not. I ran inside straight to the information desk.

"Can you help me, please? I'm looking for a Wayne Long," I said to the lady at the front desk, extremely winded. "Is he still here?"

"Yes. He is in ICU, room 3101," she said, handing me a visitor's pass.

There was a decent amount of people waiting in line for the elevators, and I didn't have time to wait. I took the stairs, running up five floors without the thought of even taking a break.

I opened the door and continued running through the hallways until I got to room 3101.

"Dad!" I yelled as I rushed in and pulling back the curtains, praying I would hear a response.

The only response I got was from the ventilator machine, beeping and breathing for my dad. He was just lying there with all kinds of tubes and IVs hooked up to his limbs and a mask covering his face. With the tubes down his throat he couldn't respond to me, even if he wanted to. He couldn't respond now though, because he was in an induced coma. I put my hands on my face and sat in the chair near his bed. I clutched his hand as the tears started to flow. I had no control over my tears, and I didn't care, nor did I even attempt to wipe them away!

"I know I'm late Dad, but I brought your money man, plus interest. I can own up to my responsibilities. I can be a man and make my own decisions. I can even be a father if I choose to. I'm sorry Dad, I should have been a better son," I said, as the tears continued to flow freely.

My Dad would sometimes invite me over to his place to watch football or basketball when I was a few years younger. I would always decline. I'm busy, I got homework, or I'm tired, but in reality, I was just being stupid. Letting my pride and resentments control my decisions. Always saying to myself, maybe next time dad. Next time never came, and now God was showing me that taking life for granted was not a wise thing to do. Tomorrow is never promised to anyone. Time can never be gotten back once it's gone. You can't take back decisions you make, you can only live with the consequences of those decisions. I always made time for friends and video games but never for my father. I hated the fact that he missed my defining years, but I didn't want this. When I did come over, I didn't talk much. I didn't take any food that was offered. I only

Jack Williams

came over because my mom would keep nagging me about it. I was giving him the cold shoulder and didn't even realize it. I wanted to take it all back and just start over.

"Hello. Are you his son?" A nurse came in and asked.

"Yes. I am his son," I responded, sniffling and wiping my eyes. "What happened?"

"Well, we don't really know what happened initially, but after he was brought in, we ran some tests and found that he has cirrhosis of the liver and it's pretty bad. We had to put him in a coma to ease the pain and to release some of the pressure on his other organs especially his lungs and his heart. He was found unresponsive, and we suspect that was at least a day's time. At this moment, I hate to say it, but all we can do is pray. Miracles do happen."

I couldn't believe what I was hearing. I felt the sadness taking over my entire body and mind.

"He had this in his pocket. I think it's for you," the nurse said, handing me a neatly folded note titled "To my son," I unfolded it to see his old school handwriting.

> If you are reading this then more than likely, I didn't make it, and I am okay with this. It's okay, son. You have failed me. I gave you one task to complete, and you couldn't deliver. Where's my money? I'm going to haunt you in your dreams if I don't make it out of this. Nawwwww, I'm just joking. Hopefully, I gave you a smile. In all seriousness son, I'm sorry I couldn't be a better father to you. I spent too much time on the streets and became too deeply involved in the fast life and hustling and it has cost me dearly. Cost me my son and my daughter, and I hate myself for it. I've been in so much pain because of this illness, but no pain is stronger than the pain of not having my children around in my life on a consistent basis. Totally my fault and I know that now. I know I missed those defining years. The important ones, and I should have been there watching you grow up, leading and guiding you along the way. I was a sporadic dad in and out of your life. I

can't change that but just know that I love
you and Karla more than life itself. I had a
hard time sharing and showing my love, and I
guess it's because of the way I was raised
by my mother and father. Much the same as
what I gave both of you but it was all I
knew at the time. I know because I wasn't
raised with love. The streets raised me, and
the streets don't show you love you know, so
I'm a bit rough on you verbally. That's just
my way of saying I love you, Joey. Remember,
to be a man you have to stick to your
decisions. Make your decisions in your life
and stand by them. If they are the right
ones, you will reap the benefits, and if
they are the wrong ones, you will still reap
the consequences because you will have
learned a lesson. Even if nothing else comes
from that decision, you have what I call a
bought lesson because you learned something.
But, as a man, you have to make choices in
life and own up to them. You can never give
up or quit, and despite all else, you will
feel good when you stand by the choices you
make. This way you never, ever have to live
with regrets. Be a better man than me. Never
show fear. It's ok to be afraid of something
but fear is different, and fear can break
you down, son. You can never allow fear to
stop you. Be smarter than I was and most of
all take care of your responsibilities. I am
sorry I loved you so fiercely but was unable
to show this love to you. It is deep son,
and you will only experience this love when
you have a son of you own. When you do,
please don't make my mistakes with him, hug
him, tell him, and show him how much you
love him. Be there for and with him as much
as you can be. Keep my love inside your
heart son, I'll be watching over you. Know
that you were made in love and loved
entirely, completely and unconditionally, by
both your mom and myself. I am your father,

*and you are my son....do me proud boy...I
know you will!*

The tears were a waterfall, with no beginning and no end.

"Hey baby," I heard a voice say. It was my mom, coming in to console me.

"Hey, mom," I responded, putting my dad's note in my pocket and collapsing into my mom's arms.

"It's going to be ok baby," she said, trying to reassure me and telling me that I could and would get through this.

Mom and I stayed at the hospital for days on end, coming and going and praying that dad would show signs of recovery, but it wasn't looking good. With me being my dad's only child around and available, the doctor told me I was the power of attorney. It was up to me whether to keep him on life support or not. The doctor told me to consider the cost of life support with the likelihood that he would never recover as well. Life support was five grand a day which put at least a $25,000 stamp on my back. I didn't really care though, I felt like dad could pull through, and besides that, I had a lot of money. I decided to keep him alive and pay it no mind.

Vince came to visit me while I was down in the dumps to make sure I was okay. Other than that, we didn't talk much. We were losing contact. His decision to keep the money rolling in was on him. I couldn't be involved with it anymore. The fact that we decided to just do one job, and he threw that conversation out the window, that didn't sit well with me. It felt like he didn't respect me anymore, things were changing with us somehow.

I continued to go to school. I fell a little behind due to my unfortunate turn of events, but I caught right up, pulling my subpar grades to A's and B's. Everything the professor threw my way, I aced week after week. I submerged myself in the schoolwork, determined to get back into MIT. I wanted to stay sharp. I started depositing cash in a bank account and writing checks to MIT's financial aid department to get my balance cleared so I could return to school the following year.

Although, I was trying to play the out of sight out of mind game with my dad's situation, I was fully aware of how many days he had been in the ICU. It was day 10, and I decided to go visit him. When I arrived at this room, I just stood over him staring at his body doing my best to gather the strength to finish the job. I knew when I woke up that morning, it would be the day. I could just feel it. I walked over to the side of the bed and kissed him on his forehead.

"I love you dad, regardless of all the things we did or did not do and all the things we said or did not say, I love you with all my heart. I just wish you would be here long enough to see your baby boy become the man that you wanted him to be," I cried, relentlessly.

"Nurse!" I called out.

"Yes?" the nurse asked as she walked through the door.

"Pull the plug. Don't ask me if I'm sure because I am," I demanded as I walked towards the door. "Call the morgue and ask them to call me to make the funeral arrangements," I continued talking as I wrote down my cell number and handed her the piece of paper I wrote it on. "How long would it be after you cut the machines off?"

"That would be between your father and God."

I walked out the door looking back to see my dad for the last time. I sat in my car and broke down sobbing, not caring who saw or heard me. I couldn't stop thinking about the years we wasted. My dad died without knowing what my favorite color is, my favorite food or favorite car. He died without knowing me. I was still just daddy's little boy to him. Little did he know and would never know, I became a man the day he died. I grew up that day, making that decision to turn off his life support, or at least I felt like I did. No kid makes these types of decisions, do they, dad?

I finally got the strength to get home where mom was just lying on the couch watching her favorite soaps. As soon as she saw me, she knew. We sat there and cried together. She brought out an old photo binder, covered in dust, that hadn't been opened in years.

"I haven't opened this for a long time because of the memory lane it sends me down, but I think I'll be ok this time," my mom said as she wiped the dust off of the binder.

There were photos of my mom and dad during their prime years together. Happy years and happier times. It was clear they were both wild and free, the way life is supposed to be lived. They were showing off their jewelry, cars and other material items and it was obvious they had the best of everything they wanted. I couldn't help but laugh at some of the fashion they were displaying, but more so my mom than my dad. In one picture, dad was wearing an Adidas tracksuit. Coincidentally, I typically wear one, daily. Dad was known for being well dressed. Mom was sporting some overalls over a white t-shirt and some dirty converse and posing like she was the hottest thing since sliced bread in that picture. Another one showed them both dressed to kill. Mom was in a ball gown, and dad was in a tuxedo. She said they were on their way out to celebrate her birthday.

"Who did you guys think you were huh?" I asked, laughing at the photos.

"We was the shit, boy! You see all that gold, don't you?" mom said while pointing at the photo of her and dad with gold rings on every finger and gold chains on.

"We did it first. Kids in the 80s got it from us!" she was claiming.

"Sureee mom," I teased her. I knew she was telling the truth though, but I couldn't let her ride the high horse too long!

Our laughter soon turned to tears again as we turned more pages of photos of dad.

"Despite our differences, he was a good man. I want you to know that baby," mom said wiping away her tears.

"I know mom. Why didn't you guys stay together anyway?"

"Well. Sometimes you just drift apart. You still love that person, but you kind of just fall out of love you know?" Mom explained.

"Yeah, I know what you mean," I said, thinking about my own situation with Toya.

"One thing for sure," she said, "You were made out of love from the both of us. You were a surprise because the doctor told me I couldn't have any more children due to some medical problems I had. So, you can imagine our shock when we heard. But you were wanted, and we were very, very happy when I found out that I was pregnant."

It felt good talking to mom about dad, and it helped to ease the pain of dad's death. I found out more about my father that day, than I had known my entire life. I felt like I finally knew him.

Before I knew it, it was a Saturday, and the funeral was here. The day was all mucky, gloomy and wet. Not to mention a bit chilly due to it being October. Mom and I took separate cars. She left before me for the viewing and to see the guests and family that came out to pay their respect and say goodbye. Not only did I hate funerals, especially the viewing, but I hated seeing all the friends of my mom and dad who I haven't seen in ages and didn't even know. It was always the same reaction about how I've grown and no way I'm the same kid from way back. Am I supposed to reverse age, to stay the young boy they knew? The interaction just never seemed authentic. I would hear it more than ever now that my dad passed away, so I decided to just go for the funeral service and not the viewing. I pulled up the Leaks and Sons Funeral Home, and my mind started racing. It was Deja vu, and I had been there. I had seen this view in a dream some time ago. In the vision, I was parking in the lot, and everyone was dressed in black, looking sad as they exchanged hugs and small talk. I could see people that I knew going in the funeral home just like I do now. I saw my mom and Ms. Owens, even Toya came to show support. The only difference between this moment and my dream is the fact that Vince was here with me in the dream. As soon as I put those clues together, it hit me. Vince wasn't here. I continued to sit in the car and watch people going in waiting to see if that gorgeous Mercedes-Benz would pull up with my best friend hopping out. About 15 minutes later, I gave the thought a rest and pieced together that my best friend wasn't coming.

I finally went into the funeral service and quietly sat in the back about a few steps from where the doors open. I had just caught the last of the preacher's words.

"God works in mysterious ways which we all know. Your day can come in the blink of an eye. Live right because when judgment day comes, you don't want to be caught with your pants down."

Then he asked everyone to form a line and prepare for the last viewing. I watched everyone form a line and make their way around to the casket looking and saying prayers. It was a small service of about 20 people, so it didn't take long for everyone to go around. I took a look at my phone to see my mom had texted me a million and one times, asking me where I was. I figured I would make my way to the casket since it was now closed and help load the casket into the hearse. Halfway to the casket, my mom blitzed me.

"Where have you been?"

"Sitting right there the whole time," I said pointing to my empty seat in the back.

"Why didn't you sit in the front?" she asked.

Jack Williams

"Does that really matter mom? I'm here, and that's all that should matter," I answered back. She scolded me. She wanted to pop me, but it wasn't the time or place.

"Just go over and say hi to all of your folks," she ordered. I let out a huge sigh as I walked past her slightly afraid she was going to whack the back of my head.

"Fine," I obeyed.

Everyone had the same response when they saw me. "Is this little Wayne!?" or "man you were the same height as my knees last time I saw you," and I hated it. It all seem so superficial and phony. Not to mention the questions about college and the worthless advice everyone wanted to give with no college education of their own to back up their advice. But, because my mom asked me and for my dad, I stayed and made real small talk with everyone, with a smile on my face. Soon I broke away to be a pallbearer. I wanted Vince to be here with me, helping carry this casket but since he was a no show, I got someone I don't even know helping me. I wanted to just carry it myself. After we had loaded it into the hearse, I looked for my mom to tell her I wasn't coming to the burial.

"Mom. I'm going to head home," I told her. "I got some stuff to do."

"So, you not going to come to your own father's burial?" she asked, attempting to guilt trip me.

"My last sight of my dad will not be laid up in some casket nor will it be of him being lowered into the ground. Sorry but my conscience is clear. And if it were my funeral, I imagine he would do the same," I explained.

She turned away and walked off and so did I in the opposite direction towards the parking lot. I started to squat down to get in my car when I heard "Hey" from a short distance behind me.

I turned to see who it was. It was Toya.

"Hey. How are you?" I replied back.

"I'm cool. I'm good. I just wanted to check on you and make sure you were ok and if you needed me for anything I'm here for you," she said as she hugged me tighter than usual.

"Thanks, I appreciate that."

"I actually wanted to talk to you about something if you got some time," she said.

I opened my door, and I took off my blazer, throwing it in the car, letting her know that was not about to happen. I had no idea what she wanted to talk about, and I didn't care.

"Maybe some other time. I really just want to go home you know," I responded.

"Yeah. No, I totally understand. Just call me whenever you get a chance, okay?"

"Sure," I said as I turned my key, firing up my Malibu's engine.

I had no intention of calling her. I didn't want to lead her on in any way, for her to think I'm attempting to get back with her or she has a chance at getting back with me. That time frame has ended, and I wanted her to know and understand that.

I sat in my car a little while longer while I called Vince. I didn't want to jump to conclusions so I thought I would give him a call and to my surprise, it went straight to voicemail. I started to get angry but also a little worried. I wanted to be angrier than I was but I didn't know if anything happened to him or not. I figured I'd give it a rest for now. I went home to study for midterms. It was a good opportunity since my mom was gone and the house was empty. I could study with no interruptions. I pulled in front of our house, and an odd vibe was in the air. I noticed an unmarked squad car two houses down. When I got out of the car, so did the cops.

"You're coming with us mister," one of the cops said.

"For what?! I said defensively.

"You've been chosen for a line-up. We can do this the easy way or the hard way. Your choice. I don't want to have to rough you up kid. Just come on," the other cop warned.

I wanted to deck one of them and run. If I was going to go down, I was going to go down fighting. That was my mindset, but I was too emotionally drained. I did what they asked of me, and walked to the back of the squad car.

Jack Williams

Homecoming

It had been about four months since the cops had me in that line-up. I was scared to death that the cops were going to kick my mother's door in and scoop me up like a cup of ice cream at any moment. I had been low-key ever since, taking my mother's advice since she had been in this position plenty of times.

I also visited Renee as many times as I could in the different cities she was in for modeling jobs. We were practically dating long distance now. I told her about my escapade as a criminal, and to my surprise, she was cool with it as long as I was done with that life, which I was. Only thing Renee didn't know was that I was broke. Renee was a very understanding woman so I'm sure she would understand my position and help me, but I would feel less of a man if she had to help me financially.

After paying for my dad's hospital bills, funeral, my school tuition and my mom's treatments, I was in financial trouble yet again. I had about two grand to my name, and I was awaiting my re-admittance letter from MIT that seemed to be taking a lifetime to arrive. It should come any day now. I was so ready to go back to school to get my life completely back on track. I was lying on my bed looking out my window thinking about it all when a knock on my door interrupted my thoughts.

"Hey, where is your mom?" Ms. Treaty asked.

I hired Ms. Treaty a couple months ago as a live-in assistant for my mom when I'm gone or out and about so she wouldn't be on her own. She helps my mom in everything from cooking, to chores, to taking medicine, and even conversation. She was awesome, and she wasn't that expensive. Well, when I could afford her she wasn't. Her $40 an hour rate was running my little two thousand dollars dry. My two grand was enough money to last until I got back to school but where was I going to be working, and how I was going to be sending funds back here for my mom was the big question. Would I even be making enough? I constantly wondered.

"She should be in her room or maybe the backyard. She wanted to plant some flowers or something like that," I answered.

"Okay, I'll find her."

Ms. Treaty left my room in search of my mom, and I put my head back in the clouds. I decided to truly put my head in the clouds as I looked over at my half smoked joint from a couple weeks ago. I grabbed it and headed to my car out front.

"Found her! She's in the backyard planting some tulips," I heard Ms. Treaty say as I headed downstairs. "Where you going? I'm about to make some salmon croquettes for lunch!"

"I'm just going out to my car for a second. You know I can't miss those croquettes!"

Ms. Treaty was a complete beast in the kitchen. Her salmon croquettes were so good, they should be sold globally. She made them with just the right amount of crisp to salmon ratio. It was perfect timing because after I finish a joint, I'm usually instantly hungry and those salmon croquettes were going to do more than just hit the spot. They were going to beat that spot down.

Soon as the fire touched the joint, the smell of cannabis instantly filled the Malibu. I cracked my window about halfway down so the smoke would clear. I hated the smell of smoke in my car. I took my first inhale, holding it in for a few seconds, then exhaled, causing me to cough like a flu victim. I looked over at my passenger seat, and I couldn't help but think about Vince. I only smoked when he was with me. I took another toke, much smaller than the first for my chest's sake. Another puff and wondered what Vince was doing, was he okay and taking care of himself? I must have thought him into existence because after that puff, my phone buzzed and to my surprise it was Vince. I thought about not answering. Part of me just didn't want to be bothered. I decided not to act like that, and if he was calling me, it had to be for a reason. I picked up probably on the last ring barely catching him.

"Hello?" I asked, pretending not to know who was calling me.

"What's up, man? You know who this is?"

"What makes you think I wouldn't recognize this voice?" I asked, with a confused face.

"I know we haven't talked in a while, so I just wanted to be sure you know?" Vince explained.

I took another toke on the joint and paused for a second before responding. I had known Vince since we were kids. It was the stupidest question I had heard in a while.

"You do know I have known you since you were a kid, right? Don't mind me. The weed is talking," I explained after realizing I was probably using too much brain power from effects of the cannabis. "So, what's up bro?"

"Nothing man. Just miss you. Want to hang out?" Vince sounded weird to me, like off.

His voice was a bit shaky and he never really gets straight to the point. He had me slightly worried, so I figured I'd meet up with him.

"Uh yeah, sure man. Our burger spot?" I asked.

"Yeah. How fast can you be there?" Vince asked.

"I mean, I can leave out now and be there in about 15 minutes. That's fast enough?"

"Yeah. Love you, man. See you there!"

I took one last puff as my joint was now a roach and flicked the remains in the street. Vince is acting strange, I thought to myself. I ran back into the crib to grab my wallet with my driver's license just in case the cops wanted to act a fool today, and my sunglasses. I ran by the kitchen to kiss my mom on the head and to let her know I was leaving out for a bit and I snuck one of the freshly cooked croquettes out of Mrs. Treaty's basket. I burned my hand and parts of my tongue, but it was worth it.

I got to Sparky Burgers, and I saw Vince's Benz out front but no sign of him. I was scoping the outside seats and the inside from my car.

"Where is he?" I said to myself as I pulled out my cell phone to call him.

Soon as I pulled my phone out, Vince popped up on the side of my window, scaring the life out of me. "Hey! Sorry man. Didn't mean to scare you. I saw you pull up from across the street. You, alone right?" He asked me.

"Yeah. Why would I have someone with me? What's your deal? Why you acting all weird? I took my sunglasses off to look at him. His eyes were shot looking, slightly dilated and baggy. He was sniffling every minute. I jumped out of the car.

"Look at me!" I said with bass in my voice.

"I can't. The sun is extra bright today man."

I grabbed his face and turned it towards me, shouting again. "Look at me! Are you doing cocaine bro!? Are you serious right now!?"

He pushed my hand away and stepped back with a disgusted look on his face.

"You can't judge me, man! Yes. I've been doing a little Coke here and there. Yeah. So, what! I've been getting rich at the same time so what's the problem?!" he explained.

"That money shit doesn't matter man when your brain is all messed up. What's the matter with you?!"

"You not my father man!" he shouted at me.

He had a point. He was free to do as he pleased. I wasn't his father.

"Yeah, I'm not your father, but I'm sure he would be disgusted with his son right now!" I shouted back.

"What you say to me?!" Vince screamed as he charged towards me.

I ran around my car to escape the direct path he made towards me. I didn't want to fight my friend, and I definitely didn't want to fight someone charged up on cocaine. That's just a quick way to be killed.

"Relax!" I yelled.

"I'm going to kill you!" He yelled back as he tried to jump over the hood of my car to get to me.

I ran on the other side. My heart was beating a thousand beats per minute. He had the look of a wild animal in his eyes.

"Relax! I'm sorry! I should not have said that to you! C'mon man. We're friends. Let's hug it out and talk. You wanted to talk to me, right?" I reminded him. "Let's go over there and talk."

We were both breathing extremely heavy like wild beasts after a chase for a game. I started to walk towards him as he was just starting to seem a little calmer at the moment.

"C'mon. Let's sit down and talk," I said while pointing to the outside seats at Sparky's.

He followed me to the seats, staring at me the whole time as if I was planning to stab him in his back as soon as he looked away. I sat down, and he continued to stand. "You don't want to sit?" I asked.

"No, I need to stand. Just in case I need to run."

"Run from who?" I said with a confused look.

Vince started looking behind him and around us. "I don't know. I just feel like someone is following me," He explained. "I got a lot of money, man. They are after me," Vince continued.

"I can see. Nice threads," I said, waving my hand up and down at him.

Vince was dressed like he was straight out of Miami. Everything was Versace. Literally from head to toe. Glasses, his black and gold silky button-down shirt that he left unbuttoned exposing his slightly out of shape body, black slacks, and black loafers. Even his rings. All Versace. The only thing that wasn't Versace was his watch. That was a gold Rolex. So yeah maybe someone was following him, but I was almost sure the coke had him paranoid.

"Hey, guys! Can I get you guys anything?" A waitress came up and asked, startling Vince and causing him to jump like a cat.

"Don't you see us talking!! Get the hell outta here!" a startled Vince yelled at the poor waitress.

I put my head down in embarrassment. People around were staring now, and I wanted no part of it.

"Hey, what's the matter with you? Lift your head up. Dumb girl got what she deserved for coming up behind me," Vince said while looking at the waitress walk away.

"She was just doing her job man," I said as I lifted my head up. "So anyway, why did you want me to meet you here?"

Vince finally sat down. "I told you. I miss my brother."

"You miss your brother, huh? Did you miss your brother at his father's funeral?" I asked, looking into his eyes attempting to look into his soul.

He just sat there quiet. Looking down.

"I am sorry. I can blame it on a lot of things but I won't. I made the decision not to go. I wanted to do a job for some money. I have to live with that, and it eats at me," Vince explained. "I hope that you can forgive me?"

I looked away as I thought about what he said. "I don't know man. I just thought that seeing as though you lost your dad, this would be something you would be there for because you know how it feels. So, I don't know right now," I explained, giving him a detailed answer.

"I know man. I'm truly sorry."

I truthfully wanted to forgive him, but that hurt me to the core. And his pathetic reasoning was just money. I had to think about it.

"Are we cool?" Vince asked.

"Yeah," I said. "How is your mom? What have you been up to?"

"Mom is cool. She's happy again. She has a boyfriend now. She thinks she is doing something now," He said smiling at the thought of his mom. "As for myself..." he paused for a second. "I'm living life baby!" He yelled with excitement giving the impression of someone with a bipolar disorder.

Vince reached into his pocket, retrieving his phone.

"Look at these bro. All mine," he said. He handed me his phone.

"These women?" I said looking at his photo library of him laid up with plenty of women.

"Shit. Naw man. Keep scrolling. But they all mine too," he said smirking.

There were photos of all his cars. He went from having just a Benz to a collection of vehicles, six to be exact. He had two Mercedes-Benz, a Porsche 911, my personal favorite car, a Nissan GT-R and a Kawasaki Ninja Motorcycle. He was posing in each photo next to the cars letting everybody know they were his and nobody else's. It was an amazing collection, to say the least.

"This is amazing bro. Where did you get these and where do you keep them all?"

"Well Pauli hooked me up with the cars of course, and he hooked me up with someone that could get me a little condo downtown with as much garage space as I need," Vince explained, sniffling every other word. "Cost me about, one, no, about 250 thousand for everything," Vince continued and correcting himself of his lavish but carelessly spending.

He showed me the photos from his condo as well, and it looked very nice. We grew up used to wooden tables and counters and default faucets. His condo had granite and marble accents everywhere and faucets that appeared to be anything but faucets.

"I'm really happy for you man," I said, scrolling through his photos.

"Thanks. It's the life I always wanted man. I'm not done though. But like you should come by and visit me. I don't get a chance to get online no more, but I have a 55-inch flat screen TV we could do some damage on Call of Duty!"

"Yeah I just might do that. Probably can break a new record in kills with 55 inches," I responded. "Hell. I need a 55 inch at the crib."

"Come back, and you can get one," Vince said then sniffled.

I didn't respond to that as I was done with that life. I didn't want to risk my freedom anymore. But I was curious.

"Come back to what? What's changed?" I asked.

"Well after you left, we had to get a replacement, and a few others left too. The Team is nowhere near as solid as it was when we did the first job but everything is different," Vince explained. "We can't do big jobs anymore because we don't have an inside man. So, we kind of just been doing gorilla style stuff where we just run around scouting for old school cars. Hotwire, drive it back, strip, rebuild and sell," He continued.

"See," I uttered.

They got sloppy, and that's why I wanted no part of it. People get a taste of something, and they get spoiled. They weren't using their head. They were raising eyebrows doing it that way. The more cars you steal off the streets, the more you got to watch your back. They could do a big job and retire. They didn't need an inside man. I guess I really was the brains. Makes sense why they would want me back. I had the masterplan again.

"That's cool. I see it's paying well. So, what's next on the list?" I asked.

"Yeah. I've made like five hundred thousand. The team has done like three million so far. Our goal is ten million," he said sniffling his nose. "But yeah, anyway, we're laying low. We got too much heat in the streets," he continued.

"That's because you guys are stupid. Doing too much too fast," I said smartly, then turned my head away as I realized I said more than I wanted to.

Vince smiled as I turned back to look at him. He knows me too well I thought to myself. I shook my head from left to right like a kid being asked to eat vegetables. "No. My answer is no. I was just thinking aloud."

"Aww come on man. Come back. We need you, and I don't know how your money is, but everyone can always use more money. I'll give you one of my cars. And Viktor will even give you 100k," Vince assured, attempting to bribe and reason with me.

"Is this why you wanted to meet with me? Did you and Viktor and the crew come up with some plan to get me back?" I asked defensively.

"No," he responded. "Well, not exactly. I do miss my brother, and I mentioned that in the meeting. Then Viktor was all like go see him and try to bring him back," Vince explained.

"So, I figured I could see my brother and maybe recruit him," He continued.

I scolded him and even thought about reaching across the table to smack him for even considering using me.

"Get the hell out of my face man, I don't know this person you've become," I said as I pointed up and down towards him. "When my homie Vincent Owens returns, then call me. I don't know you, dog. You hear me? I don't know you!"

He just stood there looking at me as if he didn't understand. I got up from the table and walked off towards my Malibu.

"Yo! Come back, brother! Come on, it's not like that!" I could hear him yelling in my direction as I kept walking.

"Dammit!" I yelled as I punched the passenger seat in my Malibu. I felt like it was my fault. I stayed in the car for second, contemplating the possibility of doing one last job. One last job and retire for good. Go back to school. Be happily off with Renee. Life's good. "No way dumbass," I said aloud to myself. Some part of my brain was trying to talk me into it. It was like having an angel on one shoulder, and the devil on the other.

I looked at my casio to see what time it was, 1:10pm it displayed. I started the Malibu up and sped home, hoping to catch the mailman like a stray dog. I have been searching for my acceptance letter for weeks now. I called the admissions office at MIT last week which confirmed that the letters were being sent out. I didn't want to know whether I was accepted or not over the phone. It ruins the surprise. I called the local post after calling the admissions office, and they confirmed it was some kind of screw up with the mail, but that should have been fixed by now. My mailman had to have that letter today.

Driving down our block, I didn't see the mailman walking the street. Must have made an early run today I thought to myself. I got home and frantically ran into the house.

"Mom! You got the mail?" I yelled. "Yo Mom!" I yelled again. I walked to the kitchen. There were croquettes still left out on the table. I grabbed one as I opened the back door to peek out in the backyard.

"What the hell man?" I said irritably as I chewed on some of the croquettes. "Well. Her car is in the driveway," I uttered. Something's up I thought. Mom or Ms. Treaty wouldn't leave this food out like that.

I pulled out my phone to call Ms. Treaty. I had three missed calls and three text messages. One of each from Vince and the rest from Ms. Treaty. I disregarded Vince's message and opened Ms. Treaty's texts. My heart rate accelerated and I deeply swallowed the rest of the croquette as I read her texts.

"No! No! No!" I said, progressively getting louder. I shot back out the house to my Malibu. I started her up and mashed on the gas down the block making a loud "*skrttt*" noise. Ms. Treaty said mom had a flare up that was worse than usual and started coughing up blood. They were at Trinities hospital, about 15 minutes away. But the way I was driving I was on arrival in 8 minutes. I made my way to the hospital only to wait in line for the elevator as someone on a stretcher was being entered. I was trying to get to room 781.

"I am so sorry but can you guys hurry up?" I asked. I couldn't stop pacing back and forth. I couldn't stop my mind from racing. I had just lost my dad, and I didn't know what I would do if I lost my mom. I couldn't stop thinking about her coughing up blood. She had never done that with me. And my wild imagination didn't help. I imagined her spewing blood everywhere like an overdone horror film. Then I imagined Ms. Treaty poisoning her. I started smacking the palm of my hand against my forehead to stop the wild thoughts. I just needed to talk to a nurse or a doctor.

I finally got to her room. Ms. Treaty was there next to her. She was resting with an oxygen mask and an IV in her arm. The scene was so reminiscent of seeing my dad in the hospital. I teared up instantly at the sight. Ms. Treaty stood up to give me a hug.

"She's gonna be okay. Don't worry. She's a trooper," Ms. Treaty said.

"Yeah. I know. You're right," I responded. "So, no word on what's going on?" I asked.

"The doctor should be in shortly with something."

I went over to my mom and lightly rubbed her head. I pulled up a seat and sat by her side.

"I know you probably got some other clients Ms. Treaty. You can go if you need to, I'll stay. Thank you for helping her, you're a blessing," I told her.

"As long as you keep me posted?"

"Of course,"

A half hour went by. I could hear loud footsteps coming this way. A couple knocks on the door before it opened all the way up.

"Hey! You must be Ms. Long's son. I'm doctor Glass. You got a strong mother here," He said with a strong, loud voice.

"Yeah. What's wrong with her?" I asked right away.

"Well. She has something called Lobar pneumonia. It's pneumonia that can be found at least in one of the lobes of the lung and is considered a more severe form of pneumonia," Dr. Glass explained.

I put my head down. I couldn't believe what I was hearing. It felt like my mother just can't catch a break for once.

"But not to worry, I have good news. Not only have we fixed this issue plenty of times, she only has it in one of the lobes in her lung. With a prescription of some antibiotics, she's going to be fine. She's going to be able to run home if she wanted. I promise. But you have to promise to get her to stop smoking cigarettes. Deal?" I wiped my tears.

"Deal!" I said.

"Hey baby." I heard a weak voice whisper.

"Hey, mom!" I said with excitement. "I'm here with you. Doc says you're going to be fine and you coming home in a couple days. No talking, just rest," I told her.

She shook her head and went back to sleep. I sat by her side watching TV. The only thing interesting was the gaming channel. I imagined myself on one the shows. I would have loved to be on Wheel of Fortune, winning that easy paper. Things would be a bit easier in life. Felt like I was watching TV forever. She slept for about five hours. I thought she had never slept before. It's what her body needed though. She was always doing something whether it was moving furniture, planting a garden or driving to help out a homeless shelter. She never stayed still long enough to rest.

"Wake up boy." I heard the same weak voice say.

I opened my eyes to see my mom staring at me.

"Take me home," She asked of me. "You know I hate hospitals."

"Well yeah but I didn't bring you here, and I can't take you home because you need to be here," We had a brief stare-down to see who would win.

"If you hadn't come here, you might not be here," I continued, winning the stare-down as she looked away. "This will be over before you know it. You'll be home in no time."

After arguing with her on why I wasn't going to take her home, she insisted I go home and rest in a bed rather than resting at the hospital in a chair. I let her win this one, and went home. Once I got there, the first thing that stood out was how quiet it was. No TV was on. No random laughing in the background or phone conversations. No dish water running and no calling my name out for random tasks. The silence made me realize how much I loved my mother. I couldn't live without her.

My thoughts went into the backyard where mom was starting her garden. I started digging a hole a few feet away from her garden but behind the garage where it can't be seen. I wasn't sure about what I was going to do but I wanted to prepare just in case I decided to go back to work in the crime circuit. It was dark outside as I was digging, but I had been digging for an hour, so I figured the hole was deep and wide enough to hold any amount of cash. If I was going to go back to doing jobs, I was going to leave my mother with something. I had worked up a good sweat. I figured I would get some rest now. I walked back to the kitchen and sat down at the table. As soon as I got my little bit of relief, my phone buzzed. I looked at my phone to see it was Renee.

Can't wait to see you in a few hours.

"Dammit!" I yelled. I forgot she was going to be in town and visiting.

Can't wait till I'm hugging and kissing you!

I figured I would get some rest, since I remembered I needed to pick Renee up from the airport in the morning.

I woke up a few hours after I closed my eyes. Still tired and confused, I opened my eyes a little wider to see some messages from Renee. I ripped the covers off my body and sat up, panicking, thinking I overslept. Her flight was delayed a couple hours. I laid back down in relief.

I got up and headed to the kitchen, dragging my feet like an overworked slave. I took the plate on the table full of croquettes and scraped them into the trash and placed the plate in the sink. All of a sudden, my body jerked from the sound of our loud buzzing doorbell. I crept to the door like a ninja as I had no idea who would be at my door at 8 in the morning. I peeped out the window like the iconic Malcolm X photo minus the assault rifle. It was Vince, and he had someone with him holding a briefcase who looked to be Viktor.

"The hell!?" I said confused. I cracked the door peeping my head out as I only had on my basketball shorts. "Vince and what a surprise, Viktor!" I said sarcastically. "How can I help you guys?"

"May we step in?" Viktor asked.

"I'm not decent."

"We're all guys here," Viktor added.

I had no rebuttal, so I stepped back, opening the door for their entrance. I took a deep breath as I was annoyed.

"Eh. Nice place," Viktor said.

I lived in the hood. The ghetto or slums as some people will call it. It was a small little two-bedroom duplex. I didn't know if Viktor was being genuine or a douche.

"Eh. Save the compliments," I responded, waving my hand. "Hurry up, I got stuff to do," I reminded them of my time.

"It's simple. We want you back," Viktor said. "We just need to do one last job, and I swear you'll never hear from me again," he promised. "You were all for this at one point and now such a strong change of heart?"

"That's what happens when you smarten up," I said. "You guys counting money, living the good life and I'm living in paranoia-ville. Looking over my shoulder, jakes coming to my doorstep, snatching me up for questions!" I continued angrily. "I didn't sign up for that." There was a long drawn out silence from both of them as if they were thinking hard about what I just said. "Besides that, I've already been informed of what you guys have been doing, and it sounds too much like a day job to me," I said, breaking the silence. Viktor put his hands on his head out of frustration.

"Things will be different. We know you can bring something to the table. We're missing a variable, and you're that variable," Viktor said as he looked over at Vince who was shaking his head for a visual co-sign.

"What he is saying, is that we are stuck. We hit a roadblock," Vince chimed in. "Cops got us at a standstill, and that's why we are here. We know you can figure something out," He continued.

I was growing tired of talking. I didn't feel the need to explain myself any further. "Listen. I have stuff to do, okay. I'll tell you what. I'll think about and get back to you," I explained. I walked them to the door, shooing them away like stray dogs. At the door, Viktor turned back around reaching into his suit jacket.

"Seriously. Think about it. I'm going to leave this here with you," he said laying down a thick brown envelope on the table near the door.

"No. No, I don't want-"

"You don't have to spend it. It's fine. Just think about it," Viktor said before heading back out to Vince's Mercedes.

Vince was right behind him but then turned back around to walk towards me signaling to Viktor he would be right back. I rolled my eyes out of irritation as he approached me.

"Hey, man I know we got this rift between us now. But I'm only in this game because of you," Vince said. "When you asked me to help you, as your brother, what did I say? No problem. No hesitation because I got your back. And now I'm asking for the same in return."

I stared at him speechless; he was right. But I wasn't wrong, either for refusing their offer. Things were different when we first started. I looked down out of slight embarrassment. I looked back up at him before talking.

"I will think about it. My life is upside down at the moment, and if you weren't so obsessed with this new life of yours, you would know and understand that," I responded defensively.

Vince turned and walked away. I watched as he sped off down the street out of anger. I sat down on the couch looking at the envelope

Viktor left. I thought about taking whatever money that was in the envelope and move my mom and me to a different state. After seeing me hypothetically being hunted down and tortured, I quickly shook those thoughts away. What was I going to do, I kept thinking? I told my mom I was done with that life and not going back. I told Renee I was done as well. I could get my mom to understand, but I know Renee wanted no part of it.

"Hello?" I heard a voice say from the front door. It was Ms. Treaty. "Got a surprise for you," she said pointing outside to her car.

My mom was getting her things and making her way to the house.

"Mom? But, How did she?" I said confused and excited.

"I don't know! The doctor said she got better sooner than expected and cleared her for home so here we are!" Ms. Treaty explained.

I went over to help my mom. She was better, but you could see she was still weak. I was almost sure she signed herself out against doctor's orders. That's why she called Ms. Treaty to pick her up instead of me. She knows I wouldn't fall for that. There's no way you could get that much better in a matter of hours. But if this is what she wants, so be it.

"Hey, superwoman!" I said pretending to not know what she did.

"Hey, baby! Here, take this," she said, handing me her stuff.

"Let me straighten up for you guys," Ms. Treaty said as she headed to the kitchen.

"Why didn't you clean up boy?!" my mom screamed.

I kept quiet while my mind flashed back just 15 minutes ago to when Vince and Viktor were here. I wish one of them was here now so I could deck them for interrupting my cleaning. This reminded me, there was a stack of money on the table right in front of her. My heart started sinking slowly but surely. Mom always grabs the mail on the table when she walks in.

"Hand me that mail on the table," Mom instantly asked.

My heart was somewhere in my lower abdomen at this point, and I did the first thing that came to mind.

"What in the hell is that outside," I said, pointing and twisting my face up. As soon as she turned to look I snatched the brown envelope up and slid it under the couch.

"I don't see nothing. What you see?!" Mom frantically asked.

"I thought I saw some type of raccoon on your car. I have just been tired. My bad," I responded.

"Mmhm. Probably playing them damn video games all night. Talking about tired," she said after formulating her own thoughts.

In the plastic bags, my mom handed me, was a folder with all the doctor notes and prescriptions. I started looking through them as she went to her room to change clothes. First thing I read confirmed what I already knew.

`Patient signed herself out against doctor's orders but agreed to the prescription.`

I wanted to thump her on the head for being so stubborn. I continued to read to see what else I could learn.

`Total due = $5700.00.`

My eyes almost fell from my face to the folder while looking at that. It was an instant depression. I wondered how we were going to get that kind of money. I still wanted no part of that brown envelope.

As if there weren't enough surprises already, I heard a car door shut outside. I got up and peeked out the door to see an angel approaching. It was Renee.

"Dammit. What is she doing here?" I said to myself.

I was unprepared. Had nothing but shorts on. My mom was just returning from the ER, and the place was a mess. I panicked and opened the door meeting her outside doing my best to stall while my mom was changing and Ms. Treaty was cleaning.

"Heyyyy! What are you doing here?" I said, doing my best to pretend I was more excited than nervous.

"Surprise punk! Where are your clothes, weirdo?" she asked after giving me a hug.

"Oh! My clothes. Yeah, there in the crib, of course,"

There was an awkward silence. My brain just couldn't work. I couldn't think of anything to say. Then I started thinking too much. Am I being weird? She is going to think I have another woman in the house? I was tweaking out.

"Oookayy. So, are we going in there or what?" she asked after standing through the silence.

"Yeah! Of course," I opened the screen door, peeking through the house door. The house was still a mess, but at least my mom changed clothes.

"Why are you acting so weird? You got another bitch in there? That's why you got on no clothes!?" she stared at me, asking aggressively.

"What?! No! And I'm not acting weird!" I said in defense.

After sighing, I opened the door.

"Mom! Can you come here for a second?"

My mom leaned back peeking from the kitchen looking in our direction.

"Who is that?" She asked.

This day was going backwards. I never got to prepare my mom for this exact moment today. I told my mom about Renee and showed her pictures, and while she thought she was cute and all, my mom loved Toya. I was about to faint at the thought of her acting a fool and rejecting Renee.

"Mom, this is Renee. My girlfriend I've been telling you about-"

"Ahh, my son she's beautiful!" She responded.

My soul returned to my body, and my mind relaxed when she said that.

"Aww Thank you Ms. Long, and I see where your son gets good looks from," Renee complimented, looking and smiling at me. This is working out just great I thought to myself.

"Sorry, the place is a mess. Someone didn't clean up," My mom said, staring at me like she wanted to give me a knuckle sandwich. "And go put some damn clothes on!" She yelled, then smiled back at Renee.

I shot upstairs to my room. I took my time putting on my clothes, giving Renee and mom time to get acquainted best they could. Every couple of minutes I could hear them laughing and such. Probably was dogging me out, but I didn't care as long as they were enjoying themselves. I emerged from my room dressed in my Burberry button-up I got at the mall in Vegas. I took a break from my usual Adidas tracksuit for once. I was dating a fashion model, so I had to act like it.

"Oh good. Glad you're back. Wait a minute, where you think you going? Your little girlfriend here, you trying to show off huh?" My mom called me out. "Chill mom!" I yelled as I wanted her to refrain from embarrassing me any further although she was right. I wasn't a flashy guy by any means.

"Mhm. Anyway, go up to the pharmacy and pick up my medicine," My mom ordered me as she dug into her bag looking for the script. Shaking my head to my mother's demands as it was another errand I had to run, I grabbed my keys. "Wanna come with?" I asked Renee while twirling my car keys on my index finger. "Be back mom." Renee and I walked over to the Malibu.

"Nice pipes," she said, looking at the back of the car. "And nice interior. I see you switched the gear shifter around for a better feel."

I was just standing there with hearts in my eyes as she spoke about my car. She knew something about cars, and she's beautiful?! I was thinking to myself. My crotch area was starting to bulge a little.

"Can I drive her?!" she asked.

The bulge deflated like a pierced balloon.

"Uhh, sure I suppose," I said uneasily as I tossed her the keys. "You got a car back home?" I asked her.

"No, but I want to buy one."

"So…when's the last time you actually drove?" I asked concerned.

"I don't remember actually, but it's like riding a bike! Get in punk, let's go!" She commanded.

It felt like I was entering the car that takes you straight the dungeons of hell. "This must be what it feels like when parents teach their kids to drive," I said audibly, both of us laughing.

"Oh, hush. I can drive!" She reassured me as cranked the Malibu's engine. "Oh, she sounds great!" Renee whispered, listening to the gurgle and rumble of the engine and pipes.

"Ok just ease on her because she's-"

I was instantly thrown back against my seat as she mashed on the gas pedal. She had a lead foot, but she was handling the Malibu just fine, surprisingly. I could tell she was a bit rusty as I navigated her through the streets. I smiled while she was having fun. She was always working and traveling so this was more than likely a breath of fresh air. She threw her all black oversized ray-bans on embracing the drive. I was trying not to be a weirdo by staring at her, but I couldn't help it. She was so gorgeous, the wind navigating through her long black hair, the sun beaming on her perfectly brown skin.

"This the Walgreens right here right?" Renee questioned.

"Yep. You can park, I want to go in and get a protein shake," I told her.

"Cool. I need some lip balm, too."

"And I'll take those keys off your hands as well miss lead foot," I jokingly said but reaching my hand out while we stood on opposite ends of the car.

"If you want them back you gotta take them from me," she uttered as she bit her bottom lip, giving me a seductive glare.

I jumped over the hood of the Malibu before she could even react, catching her as she turned to run and picking her up, throwing her over my shoulder while tickling her to death until she dropped the keys to my most prized possession. She let out the loudest scream and laughter mixture that screamed out I'm having the best time ever right now. I sat her on the hood of my Malibu and picked my keys off the ground.

"I hate you so much," Renee said giggling.

"I had to get my keys back without inflicting pain on you," I said, matching her laughter.

"And I gotta get something from you," she mentioned, hooking her index finger between buttons on my shirt. She slowed down, reeling me in, with each tug pulling me closer to her. She opened her legs to fit me in her personal space like a puzzle piece then closing her legs behind me, locking me in. Without any further hesitation, we rammed our lips together in attempts to kiss each other's face off.

"Get a room!" A woman driving past yelled out interrupting our love session. We laughed in response. Lucky for her this isn't my ideal world because if it was, we would have been undressed already.

We went inside Walgreens and grabbed my mom prescription and was lounging around looking at candy and magazines. I was looking at the auto magazines, and she was, of course, looking at the fashion magazines. I could feel a weird energy in the air. As soon as I felt at, I heard it.

"Joey?" An extremely familiar voice said.

I turned to my left to see Toya standing there in an way oversized Georgetown Hoyas hoodie. I haven't seen Toya since my father's funeral. She's been trying to reach me, but I've been avoiding her. I know she just wants to get back with me and I just don't want that route again.

"Hey, Toya," I nonchalantly responded.

As soon as Renee heard another woman's voice mention my name, she came over and rested her head on my shoulder, staring at the same-sex species in front of us with curiosity.

"Hey. I'm Renee. Joey's girlfriend. You are...?" Renee said as she attempted to interact with Toya.

Toya looked at Renee then back at me to stare into my soul before breathing heavy. You could see her jawbone muscles flexing from gritting her teeth so hard.

"I was just leaving," Toya said with her eyes never leaving mines. She walked in my face.

"To hell with you!" She screamed before shoving me. I took the shove and stepped back. Staring back at her with a face that says what the hell. I looked over at Renee who was taking off her earrings.

"I don't know who that bitch is, but I'm about to knock her head off!" Renee said as she geared up to chase after Toya.

I snatched Renee up before she could chase after her, letting her know it wasn't worth it. If this was some chick I met in the club or some one-night stand, then I would have let her go. This was Toya who was someone I had a history with, still care about and ultimately still loved. I'd never allow physical pain to come to her as long as I had the power to stop it.

My day was going from sugar to shit quicker than I could process it. I had Renee yelling at me now because she thinks Toya was some random woman I was cheating on her with. Everyone in Walgreens was staring at us. Some more intensely, like they were watching a movie and others on a sly as if they were afraid to be caught.

After arguing for a few minutes, the manager eventually came over to escort us out.

"Just take me to my hotel please," Renee demanded. This was the first time I've seen Renee upset and it just so happens to be directed at me. The nice guy in me wanted to just say okay and take her home and forget the whole thing, but I didn't allow myself to back down that easy. I wasn't given a fair shake. My side of the story never made it to the air, and it needed to.

"Listen! If you want to act a fool, then go ahead, be my guest but at least know what you acting a fool over. Do you even know why you're acting like this?" I asked her. "Don't worry, the answer is no," I abruptly answered for her. "You think I'm out here just slaying women left and right or something, but I'm not. You're the only woman I'm seeing and that I want to see," I explained.

She was standing by the passenger car door frowning with her arms folded, looking like a spoiled child who was just told no for the first time. "That other girl, that was my ex okay. I left her months ago, and she's still upset about it because I've been ignoring her. Just so happens that with my luck we'd run into her," I pleaded my case. She didn't say anything, she just got in the car. I paused before entering the driver's side, shaking my head at the madness. She sighed heavily as I started the car.

"I'm sorry, baby. I overreacted."

I looked over at her after she said it. She looked sincere about it.

"It's cool. What hotel you at?" I responded, pretending not to care.

"You mad at me?"

I wanted to say, 'Hell yeah I'm mad at you, what do you think?' But the little angel on my shoulder told me to do otherwise. Be the bigger person.

"No, I'm not mad. It's cool," I repeated dryly. "I understand."

"Want to get something to eat?" I offered, preparing to bury the hatchet and move on.

"Yeah. My hotel is the Blackstone Hotel," Renee told me as she scrolled through her emails on her phone.

The Blackstone Hotel was in the heart of downtown. I figured I'd take the thirty-minute scenic route which pretty much showcased the inner city before you got to the uppity rich downtown area. Driving on the route, you could see all the abandoned homes and properties as well as the severely poor people. Most of them were drug addicts that got lost in the system via jail or military veterans, whom the government simply turned their backs on and forced to the street.

"Wow. This is where you're from huh?" Renee asked out of curiosity.

"Yep. I won't lie though, never had it quite this rough.

A stray man in dingy clothes ran up to the Malibu frantically with a bucket of water and a squeegee to wipe my windshield down while I was stopped at a red light. Renee eagerly raised her window out of fear. I reached into my pocket and gave him a couple bucks and whatever loose change I had.

"God bless you," the man said.

"You too, family."

I looked over at Renee who was staring at me like I did something wrong. "What's you wrong with you," I laughed.

"Why do you give them money when you know they are going to buy drugs with it and only do themselves more harm."

"Wait a minute," I paused her. "Who said they were on their way to do drugs. They are people just like us and yeah some just might be on drugs, but a lot of them were forced into these circumstances," I explained.

"What if that was you, wouldn't you want someone to help you?" She looked at me with her lips turned up like I was talking out of my ass.

"Well yeah, I guess. But come on. They all just trying to get a hit," she responded.

"We will have to agree to disagree on this one pretty lady," I replied. I shook my head.

"Look! See!" Renee shouted out, pointing to our left. Two junkies less than 3 blocks away from where I gave that guy some money, were shooting up under a viaduct. "Wow" was all I could say. I lost my case. It made me think about Vince a lot. He was embracing this new fast life which was cool minus the drugs. Renee had a point.

I wanted to believe some of those homeless people had humanity left but maybe there were just looking for a hit. I couldn't imagine that happening to Vince but then again, I could. He already ditched me for the lifestyle. One day you are riding clean and the next day you strung out. I couldn't let him ditch himself.

"Uhh earth to Joey! Red light!" Renee yelled out as I was approaching a red light with no intentions of stopping.

"My bad," I said as I made the stop just in time.

"You okay?" Renee asked me.

"Yeah, I'm cool," I responded. I was contemplating doing the job with Vince. Maybe if I did the job, he'd change his new ways. In fact, if I do the job this has to be the last job and no more Coke. My mind was made just like that.

I was ready to drop Renee off and get to work. But I promised her food. I valeted the Malibu at the Blackstone, and we went in to dine at their in-house restaurant. The staff thought we were famous models how way we were dressed. I overheard one of the workers wiping down a table say she saw us do a shoot together. She was mistaken because I had never posed for a magazine in my life, but I was sure she had seen Renee before. If they only knew how much money I really had, they would know for sure it wasn't me in that photo shoot.

For the first time in a long time, I had no waiting time to be seated. We were presented with menus and a very nice seat by a window. Once seated we were given enough warm bread and salad to feed the homeless. The salad was decent, but the bread was scrumptious, warm and fluffy with just the right amount of crisp on the edges. Most restaurants that bring bread come with butter, but at the Blackstone, their bread came with a sweet cinnamon butter that complimented the bread so well. Combining both sweet and salty flavors perfectly. I didn't even want to order an entrée. We enjoyed the bread so much, we had three baskets worth, and in each basket, there were five buns.

Renee ordered a chicken Caesar salad, and I ordered the Blackstone burger with a side of fries. When the food came, neither of us could finish our meal because of the bread and cinnamon butter gluttony. My belly poked far out enough for everyone to notice. I was sure if I had a wig on, someone would mistake me for a pregnant woman.

I figured since we had eaten, and Renee basically has to go rush to get ready for her shows, it would be a good time to let her in on my plan to return to my old ways in order to save a friend.

"Babe. So, I've been thinking," I said after taking a small sip of water anticipating a long explanation.

"About?"

"Going back to work," I said, looking at her, ready to face whatever consequences coming my way.

"I thought you were waiting for your acceptance letter before you decided to find a job," she responded.

She wasn't following me. She thought I was talking corporate. That's when I realized this was going to be tougher than I thought. "No. Not that kind of work. I'm talking about my old work. Work, work," I explained, putting emphasis on work to let her know which work I was talking about.

"You're joking right. Tell me you're joking so I can tell you you're not funny," she responded with a straight face.

"I wish I could. Vince needs my help. My mom and I need money. My back is against the wall here," I explained.

"I know this is kind of random and sudden, but until we had that talk in the car earlier about those drug addicts this wasn't really on my mind, but then it hit me. Vince is on drugs, and I can't let him go out like that."

Renee was just sitting there with a straight face, staring at me. I couldn't tell if she was listening or thinking or what. After a brief moment of silence, she started to tear up.

"So, what's going to happen to us? I told you if you went back to that life I wouldn't be here for that. Does that no mean anything to you!?" She whimpered.

"It means everything to me. But I have to save my best friend. I have to get him out of this life he thinks is so right. In that process, I will be saving my mom and myself as well. One last job, then I'm yours for life. We can get married, I'll go to school and be a stay home dad if I have to, to prove my love to you. I have to do this though."

She got up from the table, throwing her napkin down before storming off. I just sat there in silence thinking to myself, wondering if I was making the right choice. After about five minutes of silence, I sent Renee a text that simply said "I love you. Trust me." I dug in my pocket and left three twenty dollar bills on the table and proceeded to the valet area to retrieve my Malibu. Once inside my car, I pulled out my phone called Vince before heading home.

"Hey. I'm in."

Friday the New Plan

Right after leaving the Blackstone hotel, I drove over to Vince's condo to meet him and Viktor. I found parking about a block away from his place. I knew I was in the right place because I saw his Mercedes parked out front. "Damn. This guy has a doorman now," I whispered to myself.

"Who are you here to see Mister?" the doorman asked me as soon as I entered the building.

"Vince-"

"1206. Elevator on your left," the doorman said, in his monotone voice after making a call to Vince.

Vince's new residence was impressive. The lobby looked like something out of Rome or Greece. It was like he bought a piece of Vegas here. Gold accents and statues everywhere. Even a small wishing well that was stuffed with pennies probably from people wishing for a place of such magnitude.

My thoughts ceased as I stepped off the elevator onto the 12th floor. I could hear loud noises resembling gunshots and explosions. Either someone was watching a war film, or D-Day was upon us. To my surprise, it was coming from room 1206. I got a text from Vince saying it's open. I slowly opened the door as I thought I would need to take cover from an explosion once entering.

"Yo! My main man Joey!" Vince yelled with excitement, once seeing my face.

He was playing Call of Duty on his huge 55-inch TV with a surround system that could shame a low budget movie theater.

"Grab your sticks man, come on and run a match with me. Catch online bodies," he asked of me. "Live a little!"

As much as I wanted to decline in order to get straight to business the gamer in me couldn't resist. I had to give it a shot.

"Okay. Just one match because we have to talk business. Where's Viktor?" I asked with my arms folded to show I meant business.

"He's on his way. Should be here any minute with his bean headed ass," Vince joked. He made us laugh hysterically.

"Alright load us up. I haven't played in so long, let's see if I still got it," I said to Vince as I picked up the controller.

When Vince and I would play COD together, we'd usually play against each other with random teammates to even the playing field because we were that good. On opposite teams, whether he won or I won it always be a close match, often a kill or two apart. With us being on teams it was a total slaughterhouse on the opposing force. This time was no different. We still had the juice. The sound system really put me in the game. You could feel each gunshot, each explosion thump through your chest. I was an experience that made me never want to go back to regular TV speakers ever again. Our five-minute match was up, and Vince and I were high fiving in victory as we obliterated the opposing team 75-47.

"Not even close!" Vince said aloud.

"I bet with some practice I could take both of you guys on," Viktor said from behind us, standing there with his hands on his waist as if he had been watching the whole match.

"I doubt that, but I'd love to see you try one day," I said, back to Viktor.

"Perhaps one day. For now, let's get to work."

Vince walked us around to his dining room table where he had some paper, pens and a few refreshments laid out for us.

"Pass the pitcher, please. I'm extremely parched," Viktor asked of Vince.

"Sure. I don't know if you've ever had what's in here though. I can't be responsible for you becoming addicted to this," Vince said as he passed the big dark green pitcher to Viktor.

"Really? Kool-Aid?" I whispered at Vince.

Viktor looked confused as hell as we watched him pour himself a glass.

"Why are you guys staring? What is this "kool-aid" stuff?" He asked, cautiously.

"Powdered flavors with water and sugar basically. Drink up," I told Viktor, as I grabbed the pitcher and began to pour myself a glass.

"Whoa! This is crap!" Viktor asked, twisting his face up and sideways as he made a commotion. "Why is it so sweet? I hate it! But I kind of like it," He said, sucking his teeth as if he was cleaning the liquid off each tooth.

Vince and I were cracking up laughing at Viktor's reaction. "Take him out the hood but can't take the hood out of him," I uttered and laughed with Vince. The COD and clowning reminded me of how much I honestly missed my best friend. If I was going to get him back, I couldn't lose track of the mission. "Okay, let's get to work. So, you guys are basically scouting and then boosting, right?"

"Basically. But the rest of the process is just like the heist we did. The VIN numbers, the restorations and all," Vince said, like he was running things.

I turned and looked at Viktor. "So, who came up with this plan?"

Vince and Viktor looked at each other as if they didn't know who came up with the plan. There was a two-second silence before they both answered.

"We all did!"

"So, here's the new plan. Demand is too high to be scouting for a couple cars here and there. The reward isn't worth the risk. You guys probably got every cop in the land on high alert. No more scouting small time. Time to scout big time. Big money!" I explained with infomercial excitement. Vince and Viktor were fully attentive as I spilled my pitch.

"For someone who doesn't want to do this, you sure seem ready," Vince added.

If he only knew I was only showing interest because I am trying to save him. He was about to find out. "If I'm going to do anything you of all people should know I'm not going to half-ass it. Two feet in or no feet at all. So, listen up. We have to scout for lots. Old school car lots to be exact. We find the best lot and take it," I explained, like a professor giving out the syllabus of the first semester. "How were you guys scouting before?" I asked.

"We drove around. Guido, King Kong, Tony, and myself," Vince answered.

I drew a total blank. I scratched my head. "You kidding me?! You drove around? And who in the hell is Tony?" I asked perplexed.

"Yes. Why don't you fill your friend in on who exactly Tony is, Vince?"

Viktor's thick German accent filled the room. I turned from Viktor to look at Vince who now had a blank look on his face.

"Well…So, I don't know who he is, like I don't have years with him and stuff. Look, D and Jean dropped out, and we needed two more people. Hence, King Kong and I found Tony."

"Okay, but how? How, when, where?" I asked. He looked down like a child faced with guilt.

"Online chat room," he uttered.

"What!" I questioned.

Viktor was laughing in the background.

"It's an underground chat room to link people together that's trying to do some work. He's been hitting cars with us, and he's a good man. Trust me."

I was lost for words at the fact that he would bring someone in on jobs like this without knowing them. It didn't make sense to me. The more I was finding out, the more I wanted out of the game and I had just stepped back in.

"You know what. Fine. But that guy is your problem."

"My words and thoughts exactly," Viktor said, adding his two cents in.

"Okay, moving forward. No more driving for scouting. We're going to use the internet. We can find everything we need on the net. Except friends!" I shouted and nodded at Vince, giving him no doubt that I was talking to him.

"We find a lot with as many of the cars we need and juice them. I'll find the lots, don't worry about it. Other than the new team and sloppy technique, is everything still the same Viktor?"

"As far as I know. There is more money on the table now of course which is why we are so anxious," Viktor said.

I looked down at my phone to see if I had any missed calls or texts. Mainly, from my mom and Renee. Neither of them hit my phone. In the midst of looking at my phone, I wondered about my soon to happen departure from home away from my mom and disconnect from Renee. My stomach turned as I could feel the future heartache.

"Distracted?" Viktor questioned.

"Uhh no. Actually, I was just thinking of my terms," I said quickly, to throw off the fact that I was indeed distracted by my thoughts.

"Your terms?" Vince said with a hint of confusion.

"Yeah. My terms," I confirmed. "Check it," I said, after clearing my throat to voice my demands. "I have accepted you guys' offer. Viktor, you have provided me with 100 thousand dollars as promised. Vince, I will need the keys to the GT-R at your earliest convenience. Now, I need you guys to accept my offer. I will NOT do this job if you show up at my home again! I will not do this job if I cannot be compensated twenty-five percent of my total earnings up front. Most importantly, I will not do this job if Vince continues to do coke. I need you off of that immediately, like starting right now and in fact, you will be going to rehab."

Total silence. This was clearly an outrageous demand for them.

"I'm not done yet. If you don't accept, I will gracefully return the hundred thousand and forget this meeting ever happened. If you accept and then breach my contract for whatever reason, then I will keep all possessions and disappear," I explained. "So, do we have a deal or no?" I asked.

"This is horse crap! Why do I have to go to rehab for!? I don't even use coke that often man!" Vince shouted.

"I would believe you if I hadn't watched my parents and their friends use it for many years. I know the signs and facial looks. Besides that, I know what little bottles they come in, and they look just like the ones on your counter over there," I said, pointing to his granite counter in the kitchen. "So, I'm going to ask again, do we have a deal or not?"

Vince sighed and grunted out of anger.

"Okay. Let's move on. Vince will keep his nose clean. I'll keep an eye on him in addition to yours. When do we start?" Viktor asked.

"Right now," I uttered, fiercely. Vince and Viktor shared eye contact and then nodded, agreeing to my terms.

We were to meet at our garage where we originally started to meet and inform the rest of the team and sketch out our plan before executing. Viktor headed out first. Before Vince and I were leaving the condo, I had Vince flush all of his cocaine supply down the toilet. He was so mad, but I didn't care. This was for his own good, he just couldn't see it. After flushing his precious powder down the toilet, we headed to his garage to get my new car.

"Wow. I can't believe it. Here she is. Godzilla in the flesh!" I whispered to myself.

"Do you know why the world refers to her as Godzilla, Vince?" I asked in my dramatic voice as I was in a trance from looking at her beauty.

"No, actually, I don't. Had no idea her name was Godzilla," Vince answered.

I heard Vince's response to my question, but I wasn't ready to school him just yet. I was occupied by Godzilla's beauty, rubbing her coupe steel gray body, following and caressing each curve all the way to her behind, waiting the moment she would let me inside her and accept my love.

"What the hell. Stop being weird bro! Before I send you to rehab," Vince pleaded. I laughed, but Vince was ignorant. He didn't deserve her. Godzilla deserved someone that knows how to appreciate her. Someone to treat her right, and loves her like she's the only one in the world. I continued to marvel at her rear-end. It was the biggest part of her body, fitting four circular taillights and a double duel exhaust, each wide enough to fit a softball.

"I know you have at least seen some of the Godzilla films, right? Not the American remake crap. I'm talking about the originals. Remember the terror in the eyes of the Japanese when they first witnessed Godzilla? Well, when Japan or Nissan introduced the Skyline to the world it was such a beast, out-performing all cars in its class, the world was forced to name her Godzilla," I explained to Vince, with a short story.

"You know how many horses she's putting out? Engine type? What kind of...you know what? Never mind," I stopped, cutting my facts list short because I knew Vince wouldn't appreciate them.

"I just know she's fast, man. And she looks good. That's all that matters to me," Vince responded.

"Yep. She's fast, and she looks good. Keys, please," I said abruptly. "Here, take my Malibu and follow me."

I have to get a room for the night. I can't go back home until this is done," I explained to Vince.

I pressed the unlock button on the key, opening her arms to let me in and she did with warmth. I pulled the latch to pop the hood to see if what I read was true. It was just as I read. She was sporting a mere hand built V6 engine, but that was the kicker. She's a sleeper. If a Ferrari was to pull up next to her, anyone would bet their home that the Ferrari would smash Godzilla, but that would only leave those gamblers homeless. Godzilla has two twin turbochargers in her V6 that gives her 545 horses to play with and all-wheel drive that allows her to hug the pavement and accelerate beyond belief. I stared at her engine for another ten seconds before starting her up and taking her on the road to see her performance entailed. I was used to the typical key in the ignition, turn to start system, but Godzilla uses a smart key, a push to start system. By my quadriceps, lied the handbrake and next to the handbrake was a bright red button that read "start, stop," It looked like the kind of button that screamed Press me! So, I did. For a two-year-old car, she started right up with no signs of a hassle. I was so used to my Malibu, that I was shocked at how quiet Godzilla was in comparison because she was such a monster. She didn't have that deep and loud V8 engine gurgle noise. Instead, it was a quiet and subtle hum. I was ready to take Godzilla out on the streets and tame her.

"Hey! Let's shake!" I yelled out the window to Vince who looked like he had been waiting for me all along and quite annoyed.

"I thought you would never ask," he yelled back. We crept out of the garage slowly as if we had just stolen our two cars. I rolled up to the first stop sign with Vince closely behind me as I waved out of the window for Vince to drive around. I had to tell him something. He pulled up right along the side of me.

"Yo. While there is no traffic and not a cop in sight, I want you to race me down this block really quick. I know the Malibu can't win, but I want to put this in perspective," Vince nodded, revving the Malibu's engine, giving me the okay signal.

I revved Godzilla's engine giving Vince the okay signal right back. With both of us revving the cars, you could feel the ground shake. I held my hand up, dropping my fingers from five to four, to three to two and before I could get to one giving the green light signal, Vince shot from the stop sign, cheating me out of two seconds. I quickly stomped the throttle and took a ride on what felt to be the closest thing to a rocket ship that I could imagine. The two-second advantage that Vince had was made up instantly. In what seemed to be in the blink of my eyes, I was at

Jack Williams

70mph, and Vince was in the rearview mirror playing catch up. I quickly pounded the breaks to make the next stop sign.

"WHOO!" I yelled out of pure excitement and adrenaline.

"Man that was no contest! Let me get my Benz then we'll see who's the fastest!" Vince said, while mean mugging me.

I couldn't help but laugh at Vince's competitive spirit. The race didn't mean anything, I just wanted to see what the GTR could do up against another fast car.

"You cheated and still lost, punk! But it's cool, man. You got it. It's a no match for the Mercedes!" I said, stroking Vince's ego and also lying through my teeth. Godzilla would smoke his Benz with ease. Vince would need a Lamborghini to have a chance at passing Godzilla.

"You damn right, it's a no match," Vince responded.

I shook my head and continued on my quest to the motel before going to meet with Viktor and the rest of the team. Thirty minutes later, I had yet again arrived at the Just Sleep Motel. This time around I figured I would be there for a bit longer, so I got the deluxe room. Instead of a twin bed, I got a queen size, and I also got cable TV. Wasn't the cleanest looking place nor the best smelling but for no contract and twenty-eight dollars a night, it wasn't bad at all.

"You know, you can stay at my place man. You don't need to be in no rundown motel like this," Vince reminded me.

"I know man, but you know me."

"Yeah. Prideful," Vince uttered.

"That's right," I said nodding and smiling. "Besides that, I can't go too far from my mom you know. I need that medium between mom and our HQ, just in case she needs me," I explained to Vince.

"You the only person that knows I'm here so if you ever feel the need to surprise visit me, I'll be here. Not at my mother's crib," I continued to explain.

"Ok, are we headed to the garage now where the team is?" Vince asked.

"Not yet for me. You go ahead. I'll be there. I got to pick some stuff up, and I have to fill my mom in on my decision. I can't leave her in the dark you know," I answered.

"Yeah. I hear you. Well, I'll see you when you get there," Vince reached out for a dap as we parted ways.

"Oh wait, switch cars with me. I can't show up with a new toy like this. I will be needing her back though so don't enjoy her too much," I said to Vince, with a smirk as we swapped car keys.

I jumped in my Malibu and instantly twisted my face up upon turning my key in the ignition to turn my car on. She felt so outdated, so plain and so simple. When I pulled out of the parking lot I headed to my mom's place, she felt so slow. Going from my Malibu to Godzilla and back was like an old man, finding some new young love. Once you get a taste of what that's like, you don't want to go back. I removed those thoughts from my mind as I got close to home thinking about what I was going to tell my mom. The truth shall set you free Joey I sarcastically thought to myself. There wasn't a better option anyway.

I saw her car in the driveway as I got closer to the house. I pulled into the driveway behind her Camaro.

"What's up Jo!" I heard some nearby kids that were shooting hoops yell out.

"What's up little homies!" I yelled back, showing them equal love.

"Come shoot some hoops! Come play!"

"I can't today y'all! Maybe tomorrow I'll show y'all a thing or two!" I continued yelling out. They were lucky. I would do anything to be in their shoes again. To be a kid again. To be that little kid selling fireworks around the way and capping my days' worth of hard work with Super Nintendo, Sega Genesis, and cartoons.

"Boy where you been?" mom yelled as soon as I grabbed the screen door, bringing me back to adulthood.

"Uhhh nowhere really! Why you all in my kool-aid lady?" I asked with attitude as I walked in the house.

"Excuse me? Boy, drop that attitude because I brought you into this world and I will take you out if I need to," she proclaimed as she stepped into my personal space waving her hands up in the air.

"Mom, what are you doing? Quit playing!" I said, with a huge cheesy smile on my face.

She quickly pushed me down on the couch and tickled me like I was once again, an eight-year-old. I instantly lost my breath from laughing so hard.

"Okay, okay! You win! I'm sorry!" I yelled.

Jack Williams

"I thought so! I'm your momma boy!" She said with the confidence of an undefeated championship boxer as she walked away to her room.

That's when the pain hit me. How could I do this job against my mother's will? How could I pain her like this especially after I told her to her face that I was done with that life? Vince was my best friend but so was my mother. I sat there on the couch for at least a half hour fighting with myself. I got the team waiting on me to pull off the biggest and last job of the contract, and on the other end, I got my mom wishing the best for her son.

"This isn't for me or about me. This is for Vince and Ms. Owens," I reassured myself. I convinced myself that doing the job was the greater good that needed to be done. As much as I wanted to make my mother proud, I knew if need be, she would forgive her son. But, I can't live with letting Vince, someone who I call a brother just throw his life away. I couldn't let his mom, who is like a mom to me, lose another part of her. That would haunt me to the grave. I decided I was just going to just leave. I didn't have the guts or the heart to face my mom. I reached under the couch for the manila folder Viktor left me. I peeked inside of it, double checking to make sure it was all there. After the eyeball count, I made my way to the backyard shed where I dug the hole for my mom. My only expenses were room, board and food when I thought about it. I took five grand out of the hundred for my pockets and tossed the envelope in the hole and covered it up.

I went back inside to my room to pack a few things. Everything was to fit in my duffle bag which kind of pained me because I couldn't fit my PlayStation and my TV in there. I hoped to stay busy so I wouldn't think about my PlayStation, and I could do without it. I grabbed some clothes, about one week's worth of underwear, socks, t-shirts, a hoodie and two pairs of my favorite Levi 501 black denim jeans. I went over to the bathroom to grab my toothbrush and deodorant. My bag was getting pretty stuffed quickly, but I had one more thing to stuff in there; my money counter.

I headed to my room to retrieve the counter only to be scared to death by Ms. Treaty.

"Jesus! I didn't hear you come in Ms. Treaty, you scared me half to death," I said as I gathered myself back together.

"C'mon. A tall and big guy like you, afraid of little ol me? No way," Ms. Treaty said, as she laughed at my mishap. "Just doing my daily routines though. Where's your mom, in her room?"

I had to think of something quick because if Ms. Treaty knocked on my mom door, my mom would come out and I would be busted. I did the quickest thing my mind came up with.

"Um. Yeah, she's in there but before you do that, can I talk to you for a second?" I asked.

"Sure hun, what's up?" I took her to the living room where it was safer for us to talk as it wasn't so close to my mother's room.

"Well, I'm kind of sneaking out for a few days away on vacation. Mom doesn't know, and I want to keep it that way. I'm going to write her a letter, so she will know, but I'll be gone by the time she reads it. I'm going to put it in her car. I just need you to make sure she gets it and check on her more frequently you know. Maybe y'all can go out or something a few days out the week," I nervously explained. She looked at me like she just knew I was pulling her leg.

"Oh, I don't know. I really don't want to-"

"Please Ms. Treaty. I need this from you. Here, I'll even pay just for this small favor," I said, digging in my pockets for cash.

"Seven, eight, nine, a thousand," I counted aloud, peeling back hundred dollar bills. "Thousand dollars okay?"

Her eyes brightened up, looking at the cash, I was sure she had to say yes now.

"Fineee," she said, as she looked away then back at me signaling she really didn't want to be involved but she'd be silly not to take the money.

"You lucky I got bills boy," she continued as she took the stack out of my hands.

"Thank you so much. I'm so grateful for you. I only got one mom so watch her for me," I told her as I held her hands.

"Then why don't you watch her, instead of sneaking off on her?" she countered me.

She hurt me with that statement. I wasn't expecting such a heartfelt response from her. I stared at the ground holding my silence.

"I have to do something for the greater good. I know she would understand, but I also know she wouldn't want me to do it, so I have to do this for me," I explained. "I have to run though. One day, I'll explain everything to you," I said as I went back to my room to grab the money counter.

Surprisingly, the money counter still had some cash in it. I counted it quickly up to five hundred dollars and stuffed it in my pocket and sat the money counter in the duffle bag. I stood by my door, scouting my room making sure I wasn't forgetting anything. 'Ah, of course' I said to myself, almost forgetting how dingy my motel room was. I snatched my pillow case off my pillow and stuffed it in my bag too. I nodded at Ms. Treaty on my way out the door, thanking her for what she's doing. Thanking her for helping me be a coward. Thanking her for looking out for my mom and for keeping my secret.

Once I got to my Malibu, I opened my passenger door sitting my duffle bag inside and reaching inside the glove box for a pen and paper. I decided I was going to write my mom right there on the roof of my car.

> Hey, Mom. I have to start by apologizing. I said I would leave the game I was playing behind, but something has come up, and I have to go back in. I have every intention of quitting this game. I know if we spoke about it prior, you would have tried to talk me out of it just as I tried to talk you out of the game you were playing when I was just a kid. You had your reasons for being in the game, which was survival and I kind of have the same reason. I will be frank with you as you have always been with me, mom. I started this game alone but quickly found I needed a partner. I dragged Vince into this with me. After our first talk, I quit the game, but Vince didn't. He loves the game. Remember what that felt like? Remember what came with loving the game? I know you do so I know you will understand when I say I have to go in and get him out of this. It's my fault he is as deep in the game as he is. He is on drugs for Christ's sake. Little innocent Vincent as you know him. I have to do this last job, and he's out. I can hear your voice telling me no the more I write. Hell, I can see your

fists of fury coming towards my head. With that being said, I will end this letter. I cannot disclose where I am staying but know that I am safe and I love you. Check the treasure box inside the shed when you get a chance. If anything should happen to me, which it won't, you will be taken care of. See you in a few days.

I folded the letter and slid it inside her Camaro. Thank goodness, she left the Windows cracked because I didn't want to trouble Ms. Treaty for even the slightest issue.

Once back in my Malibu I stalled before leaving, tapping the steering wheel with my ring and middle finger, contemplating if I was making the right decision. Started the Malibu up and pulled out my phone, pressing call Mommy. She picked up on the second ring.

"Hey. What's up? What you want boy, you are interrupting my show."

Although I was feeling blue about it all, I still cracked a slight smile. She always knew how to make me smile. "Hey, mom. I uhh. I didn't want anything. Just wanted to say I love you."

"Aww, I love you too baby. You must want to borrow my car or something?" My cracked smile turned into slight laughter.

"No, I'm cool with mines. Love you. I'm gonna go for a drive, okay?" I told her.

"Okay. Just be safe. Love you, too."

I hung up the phone and made my way to the garage. It was 6:37pm. The sun was just starting to go into hiding as I pulled up to the garage. It has been some time since I have seen the garage last, but everything looked and felt the same. The atmosphere even smelled familiar, like fresh asphalt and with traces of gasoline from all the semi-trucks that go through the area. *Boom! Boom!* I knocked on the door. The peephole chamber slid back.

"Surprise," I said with no emotion. "Let me in." There were about three unlocking noises before the door unlocked. "Well if it isn't my pal King Kong!" I said in a joking manner. "How you doing man, let me get a hug!" I continued, before being pushed away from my hug.

"Go over there. We have been waiting for you," Kong said, pointing to where the team was. Vince, Viktor, Big G and Guido were all around a round table conversing.

"Ah. Nice of you to join us," Viktor said, with his arms opened wide as I approached them.

"What's up everybody," I said to everyone, as I pulled up a chair to sit at the table.

"Just one more and we can start," Vince informed, as he pulled out notepads for everyone.

He was referring to his new recruit Tony who I couldn't wait to meet since Vince was so sure of this guy. He had to be a class act. I couldn't help but wonder why Vince liked this guy and why he picked him. Did he look like me? Was he tall or short, big or small, handsome or funny looking? Was this my replacement? Couldn't be, because I wouldn't be here if so.

After twenty minutes, I pulled my laptop from my bag to get to work and search for our lot to heist.

"Looks like your new recruit can't tell time," I voiced, staring at Vince. He didn't have anything to say as he pulled out his phone to call him. I was narrowing down my searches, giving directions and speaking aloud for everyone to take notes.

"We got some decent lots on Halsted Street and Western Avenue. I think the Western Ave lots works better though," I explained. "I think we can blend in," I continued.

The lots on Halsted Street were easier to hit, because they were more privately owned so it could be an in and out job. The area was a bit empty, so by driving multiple cars out that lot would stick out like a sore thumb.

"This is the one right here, Retro Autos," I said, spinning the laptop around.

"Let me see that," Viktor's German accent commanded. "Okay...very nice selection of automobiles. Okay, let's-"

Boom! Boom! Boom! We all looked at Kong to go get the door. Kong rolled his eyes and sighed as he went to see who was at the door. "It's probably just Tony," Vince said.

Kong looked through the peephole and opened the door. In comes this Hispanic guy rocking a buzz cut, about 5 feet 10 inches tall,

175 pounds and looking to be about than 27-28 years old. At first glance, this guy seemed familiar. Disturbingly familiar. To the point that my glance turned to a hardcore stare that was analyzing every facial feature he had. My heart rate started to elevate as, 'You lucky I don't have my car, I would smoke you kid' started playing through my head over and over at the speed of light. My mouth dried up like a desert, and then it hit me.

"Shit!" I said aloud, in a panic-like manner. I grabbed my laptop, shut it and stuffed it in my duffle bag. "Vince. Next room, now!" I grabbed him by his shirt, damn near dragging him into the next room.

"Yo, what the hell man, chill! This is a 400.00 shirt you yanking on!"

I slapped him with medium strength letting him know I was serious but not strong enough to hurt him. "Shut up!" I said to his face. "I knew I shouldn't have friggin trusted y'all man. Damn!" I paced back and forth.

"What's the deal?!"

"Tony! Your best bud Tony? He's a damn cop! A pig! A dick! A goddamn joke!" I said furiously.

"What?! Horseshit man, how you figure that?! He's legit as-"

"What is going on in here?! You two playing slap-ass? We got work to do!" Viktor came in and interrupted.

I peeked out of the window to see where Tony was. I couldn't let him see my face. Everyone else's cover was pretty much blown. I had to save my own hide.

"He's saying Tony is a cop, but he hasn't told me how, why he thinks this. I think he's just jealous or something," Vince said, borderline disrespecting me.

"Excuse me? Do I look some girl to you?! Listen, remember the night of the first job, when those cops pulled up on me? He's the one that was in the driver seat. So this whole time, y'all have been working side by side with the feds!" I explained. "I have to get out of here. He can't see my face," I continued.

"Are you sure?" Viktor and Vince both asked me.

"You think I would forget a face that had me almost piss myself? Hell yeah, I'm sure, I'm positive, like there is no doubt in my mind sure!"

Viktor and Vince both looked at each other and slowly nodded.

"What are we going to do now?" I asked. "Search him for a wire. If he has one, we may as well abort the mission. Like, leave the country-"

"Just relax. Relax," Viktor said. "Come on Vince let's figure something out.

Viktor and Vince both went out there and played the game as if everything was cool. I could hear Tony asking about me, eager to meet me. I didn't know if that was him being told about me through Vince and the team or him tapping our phones. Viktor hugged him and patted him down in the process as he pulled out a chair for him to sit at the table. You could see the uneasy look in Tony's eyes right after he was frisked. Viktor snapped his fingers, signaling Kong to come over. Kong then held Tony down in the chair as Big G duck taped his mouth shut while Viktor conducted a more intrusive search, running his hands over his body from head to toe and back up. That's when he felt it.

"What's this!?" Viktor yelled, as he started pulling a wire out of Tony's shirt. He touched Tony's ankle.

"Carrying a gun too, aye?!" he unstrapped it from around his ankle.

"Clean too. Looks police issued. What do you know? The police?!" he said, as he unraveled the gun from its holster.

Tony was yelling out muffled sentences. Nobody tried to make out what he was saying.

"I trusted you man, you betrayed me. Made me look like a fool in front of my team!" Vince uttered to Tony.

Viktor then whispered to Vince and Vince took to the gun from Viktor.

"No. No way," I said to myself, confronting my worst thoughts. Vince stared at the gun then back at Tony. "Don't do it, bro," I continued talking to myself.

Before I could squeeze another thought out, Vince took the butt of the gun and started beating Tony with it. Hitting him repeatedly until Tony passed out, falling over with the chair still attached to him like a backpack.

"Vince, what are you doing man? This isn't you," I reasoned.

Viktor took his black suit jacket off and sat it on a table. He approached Vince and pulled him in by his neck as if he was his father, whispering something into his ear and then bam! He floored Vince with a body shot. "Next time, think before you let just anyone in here!" Viktor yelled.

"Yo! You lost your mind? Touch him again, and I'll touch you!" I said with anger walking towards Viktor.

"Touch me, and I'll touch your mother!" he countered me with.

I froze as he said that. All I could do was stare back at him, with a Satanic look in my eyes. I never wanted to kill anyone in my life until he said that to me. I wanted to break his face and dismantle his body for even the thought of harming my mother.

"Your choice. Or, we can do this job and get it over with," I slowly backed up, keeping my eyes on Viktor, at the same time kneeling down to help Vince back up.

"You alright? Get up man."

"How we going to do this job now? This garage is compromised I bet," Vince said, bringing up an interesting point.

"Yeah, they probably watching or even headed to this place now," I added, to aid Vince's point. "Not to mention you got this cop lying here lifeless on the floor!"

"Always a plan B. Guido. Go up to the roof and look for any suspicious cars around," Viktor whispered his command.

I was sure there were going to be unmarked cars watching the place, but the coast came back clear. We all were unsure of what to make of that. We didn't know for sure if Tony against us or playing both sides but I knew he was a cop for sure and that was a chance none of us was willing to take.

"Vincent. Tie him to that chair, and you two will be with Guido, Big G, follow me!" Viktor ordered. They took Vince's and my keys and forced us to ride with them just in case we got any smart ideas, which was smart on their part because I sure felt like running and with Godzilla, they would have no chance of catching me. Viktor led us in his Range Rover, taking us to another garage in some other part of town about twenty minutes and a bit west from where we were originally stationed. Us growing up in the city, it looked familiar to Vince and me. This was the area a lot of truckers drive through, exporting and importing goods. We were surrounded by nothing but expressway and viaducts. This put us further from the dealerships we were planning to hit, but it was the perfect location for what we were executing.

"Again. Always have a plan B," Viktor said, as he walked to the garage doors.

This new garage wasn't nearly as big as the last one or as clean. From the outside, it looked like one of those old abandoned gas stations you would see on Route 66. It didn't have two levels to it or multiple bays for cars, but it was enough space to work.

"Alonso! Open up!" Viktor yelled as he banged on the garage door.

About ten seconds went by with silence. Just as Viktor was gearing to go around the back, we heard some chains swinging around followed by the garage door slowing opening, up as someone was cranking it open using those chains.

"Lange nicht gesehen, Viktor," A short, skinny and slightly feminine voice said in the German language.

"Long time no see indeed, Alonso."

"Ahh, Viktor!"

They both yelled in excitement before rushing each other for a hug. They were borderline acting like two school girls, but I kept that thought to myself. Judging from the look on everybody else's faces, their thoughts weren't too far from mine.

"Who's your new friends?" Alonso asked.

Viktor went down introducing Paul first, ending with me and Vince and giving us a dirty look as our names rolled off his tongue. We just stared at Alonso. Neither of us was in any inviting mood. What had just happened to us not too long ago was still fresh on our minds.

"So, to what do I owe such a surprise?"

"You don't owe anything, old friend, but I would be lying if I said I didn't need anything," Viktor said.

"Name it, and you got it!" Alonso replied, not knowing what Viktor would want.

Viktor paused for a second, looking down at the ground as if he was contemplating something. "I'm back in the game, and I need to borrow the garage for a couple of days."

Alonso looked disappointed, staring at Viktor. "Viktor, you know I'm out of the game for good, and I thought you were, too. I can't believe you're asking me this right now!" Alonso said, with a frown and confused expression. "I mean I thought the night clubs were booming and you couldn't have blown through all the money from the last job, right?"

The plot was starting to thicken as Viktor who was as mysterious as they come, was starting to be exposed just a little bit. I couldn't help but wonder who this Alonso guy was to him. Seemed like an old boss or running buddy he shared some history with.

"No, no. The night clubs are doing great, and I still have money, I-"

"Ah. Same ol' Viktor, huh?" Alonso acknowledged, cutting Viktor off, waving his hands around like magic wands.

"Just can't shake the thrill huh. Du bist ein Wahnsinniger!" Alonso finished his comment in his German language.

"How can I tell you no, right? Alright. A few days but then you're out of here. All of you. I live a quiet lifestyle now, and I want to keep it that way," Alonso explained to all of us. "Come on in,"

My eyebrows almost touched my hairline as we walked in his garage. The saying of never judging a book by its cover was true. The exterior and interior of Alonso's garage were the totally polar opposite. The inside was spotless and much bigger than it appeared to be. He had two exotic Ferraris in the back of his garage, one a red 360 Modena and the other a much newer black F430.

"You still have that red Ferrari I see. I missed riding with her. I see you've upgraded as well," Viktor said.

"The F430. A worthy successor to the 360. The black really makes it stand out as most Ferrari models are red. Very nice, sir." Despite the very recent turn of events, I couldn't help but comment, being the gear head that I was.

"That guy knows his stuff," Alonso chuckled. Viktor filled Alonso in on what we were doing, how we were doing it, and Alonso wanted no parts of it. Just like me but somehow, we both are here in the middle of this mess.

I pulled out my laptop so we could resume where we left off. "Look. If we going to do this, then we have to scout this spot. Like now," I reminded everyone. "I'm ready to get this over with."

"So am I. You guys take the truck and go over there. Paul, you stay here with me so we can set up. I got a couple trailers in route," Viktor assigned.

"I think you're making a mistake," Alonso said as we were gearing to leave out. "You never did know when to quit."

Viktor quickly turned around with an irritated look on his face.

"Stop. Why do you always have to put negativity in the air? We have tons of preparation for this, and if I wanted your opinion, I would have asked you for it, no offense," Viktor said, as he grew tired of Alonso's bickering.

Alonso rolled his eyes and walked into a little dining area, brewing himself some tea. I couldn't hold it in any longer, I had to ask. "So how do you two know each other?" They both looked up and at each other at the same time long enough to let an awkward silence enter the atmosphere.

"We did business together when we were younger. Then we split ways a few years ago. I went back to Germany and Alonso moved here," Viktor explained. Still staring at each other, Alonso sighed heavy.

"You never did want to admit it," Alonso said. "In addition to doing business, we were lovers."

The awkward silence grew even larger than before as we wouldn't have ever guessed that was the answer to that question. I thought about it for a second and it kind of made sense to me. The night we attended his party, he didn't have any woman on him besides working for him, and all the women in that party were gorgeous. Never seen a ring on his finger and he just got done acting like a schoolgirl when he saw Alonso.

"So, ok, you're gay Viktor, big deal. You like penis. Who cares, it doesn't affect none of us. Can we get back to work now?" I said sternly.

"See. Was that so hard?" Alonso asked.

Viktor didn't say anything, instead, he just started getting wood planks together.

"You two. Let's go," Big G said.

Vince was so quiet through this all. His face stayed mugged the whole time. He hadn't said a word since I picked him up off the ground after Viktor floored him. I could only imagine he was embarrassed and hurt. His pride and his stomach for that matter.

I usually like to scope out things on my own especially something like this because I've worked in a dealership before, but I wanted Vince to snap out of this trans he was in so I asked him to tag along once we got to the dealership. The dealership closed at 9pm, and we got there around 830pm. Usually, when customers come in at the last minute, dealerships use 'we are about to close,' as a sales technique to pressure you into buying a car as long as you know what you want. I was hoping the salesman would do that because that would allow us to come inside and see where all the keys are. After we see that, the mission is accomplished.

We parked about a block away to avoid any cameras if there were any. Vince and I walked to the dealership in silence. "I'll do the talking, and you just look out and keep your eyes open for anything useful. Cool?" I asked Vince. No words, but just nodded with a stoic look on his face. The lot was just as old school as the cars were. The classics rested on a mostly gravel and grass ground. If you were to wear all black, you would be in trouble. The cars unprotected by any fencing or gate but far enough away from the main roads which offered minimal protection.

"Hey, how can I help you guys?" A salesman asked, as we surfed the lot.

"Yeah. I was hoping to grab one of these classics if time permits it," I responded. "I am loving this Chevy Nova you got here. 1973?"

"Close. 72 actually," the salesman responded. "I'm Jim. You are?" He asked as he came down the small ramp attached to his trailer.

He had one of those thick cowboy mustaches. He favored the late Burt Reynolds and his accent wasn't too far from southern either.

"Um, Michael! Nice to meet ya," I answered as I shook his hand. "And this is my partner Abel," I said, introducing Vince's alias.

"So, this Nova has your attention, huh?"

"Absolutely. My parents raised me on old school American muscle. Would be a pleasure to surprise them with one of their own. What's the damage on this?" I asked.

He sucked his teeth and scratched his head as he couldn't give me an immediate number. None of the cars had price tags on the windshield, just a sticker that said: "ask," another technique to customers to come in.

"Let me radio my partner," he said, before pulling out a walkie-talkie. "Jeff, what the price on this silver Nova out here?"

"A dub," a static filled response came back.

He looked at me to see if that number would bother me but I kept my game face on, seeming that I could afford anything on earth.

"So how do you want the payment?" I said with confidence and shrugged.

Jim instantly had a little extra pep in his step as they probably hadn't sold anything in a while. "Cash is king. Let's go inside and grab some paperwork and keys for a test drive."

"Lead the way boss-man," I waved my hands in the path of the office. As soon as Jim stepped in front to the way I trailed behind a little to give my plan to Vince.

"Hey. As soon as you see where he gets the key from, we out of here," I whispered. "When you see it, just call my phone, and I'll pretend it's an emergency and head out," I continued explaining. "Got it?" Again, he just nodded with that same stoic look on his face.

Once in the office, I turned around looking out the window and around the office to avoid looking suspicious. Jim's partner Jeff was doing some paperwork, not paying us any mind. Looking around the office, I noticed a lot of family pictures and started to feel a slight sense of guilt. This is these guys 'business, it's how they feed their families, and we are about to take that away from them. It's them or me. My family or their family I thought to myself, and you can't run a dealership without insurance. They will be fine in due time I finished my thoughts with.

"Michael. Hey, Michael?" I heard Jim call out.

I snapped out of my daydream as I forgot I changed my name for a second. "Yes?" I said looking up with surprise written on my face.

"I got plates and keys for a test if you want to test it?" Jim said.

"Shit, hold on. My mother is calling me!"

I played like I had to be at the hospital immediately, acting hysterical, doing my best to try and force some tears out.

"Sorry guys. Hold that Nova for me I'll be back. I'm really sorry I have to go," I said, before walking out behind Vince.

My little plan worked like a charm. According to Vince, the tall gray file cabinet had a secret compartment on the side which held all the keys. One issue was we didn't have the key to open that compartment, but I wasn't worried because I was sure Viktor or Alonso would have some kind of tool to open it, so I didn't pay it too much mind.

"I'm sorry man. I messed up big time this time," Vince said, finally breaking his silence. "This was all supposed to be temporary. Now, look how deep we in this. It's up to our chest. I thought I could keep this up. All this money is pointless now. I thought I was doing well. I let my guard down. I was feeling invincible. I pulled Tony in and got betrayed. Now we even deeper in this, and it is all my fault. But I'm going to fix it," Vince assured me.

He had a lot on his plate, and I couldn't let him take all the blame. It wasn't his entire fault. I had my part too.

"Listen, man. I'm just as much at fault as you. Technically this is all my fault. I invited you out to Germany. I dragged you into this. So, chill out, this isn't your fault. We are going to fix it together."

"Yeah, but he dragged your mom into it? I put your mother at risk by being stupid. What kind of brother am I?" Vince asked.

I wanted to counter him but I couldn't. That he did do. All I could do was comfort him.

"Look. If nothing else we are family. And family sticks together no matter what. After we do this job, we're done. We're moving. My family and yours. And I'm going back to school," I said, putting my hand on his shoulder, offering my comfort.

We made our way back to Big G and headed back to Alonso's garage. On the way there, both Vince and I stared out the window, with our heads filled with cluttered thoughts. All I was thinking about was finishing this up so I could resume my normal life again. I wanted nothing more. I didn't ask Vince what was on his mind, but I assumed it wasn't too much different. I was amazed when we entered the garage. They had the ramps constructed ready to go and a little workspace for repainting and VIN stripping. I didn't think all of this would be done so fast with only a few guys.

I noticed Alonso wasn't around and his black Ferrari was missing. I didn't want to know where he was or why he left. My mind was exhausted as could be so I refrained from asking.

"Give me the recap," Viktor ordered.

"Well. We know where the keys are. Pretty hefty inventory. Most of the cars could use some work. They are in good condition but not like showroom ready," I reported.

"We can fix that. Anything else?"

"Yeah, we need some black spray paint and some masks. They got three cameras, one for the lot, and one for the front door and one for inside the cabin," Vince explained.

Viktor walked around, circling his steps, pondering something.

"Okay, so looking at the inventory on their website, I sent a list out to buyers stating what we have so here is that list of cars we need to get," Viktor continued, as he handed us the list on a sheet of paper.

```
1. 1962 Chevy Corvette C1
2. 1964 Pontiac GTO
3. 1970 Chevy Chevelle SS
4. 1973 De Tomaso Pantera
5. 1970 Buick GSX
6. 1969 Pontiac Firebird 400
```

My first thought after looking at this list was no way does he want us to do two trips again. Did he not remember what happened last time?

"It's six cars on this list, and there are four drivers, so..."

"That's right. Two trips need to be made. It's the only way," Viktor said, as he answered my question.

I wasn't a fan of the idea when we first did two trips, and I wasn't a fan now but what other choice do we have. This was a much further trip as well. The risk was too great for my liking.

"Either you find another route, two extra drivers or we are not doing this!" I said aloud to Viktor, putting my foot down.

"That's fine. I'll explain that to her when she asks," Viktor responded.

"When who asks?!" He threw polaroids at my feet. I picked them, and with one look I threw them back at him. He had taken photos of my mom's house and photos of her doing yard work.

"Leave her out of this, faggot!" I yelled with tears at the edge of my eyes.

I wanted to kill him so badly. I wanted to watch him suffer in the process as well. I had no avenues to do it. I could get a few punches on him, but his henchmen would mop the floor with Vince and me.

"Vincent. Those photos go for you too. I know where you mother stays, too," Viktor added. We both stood there staring like hungry lions.

"Nod, if we have a deal."

We both stood our ground, not giving him an inch of respect.

"You better nod damn you both, or I swear I will pay them visits tonight!" Viktor yelled. We gave in finally and nodded to Viktor's commands against our wills.

"Grab some supplies and help us secure these ramps for the semis," Viktor added a command. Vince and I both drug our feet like we were kids asked to do chores as we grabbed a hammer and nails and assisted the rest of the team in the construction of the ramps. We were working hours, sweating like pigs to finish the ramps. If I didn't know any better, I would say it was equivalent to picking cotton. The only part missing was whips to our backs. Part of me wanted to sing a negro spirit song.

Unlike the first time where we were having a blast, rocking out while we worked, this time it was silent. Nobody really said a word. The tension in the air was so thick, you could cut it with a butter knife. Once we finished, he finally let us out of his control allowing us to go home but only to return tomorrow before 5pm so would rehearse the heist. Leaving that garage gave the feeling of leaving work after the longest day imaginable. I just wanted to get something to eat and go home. Only, I was going to a crappy motel.

I sat in Godzilla and thought to myself why did I ever agree to this and what the hell was I thinking?

"It is what it is," I said to myself, as I started Godzilla up. *Tap tap*, I heard a knock on my window. It was Vince.

"Yo? What's up?"

"Squat. Tired. What you about to do?" Vince asked.

I played with my beard as I hadn't made my mind up yet. "I think I'm going to grab a burger or something and just head to the motel. I'm tired as a beat down hooker," I responded.

I was surprised to see Vince crack a slight smile and let out a chuckle as he been stone-faced for the majority of the night.

"I could go for some Cajun fries myself if you down?"

"Yeah let's do that. Meet me over there."

We drove off heading to our favorite burger spot once again. It was a bittersweet feeling. It felt so good to just drive away from that place, but it stung because we had to be back the very next day. I did my best to focus on the present moment which was enjoying some missed time with my best friend and our favorite food rather than focusing on tomorrow's task, but it was hard. We were both nervous. Even more so than the first time because this time, our backs were against the wall. Viktor had us by our balls by bringing our families into it, our running time was longer which means the risk of getting caught was higher. Not to mention, Vince beat a cop practically unconscious. This was the most normal I had seen him in a long time.

"Can I have the double burger with the Cajun fries and, a strawberry shake? And bring plenty ketchup please."

"Same thing but let me have a chocolate shake, instead," Vince ordered.

We were waiting in the outside eating area enjoying the perfect September night weather. Within 15 minutes the waitress brought us our food, and we wasted no time stuffing our faces. With all the stress of what was going on, I couldn't remember the last time I had a decent meal but this one quickly erased those empty stomach memories.

We spent a little over an hour reminiscing about high school and all the trouble we got in with girls.

"Hey man. For what it's worth, I just wanted to say I have no better time than the time I spend with my best friend," I told Vince, as I reached out for some dap.

"Don't get all gay on me now. Viktor's rubbing off on you," He laughed. "But no, seriously, likewise my brother. Thanks for always having my back. I know I'm not the easiest to deal with."

We both nodded at each other with the look of respect on our faces.

"Guess we better get some rest or try to at least right."

"Yeah, you right. Swing by the motel tomorrow. We'll shoot over to the garage together," I said, giving out the game plan.

"Yep," Vince said, before dapping me and hopping back in his car to speed off.

I hopped back in my car and headed to my old block. "Good ol' Luella street," I said to myself as I turned down my old street.

I creeped the car slowly as I approached my mom's place. Why the duplex was designed like they were, the main rooms like the living room and main bedroom have windows that faced the street, it was beyond me. I kept my distance about a house down and looked on as I could see the light from the TV flashing in the main bedroom. It was

1:30 in the morning, so I knew she was sleeping. I wanted to go in and kiss her on the head and turn the TV off for her.

"She would probably wake up and beat me," I laughed aloud at the thought of her destroying me on sight. "Love you, mom," I reassured, before pulling away to head to the motel.

I got to my motel room about 2:05 in the morning and of course I couldn't sleep. I couldn't stop thinking about the job, not to mention what had jumped off tonight with the "cop" and Viktor's threats and on top of that, I was bored and lonely. I started to think about Renee. I missed her a lot already, and I prayed she would stick by my side. I couldn't help but text her.

> Hey, hot stuff. Can't stop thinking about you. Miss, you. Wish I could kiss you. Hope all is well.

I laid down and sat my phone next to my head as I closed my eyes just in case Renee was up and decided to text me back, or maybe she just might call and want to talk.

Execution

Boom! Boom! Get up!"

I could hear some yelling and banging on a nearby door. "Seriously?" I questioned. I wanted to stay asleep for a whole year if I could. I opened my eyes, turned over and grabbed my phone to see if Renee texted me back. I sighed as my inbox was empty. The time was 1:33 in the afternoon. I slept the majority of the day away like a kid on summer break. I didn't care, either. I looked at my phone again and saw I had four missed calls from Vince. I sat my phone back on the nightstand and turned back over. A few seconds later the annoyance continued.

"Bro, come on man. Don't make me kick this door right off the hinges!"

I could hear him saying. Then it dawned on me.

"Is that..."

I got up and peeked out the blinds. I thought the voice sounded familiar. I opened the door.

"Vince what the hell man?!" I asked out of anger.

"Ohh, I thought you were in that unit! Well surprise, I'm here!" Vince said, borderline dancing his way into my room.

He seemed happier than usual. I bit hyper actually. He had on these huge designer sunglasses so I couldn't see his eyes but I had my own speculations.

"You're in a good mood I see."

"Damn right. I'm ready to take on Viktor, the world, whoever!" Vince said, passionately.

"Chill, I just woke up, so it's a bit too early for all that energy. Speaking of which, you got in late like I did, did you get any sleep? How are you this energetic?" I asked Vince, even though I already knew.

I just wanted to see if he would tell me. He got on the floor and started doing pushups, cranking them out one after another. I sat on the bed kind of collecting myself from just waking up and at the same time watching Vince crank out pushups like a machine and waiting for him to answer me.

"That's like forty unanswered pushups dude. You didn't do half of that in gym class. You going to answer my question or not?" I asked him with a settled approach. He popped up like a jack in the box and stared at his jittery hands.

"Whoo!" He randomly yelled with excitement and partially startling me.

"So, yeah about that sleep. I couldn't sleep you know? Too much on my mind, you know? So, I like started playing COD and what not you know, and then next you know boom! It's like 10 in the morning you know? So, I'm like man I really need to sleep to be at my best for today, but the sleep never happened you know so then-"

"So, then what?" I said dryly, looking at him with a stone face as he looked down, continuing his story.

"Yeah so, I got pretty tired, but it would be too late to sleep. So, then I drove over here you know and I was looking in my glove box for my heat because you never know, tonight could get nasty, so I need to be strapped, you know? But what do I see as I reach for the gun? A nice little bag of coke. So, I like sniffed a little bit right before I came over here."

"Awe, my god. You gave me this whole speech yesterday. Where's the trust? Bro-"

"No, no, no it's okay man," He uttered. "I remembered our little deal, and it's going to be okay. I only did a couple lines to keep me up. I'll be up all day man!"

I put my head in my hands as I sat on the edge of the bed pretty disappointed. Vince kept apologizing, but I just didn't want to hear it. I just wanted to go back to sleep. He betrayed my trust yet again. I wanted to knock his head off but I couldn't. I didn't have to energy to waste on him. I just wanted to speed time forward so we could get this done and resume regular life.

"Listen. Go wait downstairs for me. I'll be down in a minute. Trail me to the garage," I ordered Vince after sighing loudly as I could.

I freshened up, brushed my teeth, brushed my hair and threw the same sweats and sneakers on from yesterday. I grabbed the keys to Godzilla and headed out. Vince was reclined in his Benz with his feet hanging out the window. He was texting or something, smiling at something and looking like he didn't have a care in the world.

"Let's go jackass," I said, while smacking his feet back in the car.

With my first step out of the door, King Kong was already texting me not to be late. It was a little after 3 in the afternoon when we got to Alonso's garage. There were two trailers outside waiting to be stuffed with cars. Everything was normal for the most part. Viktor and the gang all scattered around, tightening up anything that needed to be tightened up for the night. Vince and I joined in where we could. Alonso was still absent which was odd, considering this was his place. I asked Viktor about it, but he shrugged it off. Apparently, Alonso just didn't want to be here while we were doing this, and that made sense, so I paid no mind.

I spent most of my time thinking about Renee. She never texted me back. I was just about positive she was done with me which kind of hurt because I really wanted to keep her. Maybe she didn't feel the same. I had to know for sure. I ducked away to the back away from work to give her a call. Of course, she didn't answer so I sent her another text.

Hey, can you please text me back?"
Tell me something. Anything.

After a few moments of silence, I went back to work. She was done with me.

I thought about tearing the whole damn garage up due to my anger but, I still had a mission to complete. I still had to save my best friend and my mother. I texted my mom, 'I love you,' just to hear it back. In the midst of all this, I suddenly started to feel lonely. I knew if anyone would tell me they loved me and meant it, it would be my mom. She usually texts me right back, but after about five minutes, I got nothing back from her either.

"Damn, is she done with me, too?" I said aloud, out of frustration.

"Hey bro, what's up?"

"Ah! Let's just get back to work," I continued my frustration towards my junkie best friend as he found me in the back.

Walking back towards the main area, my phone started buzzing. I reached into my pocket to grab it as if it was a ticking time bomb.

"Toya. Why is she calling me? I don't want to talk to you woman!" I yelled at my phone as it annoyingly kept buzzing.

I ignored the call and picked up a hammer and proceeded to help the crew set up the last wooden ramp for the trailers. My phone buzzed again, this time I calmly looked at it. It was a text from Toya this time.

Hey. We need to talk. Call me back asap.

I sighed and put the phone back in my pocket.

Any other day, time would drag but not today. Time was on more coke than Vince today. Before we knew it, it was 6:30 in the evening and everything was finished. The ramps to load the cars were completed, and the separators to create a lower and upper level inside the trailers were complete as well. Only thing left was to get ready, execute the game plan, get paid and say goodbye for good.

"Alright, everybody. Dig in and grab a radio. Set it to channel four. That's how all of us will stay in communication," Paul said, as he dropped a large leather duffle bag in the middle of everyone. "There should be some masks, hoodies and some black spray paint in there, too,"

"I always wanted to be a ninja," Vince said, as he held one of the masks that resembled what surgeons wear when doing surgery. "Look. Get over here!!" He said, mocking Scorpion from Mortal Kombat.

"Chill out. Focus. Can you do that for me?" I responded, with seriousness, killing his vibe. "Hey, we might have a problem," I said aloud, for everyone to hear. "We don't know what the gas levels in the cars are. We never sat in them or anything," I reported to the crew.

"Ok. Think. On the way there, let's stop at the gas station, grab some cans fill them up and boom, problem solved," Vince suggested.

"I think we should just take our chances," I concluded, after thinking on it for a while. "Chances are those cars got some gas," That place isn't in a position to lose any sales opportunities. A trip to the gas station while leaving your customer to dwell on his or her purchase can break the deal. We could have a problem, but I think we will be fine," I explained.

"Well just in case. Here. I found this in the back," Viktor came out from the back of the garage, placing a gas canister on the table.

The time was now 7:15 in the evening, and it is the go-time. We went over the game plan one last time before heading out. It was really a gorilla-styled operation. Last heist was a lot more technical. Planning weeks in advance, correct preparation, and a concrete team. This job felt sloppy and poorly planned but planned the best way possible given the time allowed and the best way possible when pressed against the wall is gorilla style. Run in and ransack the place and get out of dodge as quickly as possible.

"Ok, the truck is ready. Time to do this!" Viktor said with excitement.

Everyone was clapping their hands in excitement like they were walking through the tunnel to enter a basketball game. Not me. I was nervous. Mouth dry, clammy hands and anxiety. Felt like I was going to Normandy for D-Day. I wanted to throw up, and I hadn't even left the garage yet. I had nerves the first time but not like this. I couldn't shake the feeling, but I didn't let it hold me back. I reached into the duffle bag and grabbed a hoodie and mask which was just a black bandana and tied it around my face.

"In and out! Don't waste any time and be smart. Remember, use the radios for communication. I'll be listening in on the whole job, and I'll be right here when you get back," Viktor reminded us. "Oh, and take these photos with you. These are the cars you'll be grabbing. Six in total. Go get'em!"

We all piled in the black SUV and headed for Auto Alley. The ride there was a quiet ride; no music, no talking, just the sound of the SUV hitting an occasional pothole here and there. My anxiety got worse. I wanted to pull over so badly, get out the car and run. Maybe disappear into the woods like a wild animal. It just didn't feel right. I kept asking God to save me. I just wanted out and back into my old life. Why couldn't I just work at a grocery store or something? When did I get this deep in the game? I kept thinking to myself. My dad and my grandmother are probably turning in their grave as a result of my actions. What kind of a son and a grandson am I? The thoughts continued in my head. Am I the only one who feels this way? I looked at those around me for confirmation. Vince was deeply into some game he was playing on his phone. Big G and Guido were both talking about some fine women they had met last month. My thoughts were confirmed. Nobody was feeling the same way I was.

We had arrived. It felt like a school bully promised me a beat-down after school, and no matter how much you wanted to slow time down, it seemed to speed up.

"Bravo one here. We have reached our first destination," Vince said into his radio, mocking someone of a military branch. Everyone besides me, laughed.

"Maybe I missed the damn memo, that this job was a joke but the last memo I got said it wasn't a damn joke. Focus!" I yelled at everyone in the SUV. They all looked at me like I lost my mind.

We parked about two blocks away from the dealership just to be safe. We all got out the SUV in sync, made sure our masks and gloves were secure and huddled up.

"Vince, you remember where the keys are, right?"

"Yessir."

"Good. Ok. Now Big G and Guido you two got to bust that door down and quick. I see you got the crowbar ready. I'm going to go first. Take out the two cameras and then once you guys bust that door down, I'll go in and take out the third camera, and that's when you come in Vince and get the keys. Those keys will have yellow tags on them and will be hard to read to focus up and match the key with the car you are driving," I explained in detail.

"Ok when that last car passes us, I'm going to take off running," I said, pointing to a car that was about four blocks away and approaching fast. "Hope you guys are in decent shape because when I radio you to come running, you better come quickly. Here we go…Three, two, one. Go!"

As soon as the car I used as a marker passed us, I took off like Jesse Owens with full speed towards the dealership. It felt like I was running at the speed of sound. Cars nearby and lights were blurred, accompanied by a whoosh noise every time I passed an object. Within thirty seconds I was out front of the dealership stunned by what I saw. The light in the office was still on, and I could see at least two shadows moving around.

"I don't want to say we might need to abort mission but we might need to abort mission," I said over the radio, so everyone could hear as I walked a few yards past the dealership to miss being caught.

"We will not do such thing!" Viktor's angry voice burred over the radio. "Figure it out!"

I sighed, as I looked at the dealership. I didn't see any way in without doing some sort of navy seals type of mission.

"Ok team, get down here. Quickly!"

My hope was maybe we could all collectively come up with an idea because I had nothing. Vince showed up first followed by everyone else.

"I said fast, not slow," I told the team as they arrived but took over a full sixty seconds after I gave them the green light.

"What's the plan? We don't have all night," Viktor's voice came over the radios again. I could tell he was getting irritated due to the increasing strength in his German accent.

"We are figuring it out. Relax!" I strongly responded.

"I only see one way to do this. Ransack style," Vince said. He started smacking his palm against his forehead.

"He's right," Big G chimed in.

"What do you mean exactly by ransack?" I asked.

Vince stared me in the eyes, physically asking for forgiveness as he turned around and headed to the office.

"Hey, wait a minute!" I said as Big G and Guido followed him.

"Shit" I uttered. I had no choice but to follow since they were taking no prisoners.

I hurried and quietly climbed on one of the cars in the front to help reach the camera to black it out with the spray paint. I tried to be as quiet as possible but jumping up and down on an old-school Chevy's hood wasn't the quietest thing a person could do. The spray paint was not helping me, either, as it would shoot from the can like a wildfire, hitting everything except the target. After about four tries, I finally got the camera fully blacked out. I gave Vince and the crew the thumbs up.

Vince let out a fake cry for help while Guido and Big G crouched low below the stairs, one of them on each side. I was crouched down by the Chevy I used for a trampoline, watching everything through the window. Someone looked out the window, and I crouched even lower, almost low enough to get under the car. I couldn't make out exactly who was in the office, but the silhouette matched what I imagined the owner to look like. Another silhouette of what looked like a lady appeared by his side. I rose up slowly, peeking through the window to get a better look like a frightened kid awaiting the boogieman from underneath his covers.

"Please help. Anybody in there?" Vince yelled and pleaded. My heart was attempting to give Jeff Gordon a run for his money the way it was racing. The owner left the window and headed towards the door.

"Here he comes. It's two people in there for sure. One man and one female," I informed them over the radio.

I could see Vince putting his hands under his shirt, reaching for something.

"God no." I uttered as I saw a beam of light reflect off of his gun. Before I could radio him to put that away, they were already storming in the place. All I could hear from the outside was yelling and screaming. I got up quick as I could and before I could take my first stride a flash of light showered the room followed by a loud pop. I was frozen in my steps, stomach turning and fearing the worst. I could hear the sound of the radio, but I couldn't make out anything.

"Come on!" I heard, as my body started to calm down.

I snapped out of my trance and ran to the office. I blacked the camera right by the door with paint before going in. At first sight, the owner and some lady were laying face down and still alive on the ground. Their faces were bruised and a little bloody but it was better than being dead. It was just a warning shot I heard. I was so relieved to know nobody was hurt. I figured when going into the office, it was going to be a complete horror film. It looked like we had just interrupted a sex session, the owner's pants were down just below his butt, and the lady was wearing some skimpy little skirt. Probably was his mistress or a prostitute.

"You guys can finish as soon as we are done," Vince said, while he rattled the tall key drawer, attempting to break it right off the hinges.

"List please!" Big G said urgently.

Holding up my index finger to signal one second, I shot the last camera inside the office down with the paint. I reached in my back pocket and retrieved the four-way folded note and laid it on the table.

"Okay. Corvette C1, GTO, Chevelle SS, Pantera, GSX, Firebird 400," I said, reminding everyone of what we were looking for.

"Shit man, I can't get this thing open!" Vince yelled.

"Watch out," Big G said, as he retrieved a knife and crowbar from his bag. Big G used the knife and crowbar like a hammer and nail system, hammering the knife into the cabinet with the crowbar then twisting the knife to create a hole. Now that the hole was there, Big G jammed the crowbar in the hole and pried the open.

"Alright let's go! Find the keys!" Guido reminded us.

There were about thirty keys with yellow tags hanging, four keys going across and eight rows going down to the bottom of the cabinet. Finding the keys we needed wasn't exactly easy. The font on the keys was so small; Big G had to examine each key carefully.

"Ok, Corvette C1 and Pantera," Big G demanded, waving the keys behind him as he continued to look for the rest of the keys.

"Guido, grab those and start them up. Take this list with you, so you know what they look like," I ordered.

I anxiously looked at my watch while Big G continued to cycle through each key. I was expecting to hear of the car names with every second that went pass. I looked over at Vince who was just spaced out, looking like a lost soul while he was examining himself in the window.

"Ok, Chevelle. GSX. GTO and Firebird. All the keys are here."

"Finally! I want the Firebird!" Vince said like a little kid that usually never gets to pick what toy he wants.

"I don't care. Let's just go," I said.

I grabbed the keys to the GSX and proceeded to head to the lot.

"Wait. We can't leave the owner and that bimbo in here if you coming back. They could call the cops or something," Big G whispered to me right outside the front door.

He was right. If we left them there, Vince and I could be walking right into an ambush. I thought about it for a second.

"Okay, come with me," I asked Big G. "Help me carry them to the back. Since you bigger than me, you grab the owner, and I'll take the lady," I bargained. He stood there giving me the stone-face.

"Come on, that's why you Big G and I'm not," I said with a smirk on my face.

As soon as we grabbed them, they started fidgeting, kicking and screaming from the fear of being murdered. If I was in their shoes, I would be kicking and screaming too. Big G nipped all that in the bud as he flashed his huge blade that resembled a bowie knife in my eyes and told them to be still or else. Considering how heavy this middle-aged woman was, I wasn't sure if I got the better of the bargain as I looked over at Big G who tossed the owner over his shoulder with ease. We sat them behind the dealership, but far enough from the dealership for them to pose a threat. With their legs and arms tied together, the task of getting to the phones near impossible.

"What are those gas levels looking like?" I said over the radio.

"About a forth."

"I'm looking at half a tank," Vince and Guido both reported.

"Perfect. You guys go ahead. We have been here way too long. Big G and I will meet you at the garage."

Big G and I started to make our way towards the cars, but the thought of leaving the owner and that woman behind the way we did was weighing heavy on my mind. They were innocent, and didn't deserve what happened to them. I started to slow my walk down as Big G continued to go ahead.

"What are you doing? Come on!" Big G turned around and yelled.

"Uh, I dropped my keys back there. Go ahead, I'll meet you there."

Pretending to search the ground for my keys in the dark, I backtracked to where the owner and his mistress were.

"Hey, hey relax. I'm not going to hurt you guys," I told both of them as they tried to scoot away from me in fear. "I'm going to free you guys. I'm not a bad person, just a kid trying to save his mom and his best friend. This was never supposed to happen to you, so I apologize. I have to deliver this car. I need you both to sit tight. I will be back for you. Nod if you understand," I explained and asked for confirmation from them. After confirmation from them, I finally headed to the lot.

"I left the gas canister for you guys on top of one of the cars. You should be able to see it easily," Guido radioed in.

"This Corvette is about a little under a forth, but it should be enough to get me there," Big G radioed back.

"I am getting into the GSX now. And, all systems are a go. This one is a bit over half," I chimed in over the walkie-talkie right after starting the engine and watching to gas needle shoot to the half way mark.

After grabbing the gas canister off the nearby car, I got back in the GSX and sped off towards my destination. It was a very smooth atmosphere of a drive. It was if the town was a ghost town. Not many cars or people around, which was a good thing considering the situation. Within twenty-five minutes, the GSX was pulling up to the garage. King Kong and Vince were outside standing by the truck, awaiting me to do the last run. The trailer was outside, packed with the Firebird and the Pantera on the upper level already. Guido and Viktor were in the process of loading the Corvette on the lower level. Vince signaled me to let my window down as he was trying to talk to me. I got a small shoulder workout as I turned the stiff window knob clockwise.

"What's up?"

"Pull the car up closer to them and leave the car keys in the door," Vince filled me in on my next steps before getting back in the SUV to retrieve the Chevy Chevelle and the Pontiac GTO.

The gravel crackled under the roll of the tires as I slowly pulled behind the trailer for Viktor to load the car. I kept a decent distance just in case one of those cars came crashing down out to the trailer. I grabbed the gas canister, got out the car and put the keys in the door. Just as I got out, Viktor had just finished getting the Pantera in the trailer.

"Out, out, out. Have to hurry," Viktor said, as he brushed past me to get into the GSX. "Two more cars so get moving!"

"Where is the other trailer at," I asked him out of curiosity.

"Oh, don't you worry, its coming. When you get back, it'll be here," he said without making eye contact. I thought that was kind of weird since Viktor always made eye contact when we spoke, but I paid it no mind since he was rushing.

Kong and Vince were impatiently waving me over to the SUV to continue our mission. Looking like an arsonist with gas canister by my side, I picked up my feet a little to hurry. I didn't understand why everyone was rushing. No authorities were alerted to my knowledge, and the second trailer hadn't made it in yet. Vince and I had more of a reason to rush than the rest of the crew in my mind because I left the owner and that lady tied up.

Then I started to tweak myself out with my thoughts, what if they got loose somehow? What if it's a cop ambush when we get there all because of me?

"Hey Paul, step on it a bit. I got a bad feeling," I expressed.

"What bad feeling?!" Kong and Vince asked simultaneously.

"I don't know! I think I'm just thinking too much. Well, I left the owner and the lady tied up behind the dealership, so I was just thinking what if-"

"No! You were supposed to knock them out or kill them or something," Kong cut me off and said subjectively.

"Yeah! That's right!" Vince chimed in.

I was taken back by Vince agreeing with that notion and concluded that I truly lost my best friend if he was willing to kill. It was a point in time where Vince wouldn't have hurt a fly, and now he's beating people over the head and down to kill? It was like during our time away from each other, Viktor brainwashed him. We argued back and forth until we arrived.

"Whatever bad feeling you have, I hope it isn't true because we here now," Kong said.

"Yeah, I can see that. Maybe you should stay here until we give you the green light. We might need an extraction," I suggested.

He didn't respond at all to that idea. Just totally ignored me and grabbed his radio.

"Viktor, we are at the drop-off," he radioed.

"Perfect. You guys know the drill. Paul, I need you back here at the garage ASAP. The other trailer is having issues, and we need your help pronto," Viktor radioed back.

Vince and I got out the truck and Paul headed back to the garage.

"It's go time baby!" Vince said with excitement as we pulled up a block away from the dealer. "Time to get paid once last time!"

I shook my head, annoyed, as we got out of the truck. "Okay, be quiet and stay close," I said aloud.

We made our way down the stretch of the block towards the dealership. About thirty yards away, I decided to hop some fences and take the back way to the dealership. That way I could get a vantage point and see if anything looked suspicious and if the owner and the lady were still tied up

"I see the owner and that bimbo right there. We have to take them out or something," Vince suggested.

That stopped me dead in my tracks, when Vince said that. "What do you mean take them out or something?" I questioned him with my feet planted to the ground like a freshly built statue.

"You know what I mean," Vince tilted his head, uttered and flashed his heat.

"Absolutely, not. Have you lost all your marbles? We will not be doing that! You will not be doing that!"

"So, you would rather risk letting them find a way to get free and rat us out, I see?" Vince added.

I ignored his comment, and sped walked past him, thrusting my shoulder through his shoulder, letting him know I was serious about this. The owner and the lady were lying where I left them, almost spooning as if they knew this was their last night together alive and just wanted to sleep with each other one last time. I lightly kicked the owner on his foot, waking them up so I could give them the plan I had to free them.

"Okay I can't give you guys one hundred percent of my trust, but I will give you sixty percent. My partner and I got these last two cars to get. I'm not going to untie you but-"

Muffled screaming through the tape on the woman's mouth filled the airwaves, cutting my sentence off, mid-explanation. I looked at her with an insane look that screamed 'what the hell is wrong with you', and then the owner started to yell as well.

I turned around to see Vince pointing his gun at them.

"What the hell did I just say?! What are you doing?!"

"Get out of the way, man. This is the right thing to do in this situation. I let Tony in, and look what happened. I can't have another costly mistake on my conscious!" Vince explained. "Now move!" He yelled.

"I will not move. These people didn't do anything! This was never the plan!"

"Well, it's the plan now! They going to get us thrown in jail, now move!" He said trying to maneuver around me to get a clear shot.

I couldn't keep up with someone on cocaine. His energy was unlimited. Shuffling back and forth for thirty seconds was tough. I was getting tired, and Vince didn't even look fazed. I only had once chance to stop him.

"Look at yourself man. You are tweaking out," I barely could stand it as I was panting for air like a dog that just played more games of fetch than it could handle.

"This woman is someone's daughter, someone's mom, maybe even someone's grandmother. Same with this guy. You want to take that away? You want to kill someone's mother? Father?" I tried to reason with Vince. "Did you forget why we are doing this? Our Mothers' lives are on the line. How can you do this when we trying to stop someone from doing the exact same thing, man?" I paused for a second to recollect my thoughts. "So, I tell you what. If you want to kill them, go ahead, but I'm not moving. So, you going to have to kill your best friend, and the only witness to the crime you are about to commit!" I gave Vince the ultimatum.

A few seconds passed, we are staring at each other in silence and to my surprise, he continues to keep his gun raised as if he's considering taking my offer of killing me. Then, he finally lowered the gun and put it back in his pants.

"If this comes back to bite us, I just might kill you. And I will definitely kill those two behind you," Vince said.

"Here are the keys to the GTO," tossing the keys over to him. "Don't wait up, I'll meet you at the stop," I explained as we parted our ways.

As Vince walked off towards the lot, I turned our prisoners who looked like they had more than enough to handle for one day. I took out my pocket knife and explained the only contingency.

"Ok. You guys are free, but I can't cut you completely loose. Remember, sixty percent trust."

I cut the owner's legs free of tape which would allow him to get up and walk. I cut the woman's hands-free.

"You guys will have to use some teamwork to get totally free," I said as I walked about ten yards to the right of them. I placed the knife on the ground for them to retrieve.

"Can I trust you guys to start after I leave?" They both shook their heads, giving me the confirmation.

"Good deal. Again, sorry about this guys," I said before walking away towards the lot.

Once on the lot, I spotted the cherry red Chevelle. The bright color stuck out like a sore thumb.

"Okay Viktor, the last two cars are in transit," I radioed in. "Hello, anybody there? The last two are in transit," I repeated over the radio after getting no response.

I uttered to myself, "The hell is going on?" I started the Chevelle up with frustration.

"Viktor. Big G, Guido, Paul, Vince?" I tried over the radio again.

"What's up?" Vince radioed back.

"Where were you all? You didn't hear me over the radio before?"

"No, I just turned mine on," Vince answered.

"Ok. Something weird is going on. How far away are you?"

"Like about 10 or 15 minutes away."

"Ok, I'm leaving now," I pulled out the lot overly cautious a slightly paranoid.

I let the windows down to get some fresh air. The great smell of gas coated the inside of the Chevelle as I coasted down the street. I took a deep whiff as I came to a stop sign. "Aw shit!" I yelled as I looked at the gas meter. The Chevelle only had a pinch of petrol in her. I always looked at gas tanks like four quarters, and this was under twenty-five percent, fifteen to be exact. I looked at the passenger seat for the gas canister, and my eyes bucked wide when I didn't see it.

"Son of a bitch!" I let out; as I remembered that I placed it down when I gave the GSX to Viktor. I forgot to pick it back up.

The back roads we were taking to get back to the garage didn't offer any gas stations, and even if they did, it was too risky to stop. I thought about pulling over and having Vince grab the canister, turn around and come to me but that presented a risk as well. I didn't want to even tell Vince because I didn't want him making any stupid rash decisions. "Think!" I told myself as I hit a red light. I started twisting the hair on my head as I drove to get my creative juices flowing.

"Hope this works," I continued to talk to myself. I was going to coast the car the rest of the way there by hitting the gas only when I needed to. I gradually floored the gas pedal then let off, giving me enough speed to coast a few blocks before repeating the process.

"Man, something weird is going on. I been here for about ten minutes and haven't seen a soul," Vince reported over the radio.

"Christ. Okay, I'm almost there."

Within ten more minutes of gas and coasting, I was about three blocks away. I looked at the gas meter which read 'you better pray I don't cut off'.

I told myself screw it. The worst thing that could happen would be me pushing the car a block. I continued coasting before flooring it again. At about 45mph the Chevelle had enough. It ceased from making any engine noises. Only noises you could hear was me breathing heavy and continuously pressing the gas pedal, like that was going to turn her back on. I had a decent amount of speed coming down the block. I had two four-way intersections to go through, and I prayed no cars were coming because I wasn't going to stop.

"Thank you, God," I said as blew through the first one.

I could see headlights approaching the second intersection. I blew my horn to signal that a mad man was coming through but the driver still pulled right in front of me. I want to drive right through whoever the driver was, but I swerved right as the driver kept going straight, which cut my speed in half. Traveling at about fifteen mph and decreasing with every second, it was perfect timing as the Chevelle finally hit zero right in front of Alonso's garage.

"Pull in," Vince told me.

"I would if I could, but she's out of gas. I left the gas canister here right over there," I said, pointing to where the trailer was.

"I'll grab it. We got to get her moving if we going to get her in the trailer," Vince said.

Vince was optimistic about this situation, but I wasn't. All clues were pointing to us getting screwed over. He couldn't see it yet.

"Hey, put that down," I told him. He put the gas canister on the hood of the Chevelle as I got out of the car to meet him face to face.

"Take a look around. Have you reached out to anyone? All we have is our phones and these radios. We don't have their phone numbers, and they aren't responding."

"So, what are you saying?" Vince asked as he placed his hands on his head, preparing for me to confirm what he already knew.

"It's obvious, right? They left us. And they took the money. Viktor screwed us, brother!" I explained.

Vince was undoubtedly hurt.

"I don't understand why he would do that to us. To me! He told me I was his protégé. He told me he cared about me and we were going to go to the top together," Vince explained aloud, not directly talking to me but rather just to himself.

"Why are you so hurt over this man? He used us. He's a crook. That's what crooks do. They lie. They steal. They use. 'There is no honor among thieves', ever heard that saying before? We received all of that and some," I said but visibly annoyed. "Only thing that matters is it should be over now. We should be-"

Before I could get another word in, our conversation was interrupted by a screaming engine sound coming this way and fast. Vince and I both looked alarmed as it was dark and could barely see. Vince put his hand in his shirt in preparation to draw heat just in case. Once the car got closer, I could easily see it was Alonso's Ferrari.

"Ah. Explains the loud noise," I said.

"Maybe he can tell us what the hell is going on."

Alonso pulled up right in front of the dead Chevelle and rushed out of the driver's seat, leaving the keys in the ignition with the engine running.

"Hey! Alonso, can you tell us what's going on, please? Where is Viktor and everybody?" Vince and I collectively asked.

"I have no idea," he shouted in a shaky voice as he walked right past us.

"Where have you been all this time?" Vince asked while Alonso was entering a passcode on his door's keypad to unlock it.

With no answer, Alonso opened his door and ran inside. Vince and I looked at each other at the same time, displaying a stink face as if we took a whiff of horseshit. We both knew something was fishy. Before we knew it, Alonso came rushing back out with a duffle bag in his hand, heading to his Ferrari. Before he got to his car Vince and I both stood in his way.

"Out of our families being threatened. We were promised they would be left out of this if we did this job," I explained.

"And promised us some cash," Vince added.

"Now nobody is here. We don't know what to do man. Alonso, can you please let us in on anything?" I asked, taking a settled approach to getting some information out of him.

Alonso let out a deep sigh and tossed his duffle bag by his Ferrari. His face screamed 'I don't want to tell you anything', but it also had a bit of sorrow on it.

"Okay look. You guys probably figured this out by now that you've been used, but it's deeper than that," he explained. "You guys are going to be framed for this whole thing. Viktor called me some time ago about this. I'm not into this kind of thing, but I owed a debt to Viktor so I couldn't refuse him. I guess Viktor, or you, racked up some serious heat with the jobs you guys been doing, and he wanted me to anonymously tip the police about it. But after you guys had unmasked Tony as an undercover cop, he had me sit with him making sure he didn't die from the beating and lack of water and food. I freed him tonight, and the cops were tipped."

There was an awkward silence in the air as he finished talking. Vince and I were both stunned at what we had just heard. I was waiting on someone to come out and tell me we had been fooled. That didn't happen. Vince was breathing heavy like a wild cheetah, and he had Alonso in his sights.

"So now what? We just wait here for the trap you set for us?" I asked while my eyes filled with tears.

"Where did Viktor go?"

"I don't-"

"Where?!" I screamed, cutting his bullshit off.

I was starting to breathe heavy like a wild beast, sharing whatever angry energy Vince was feeling.

"He's probably meeting up with Viktor, bro. At his private jet or something. Straight to paradise," Vince said aloud. "Since they are lovers anyway!"

I balled my fist up tight as I could.

"Please. I have to go. Let me-"

I didn't waste another second. I threw my right fist with much fury, connecting right on his chin knocking him right to the ground. I followed up my punch by following him to the ground, getting on top of him and finishing the job. I don't recall the number of punches, but when Vince pulled me off of him, I thought I killed him. He didn't move or make a noise for about twelve seconds. I could hear police sirens nearing our location. I put my head in my bloody hands. A loud noise popped me right up. My ears were ringing as if a grenade went off near me.

"He isn't going anywhere now," Vince uttered. I turned to see Alonso's lifeless body lying there. Vince did the unthinkable. He let off two more shots, right into Alonso's chest. He still had the gun pointed at him as if he was going to fire more rounds. I slowly approached him and lowered his arm. My body was trembling with fear. I dropped down to my knees, staring at Alonso's motionless body. How could it get this far? I was left thinking.

"C'mon, we have to get outta here. Like right now." Vince said, as he picked me up off the ground. He had Alonso's duffle bag in his hand. He flashed it open. It was full of cash. "Hey, we got the money after all. I can't go to jail brother. That's not for me. We have to get rid of all the evidence, and fast!" Vince explained.

"So, what should we do?" I asked Vince. "There is a whole dead ass body right here!" "We have to get rid of it and these cars. Hand me that canister."

I gave Vince the gas canister, and he wasted no time dumping the gasoline all over the Firebird and then the Chevelle. He dragged Alonso's body next to the cars to burn with them. My mind was exhausted. I was on auto-pilot, and I couldn't make any decisions on what to do next.

"You sure this is the way?" I asked Vince.

"Yeah. It's the only way," he answered as he pulled a lighter and piece of paper out of his left back pocket. He ripped the piece of paper in half, setting one of the pieces on fire and then throwing it on the Chevelle first. As soon as the fiery paper hit the hood of the car, it instantly became engulfed in flames. It didn't take long for the flames to spill onto Alonso's body, covering him in flames as well. Vince was headed to the Firebird when my phone buzzed. I frantically opened it to see it was a text from an unknown number.

"Son of a bitch!" I yelled.

"What's wrong now?" Vince said, as he threw the last fiery piece of paper on the firebird, allowing the car to live up to its name.

"That asshole. Viktor. Look. He has our pictures all over the garage!" I explained while showing Vince the pictures Viktor sent me. Another text came in while I was showing Vince the video. Vince and I both opened the text message.

Might want to go and clean that mess up before the police arrive.

"Viktor, you motherfucker!" Vince yelled. "Oh, I want to kill him so badly!" Vince continued while reaching in his back pocket.

Vince took out another little vile and tapped some coke in the palm of his hand and snorted it. I wanted to care but I couldn't any longer. My mind was too exhausted. I damn near wanted to snort some of the coke myself.

"We have to get to that garage, man," Vince suggested.

"With what car?"

"We got Godzilla still here, but Viktor took the keys. This whole damn thing was a setup!" I said with anger.

"He took your keys, but he didn't take mine," Vince said.

"There is always a master key, and I knew a day would come when I would have to use it. Come on."

I followed Vince over to the GTR where he got down on his back going under the GTR like an alley mechanic to search for the master key.

"Got it. Come on."

"You not driving anything mister coke. I'll drive," I told him.

As soon as Vince and I got in the GTR, my cellphone started blowing up with calls and texts from my mother. I sent her to voicemail each time she called. My hands were busy. All her texts were saying *CALL ME ASAP!* Which made me feel slightly guilty about it, so I played the voicemail while I drove. She was always yelling, it was just how she talked, but this time she was screaming. I pulled over for a second so I could really focus on what she was saying as I could barely understand her through all the yelling. My heart rate started to elevate as I feared Viktor wasn't done terrorizing me yet. He had to capture my mother, too! I was thinking.

"We don't have time to be pulling over man!" Vince reminded me, but I didn't care one bit, for fear my mother was in trouble.

"Shhh!" I said, placing my index over my lips. "Something is wrong, I can't hear, be quiet!"

"Baby! I'm sorry. I went through your mail but when I saw who it was from I couldn't help it. It's your college letter baby. You got accepted!" The message played back to me.

"Finally!" I yelled. "I got back in school!"

Vince didn't say anything and was looking crazy-eyed, but he was smiling as he pointed to the road signaling me to get back focused. I could tell it was a bittersweet feeling for him, but I could also tell he was happy for me. I gave Godzilla some gas as I continued our escapade to Viktor's garage.

"I should text her at least," I said aloud, thinking about my mom. "Renee, too. She might even take me back," I continued to speak to myself but with a bit of excitement as I thought about Renee taking me back. I used my knees to guide the steering wheel as I wrote my text message to my mom.

"That's such good news to my ears! I miss you. I'm coming home tonight mom. I can't wait to start over. I'm so sorry for the pain I've caused you. I wish-"

Another phone call came in. I instantly got upset as I saw it was Toya calling me, interrupting me from spilling my heart out to my mother.

"Goddammit, why does this woman keep on calling me?"

I sent Toya to voicemail and hit send on the text message to my mom just in case another unwanted phone call came through. She called again no more than ten seconds later. Again, I sent her to voicemail. I didn't have time to get sensitive with her or did I want my happiness ruined. My happiness was becoming short-lived now that a minute after being sent to voicemail for the second time, my phone buzzed with a text message.

"I know I'm not one to talk, but you might want to keep your eyes on the road," Vince suggested.

"Hey, well read this text for me then," I told Vince to do as I handed him my phone so I could keep my eyes on the road for his sake.

"Wow!" Vince said at first glance of the text message. His eyes were looking crazier than ever.

"Wow what!? She sent naked photos or something? Read the damn thing man before you make me wrap this car around a pole!"

"I wish she sent naked pictures," Vince joked. "Anyway okay, here we go. 'Since you refuse to call me back after numerous attempts, I will just leave you with this piece of information. I am pregnant, and the baby is yours. I was hoping you would come see if it is a boy or girl with me next week but that's probably a stretch, seeing as though you can't even return a phone call. Don't be a coward, at least for your child's sake!"

The knockout blow was dealt. I was stunned. Lost for words and lost for thoughts. My mind was barely computing what was read to me. Was it real? Was she for real or just pulling my leg? I was wondering to myself.

"Hey!" Vince screamed, as he grabbed the steering wheel and directed us out the way of a median.

"What the hell! I need another hit of the caine dealing with you man. It's not the end of the world you know," Vince uttered to me while sniffling. "You will be an awesome dad. Toya will be an awesome mom. You got some money saved I'm sure, and if not, I do. The kid will be fine. You just need to focus on getting us to the garage so we can handle our business."

Vince randomly started laughing as he continued looking at my phone.

"I'd actually hate to be you right now," Vince said through his laughter, right before he took a line of coke. "Your buddy Renee just texted you and said she's willing to give you a second chance if you can prove yourself to her...That has to hurt."

I didn't even respond. I just kept my eyes on the road. I could only think what is this kind of luck I have or what did I do to deserve such outcomes. I had a split thought of driving us into a wall. Hitting a wall or flying away somehow. I didn't want any parts of this aspect of life anymore.

"You know what, if I'm really going to be a dad, then nothing matters to me anymore except making sure my kid is going to be okay. That is now my priority as a man, right?" I said and looked over at Vince for confirmation who gave me the thumbs up in return.

I put the pedal to the metal as my mind shifted gears from panic to frantic on our way to the garage. I pushed Godzilla as fast as she could go. I shifted every gear perfectly. I turned every corner with precision. I did at least 40mph over every speed limit. I ran every stop sign and red light. We reached Viktor's garage from Alonso's garage in what I felt like a record time.

"Alright, c'mon we have to burn all this shit to the ground, right? No evidence," I said to Vince, while frantically trying to open the garage door to the warehouse.

"Dammit! It's locked! I whimpered."

"I got it. Stand back," Vince said.

He attempted to kick the heavily bolted door down with some sort of Bruce Lee type of kick that he probably saw on TV.

"Ok. That didn't work. Think Vincent!" He reached into his back pocket and pulled out a little vial.

"Seriously man?!" I said, right before he looked at me with the thought of being judged. He triple-tapped the vile on his fist, dumping a tiny mountain of coke on the top of his hand. He snorted it without any second guessing.

"Ok, I got it, I got it!" Vince whispered. His eyes still looked crazy like someone glued his eyelids to his eyebrows. He took his shirt off and wrapped it around his hand.

"I will be right back. Stand here," He scurried off around the building, leaving me to look like a prime suspect, holding a gas canister. Within roughly fifteen seconds, I heard some glass shatter. Soon after that, the locks were unlatching off the door. From the time the door opened, it felt like everything went in slow motion. All I heard was 'Freeze! Freeze! Goddamnit, right now! Hands up in the air now!'

My life flashed before my eyes. I saw myself come out of my mother. The first bike I rode, my first kiss, my first drink, first joint, first criminal activity. All of the flashes lead me to this point. I had never been so scared in my life. In a single blink, it was over. I had to remember to breathe before I passed out. The first plan of defense was to just run and keep running. I was going to run to another country if I could. It seemed that Vince had the same mindset as he was already taking steps backward.

"Don't take another step!" someone from the SWAT team yelled over the portable intercom.

With no helmet to protect his face, we could clearly see, it was Tony behind the intercom. "It's over Vince. Let all three of us work something out," Tony suggested.

"One of us has to make it out of this brother," Vince whispered to me, ignoring Tony's demand, while he kept his hands held high.

Before I could respond, I was met with a grab and choke hold from behind. "Don't do anything stupid kid!" SWAT demanded.

"Vince what the hell?!" I whispered.

"Relax. This is my ticket to heaven. My ticket to reunite with my father. Deliver this to my mom," Vince explained, while discretely stuffing a note in my back pocket. "I always knew this day would come," I never thought it would be the cops taking me out though. Thought it would be some hating ass sucker in the streets, so I kept that note on me. Whatever happens next you just keep going. Don't turn around. I love you brother. Stay back! I'll blow him smooth away!" Vince yelled, ordering SWAT to step off as he'd seen them inching closer one step at a time.

"You are all coked out man. You are not thinking straight. There has to be another way," I reasoned.

"Joey, you know I can't go to that place. I can't be caged up. Either let me fly or let me die," he said, looking directly at our enemies. "Don't worry. We had an incredible run. I had an awesome time. This is what I want. You're about to be a father. Make sure you tell him or her all the stories of us," Vince said.

"Let's just talk man?"

"It's time to run brother. They're gonna shoot at us soon. Make sure you get that note to my mother. See you on the other side brother. I love you," Vince uttered.

"Vince!" I screamed. "Don't! No! Don't do it.!"

As soon as Vince released me, he reached under his shirt, and all I heard was gunfire! I turned to run faster than Forrest Gump only to realize that my legs were not operating anymore. Maybe the loud gun fire scared them stiff. I wasn't too sure. I wanted to turn around and look, but I knew if I turned around, I would see my brother lying lifeless on the ground, a sight I couldn't take. All these thoughts were processing within milliseconds before I realized something. Not only did my legs stop working, but I was the one on the pavement lying face down. I grabbed the keys to Godzilla that were lying by my waist and unlocked my doors. I was planning to get up and drive away. I still had fight in me. That's what I wanted to believe. A half a minute later, cops were all over me and handcuffing me.

"We got two gunshot victims. One alive and one believed to be deceased. We need a medic immediately!" the cop holding me radioed.

"Dispatch in route," was the last thing I heard. Sheer blackness became my friend.

Before the Box Closes

Temptation is the devil in its purest form. I devised a great master plan, but I never thought I would have to live every minute of it looking over my shoulders. That was six years ago. I've been paralyzed from the waist down ever since that fatal night. Bullet hit me right in my spine, damaging my L5-L9 nerves. Doctors said I was lucky to be alive. That must be an automated response from doctors because I say I'm unlucky to be alive. What's lucky about being young and suffering every day? What's lucky about not being able to take care of myself? What's lucky about not being able to see and raise your kid? She doesn't have a father in her life, and I want to be in her life so badly. I mean Christ, I don't even know her name, and I just know she exists. What's lucky about reading your mom's obituary every day knowing if you did things differently she might still be here? Not being able to go to her funeral. What's lucky about getting your best friend hooked on drugs and then killed? What's lucky about throwing your life in the trash? Nothing, answers all of those questions. I had it all. Promising career after college, beautiful girlfriend, and best friend only God could deliver. Now I have nothing.

Don't open Pandora's Box if you run into one. I saw my parents open the box and I got to see the effects of it through their lives. They had it all and lost more than all. I thought I could do something different. It's like to be young is to be stupid in the sense that you think you know everything. You think you are invincible. My dad told me I wasn't built like that, but I didn't listen. My mom warned me, but I didn't listen.

It seemed like yesterday when mom and I used to feed the birds. Or running around playing with kids, wrestling in the grass and playing hide and seek with girls. I would do anything to sit in my room and play PlayStation with Vince or get yelled at by my mom for not doing the dishes. I would even do anything to go back to my shitty job at the dealership. Anything beats this place I'm in. I have nobody to talk to in here. I have nobody to call on the outside either. I don't even know

233

where I am. I just know it's a prison, it's bizarre, and it's terrifying. This place is like no other on earth unless of course, it's another prison. This isn't a place fixed for mankind.

I sleep on a mattress no thicker than a Hershey's bar. Every day, I need help getting into my wheelchair. Most the inmates just look at me while I'm on the floor. I just lay there until someone with a heart picks me up. Periodically, I've heard unlimited screaming. Someone was either getting stabbed or even worse, raped. Riots happen every week. The constant fighting. They feed us garbage. I would kill for a burger and fries from Sparkys. I don't understand this place. I spent so much time focusing on complaining, I forgot that no matter how bad things get, they can be worse. Forgetting this has led me here. I have about another three or four years in this place, I can't remember. I lost count. Then when I get out? Then what? God knows I can't go back to that life I was living, even if I wanted to. If I have learned anything, its choices bring consequences, be they good or bad. And like my Dad said, you have to live with those consequences derived from the choices you make. I have learned to be thankful for what you have in life and to be humble. Though at present, all I have is the ability to breathe. Nothing else.

I don't have anything else to live for, so I've been thinking about the other side a lot lately, and how death can't be the end of the road. It's simply the next stage after life, and it could very well be my only way out of this life. I learned in school that energy can't be created nor destroyed, so if this is true, that means that my mom, dad, and my best friend are still out there. Death has to give us this new relationship with ourselves, and I believe it is to reunite us with our loved ones. Otherwise, death wouldn't exist. I miss my mother, my father and my best friend dearly. There is only one way to test out this theory. I just ask that this journal be given to my daughter wherever she may be in life...it's all I have left to give...

www.ingramcontent.com/pod-product-compliance
Lightning Source LLC
Chambersburg PA
CBHW022136240626
47153CB00007B/2392